V

By Angela Verdenius

(Book 3, Big Girls Lovin' trilogy)

Copyright 2011 Angela Verdenius

All Rights Reserved

ISBN: 978-1-4710-9254-1

Cover images courtesy of pixitive, Monkey Business Images, Istock.com, Dreamstime.com & Joleene Naylor

Cover by Joleene Naylor

No part of this book may be reproduced or copied in any form without prior written consent of the author & publisher.

This is a work of fiction and all names, characters, incidents and places are from the author's imagination.

I found with Doctor's Delight that some readers were having difficulty with the Australian slang, so I thought a list of the slang I've used will help while reading the following story. If I've forgotten any, I do apologise! Angela

Australian Terms/Slang

Got his/her/their goat – annoyed him/her/them

Dander – temper.

Golden Link Nursing Association - fictitious nursing organisation that visits patients at home. In reality, there are organisations that do this.

Moosh - slang for face/mouth

Torch - flashlight

Mobile phone - cell phone.

Bloke/s - men

Iced coffee/chocolate - a milk drink flavoured with chocolate or coffee.

RAC - Royal Automobile Club of Western Australia. Covers insurance, holidays, loans, etc.

Tim Tams - a brand of Arnott's Biscuits. Yummy!

Chemist - pharmacy

Buggered - many Aussie use it as a slang word for 'broken' (it's buggered), 'tired (I'm buggered), and 'no way' (I'm buggered if I'm going to do that). Just some examples.

Bloody - a swear word 'no bloody good', in place of 'no damned good'

Tucker - food

TLC - Tender Loving Care

Biccies - biscuits. The same as cookies.

Boofhead - idiot, simpleton, etc. It's an insult, though sometimes we use it as a term of affection. It depends on how it is said and meant.

Sheila - female.

Hoon/s - person/people who indulge in antisocial behaviour. Great explanation in Wikipedia

Primapore - sticky patch with a pad in it. A medical dressing.

Panadol - paracetamol.

Milo - chocolate malt drink. Can have it hot or cold. Yummy!

Budgie smugglers - men's bathers, small, brief and tight-fitting.

Tea - some people call the evening meal dinner. In my family, we've always called it tea, as in breaky, dinner and tea, or breaky, lunch and tea.

Donger - penis

Yamaha & Suzuki - 'brands' of motorcycles.

English Blazer – really yummy men's after shave!

Pub - hotel.

If someone's tickled pink, they're - delighted

Giggle-box - TV, television

Lug - face

Shag - sex

Pedal Pushers - three quarter pants/knickerbockers

You wally - silly,

Beaut - beautiful, awesome, great, wonderful

Crash cart - resuscitation trolley in a hospital or medical setting - used for life threatening situations such as cardiac arrest.

Chapter One

Sitting at the bar, Tim sipped from the glass of beer and watched the crowd reflected in the mirror. Music was pounding out and a group of dancers were gyrating in a corner of the bar. Bodies whirled and dipped, short skirts and jeans flashed around, and women wiggled and shook their bosoms while the men flexed their muscles and showed off their prowess.

There was only one bosom that Tim was interested in at that moment, and it belonged to Cindy Lawson. He couldn't help but watch her bosom as she shimmied and rocked her way merrily around the floor. The tight top she wore not only clung to her generous bosom, but whatever bra she was wearing had pushed it up to eye-watering level. The generous curves almost threatened to spill out of her top.

She shook her ample bottom with gusto and her generously curved hips seemed to have a mind of their own as she swivelled them with the expertise of a belly dancer.

Shaking his head, Tim closed his eyes briefly while taking another sip of beer. Cindy Lawson was an out-of-control, overblown hour glass. Most plus-sized chicks he knew covered up their curves, but not Cindy. Oh no, she had to flaunt what she had in tight tops that showed every curve to advantage, and right now she also had on a skirt that had a slit – yes, a slit, damn it – right up the length of one plump thigh. Her blonde hair, recently dyed back to its original colour from the flaming red she'd previously had it, was pulled up in some intricate knot that had wisps of hair clinging to her flushed cheeks as she shimmied and boogied and basically tore up the dance floor in a pair of stilettos that had his toes cringing in sympathy.

How she didn't go arse up on the dance floor, he'd never know.

"She is some dancer," Rick observed, sipping on a Coke.

"Is that what you call it?" Tim slid his glance back to the mirror and held his breath when Cindy dipped low and her bosom threatened to come free completely from the tight confines of her top.

Going by the wide eyes of her dance partner, he was obviously hoping she would break free. Literally.

"So." Rick looked at Tim's reflection in the bar mirror. "Not on call tonight?"

"Whatever made you think that?"

"You're drinking alcohol."

"What, you don't think I could deal with a dog when I'm drunk?"

"I can't deal with a human patient when I'm drunk, so I don't see the difference with your animal patients."

"True. Both can bite."

Rick grinned. "Amen, brother."

They clinked glasses.

"Nah," Tim said. "I'm not on-call." He glanced in the mirror again but Cindy was lost from sight. What did catch his attention now was a sultry brunette with a short skirt and pouting lips, who was gyrating her hips in exaggerated slowness and watching him while licking her lips suggestively. "Whoa. Get a load of this babe."

Rick's glance was decidedly disinterested. "Nice."

"Nice? Are you kidding me?" Tim grinned at the woman and she started to shimmy her way across the dance floor.

Oh yeah, that's what he liked. A hot looker with great legs and a nice handful of bosom just right to fit into his palms. Neat little bottom and full, pouty lips.

Rick shook his head and sighed. "You're gonna regret this."

"I doubt it." Tim grinned wider when the woman slid up onto the vacant bar stool on the other side of him. "Hello, sugar. Nice moves out there."

He couldn't see his friend, but he could imagine the eye rolling that was going on behind his back.

The woman licked her lower lip and gazed up at him from lowered, thick, and very obviously false eyelashes. "Thanks. I'm Sassy."

He just bet she was. "Tim." He stuck out his hand.

"And I'm Rick," his friend said, sticking his head around Tim's shoulder.

Tim elbowed him in the stomach and leaned closer to the woman. "And he's of no consequence."

Sassy smiled.

"So." Tim ignored Rick's chuckle, "All alone tonight? Or with friends?"

Perfume, thick and strong, surrounded him as she leaned forward, giving him a good eye-full of her cleavage. "I came with friends, but I can leave without them."

There it was, the bold invitation. No messing around with this woman.

"Really?" He slanted a glance back to the dance floor. "Male friends?" *Any problems there?*

"Just a group of friends," she assured him, and looked at the barmaid as she approached.

"What are you drinking?" Tim queried.

"Beer."

He nodded to the barmaid then turned back to Sassy. "So, Sassy. Celebrating anything?"

"Apart from meeting you?"

"Okay, that might be cause for celebration-"

Rick groaned.

"But," Tim continued, "Any other reason?"

"No." Accepting the glass of beer, she ran her fingertips – talons, really – down the frosted surface before picking it up and taking a delicate sip. "So, Tim, what do you do for a living?"

Rick leaned forward on the bar to peer at Sassy. "Puts his hand up horses' arses."

Tim mentally swore. Some days it didn't pay to keep company with friends when you were trying to pick up a girl.

Sassy raised her brows.

"Ignore him," Tim said. "The poor bastard's drunk."

Her gaze fell to the Coke in Rick's hand.

"Rum in it," Tim said. "Lots of rum. Mostly rum, actually." He looked at Rick. "Do you mind?"

"Not at all. It's always educational watching you."

"What are you, fifteen?"

Rick grinned widely.

Tim returned his attention to the beautiful brunette. "What about you, Sassy? Model? Actress?"

"Miranda," Rick called to the barmaid, "I'll need another Coke. Fast."

Jesus, why did Rick have to pick now to get in a funny mood? Annoyed, Tim glared at him over his shoulder.

Laughing, Rick turned away to take his glass of Coke from the barmaid.

Coming from the opposite direction Tim spotted Cindy bouncing towards the bar. Yes, the woman was bouncing. Everything bounced, in fact. Bosom, hips, hair, even her eyes brimmed with sparkling delight. Seriously, what was with her?

"Tim?"

Refocussing on Sassy, he smiled. "Sorry. Annoying friend and all. Let's go find a table."

Taking her elbow, he picked up his glass and steered her through the crowded floor to the table, ensuring he strode right behind her so she could feel the heat of his body and get a good whiff of his English Blazer aftershave. Nothing like a little masculine scent to help get the hot blood flowing in a beautiful woman.

Gallantly holding the seat for her, Tim waited until she sat before taking the chair opposite.

"My," she said. "A gentleman. Not easy to find nowadays."

He merely smiled a little. "So, Sassy, what do you do for a living?"

"I manage a clothing shop, Petite Creations."

"Really? Why do I know that name?"

"I sincerely hope you don't shop there." She laughed huskily.

"Never set foot in it, but I do know the name."

"It's fairly new to the city, but it's quite elite."

That would explain that. No doubt he'd heard someone talk about it. "Really?" *Booooring.* Faking interest, he smiled.

"Oh yes. A lot of the more influential women shop there." Warming up to subject, Sassy continued on for several minutes about the creations in her shop. When she finally stopped, Tim's eyes were almost glazed but he kept that smile on his dial. He was nothing if not polite, even when he was faking it.

"So," she finished, "Enough about me…"

Thank you, God.

"What do you do, Tim?"

"I'm a vet."

"Oh. Really?" She studied him for several seconds while he took a mouthful of beer before her eyes widened. "Tim? Tim Clarke the veterinarian?"

Uh-oh. Had he just hit on a client? His boss would *not* be happy. "Do I know you in a client capacity?"

Her eyes gleamed. "No, I don't like animals, all that hair getting on my clothes and things. But I do know your mother."

"Are you sure?" Jesus, he couldn't even hit on a woman without the ghost of his cold-hearted mother looming over the whole thing. "She shops at Petite Creations?"

"My mother knows your mother."

Ah, now he was getting the picture. "When you say you manage Petite Creations…"

"My mother owns it. Or rather, her company. It's one of a chain of shops that are world-wide." Leaning back on the seat, Sassy crossed her legs leisurely, but Tim didn't miss the glow in her eyes.

Gold-digger was written all over her.

Okay then, they were playing on sort-of the same team. He wanted her body, she wanted his money. He'd get her body but she sure as hell wasn't getting his money – or his phone number. A quick boink her and leave her, that was what he had lined up for the night.

Crossing his own legs, he let his gaze drift down to her cleavage. "Delightful."

"And to think," she said brightly, "My parents and I will be attending your mother's party on Saturday night and we'll meet you there. But better yet, I have an idea."

Tim was pretty sure he didn't want to hear it, the bells were going off in his head like out-of-control ringers.

"How about you pick me up on Saturday night and we can go together?"

And there it was. They'd only known each other for less than twenty minutes and she was eyeing him as though mentally measuring him for the groom's suit at their wedding. Maybe that's what the alarm bells were – the ringing in her head transcending time and space to clang inside his.

He shuddered mentally.

Time to nip this in the bud, and fast. "Well, it's been nice meeting you, Sassy. I'll have to introduce you to my girlfriend."

Her smile froze on her face. "I beg your pardon?"

"My girlfriend."

"You have a girlfriend?"

"Yes, and she'll be delighted to meet you."

"A girlfriend here?"

"Yes." Man, he really was an arse sometimes, Rick was correct. But at least his arse was his own and not in the cold hands of a gold-digging harlot who'd sell her soul for his old family money. "Did I forget to mention her?"

Sassy stared at him for a few seconds and then her eyes narrowed. The woman was on the scent like a bloodhound on a poor fox's trail. She looked around. "And where is this girlfriend now?"

"Coming. Shortly." He glanced around as well. "Any second in fact, so I better head back to the bar. Nice meeting you, Sassy." Tim got up and walked back to the bar with her eyes burning a hole in the back of his shirt.

Rick was chatting to Cindy, and he looked up as Tim took the bar stool beside him. "What happened? Did you luck out?"

"She was mentally measuring me for the wedding suit."

"Let me guess, she recognised your name."

"And monetary connections." Tim nodded to Miranda. "Another beer."

"So how did you get out of it?"

"Told her I was here with my girlfriend."

"And she didn't throw her drink at you?" Rick shook his head. "I'm impressed."

Cindy, standing silently beside him, didn't look impressed at all. In fact, those big blue eyes were studying him closely. "You picked up a woman and then dumped her?"

"Gold digger," he explained. How could she not get it?

"From what I've been told, they're just your type."

Tim's brows rose. "Who's been telling tales? Rick?"

"Maddy," Rick replied. "And Mike."

"Mike wouldn't talk."

"You'd be surprised what he tells Maddy."

"No, I wouldn't. What is it with you and Mike? Get a ring on your woman's finger and it's magically through your nose as well."

Rick grinned.

Cindy placed one hand on her generously curved hip. "That's disgusting behaviour."

"Trust me, I can get worse than that."

"You seem proud of that fact."

"You seem disapproving."

"Really?"

"Really."

"No wonder you haven't got a woman yet."

"Oh, I had one all right. For all of ten minutes before she was planning on walking down the aisle with my money."

"Money isn't everything."

"Says you."

Cindy's eyes narrowed.

"Whoa." Rick looked at Tim. "Mate, not cool."

"It's all right." Cindy moved between Rick and Tim's stools, which placed her really close to Tim. "I can deal with him myself."

Several things hit Tim straight away – she smelled nice, and she had her dander well and truly up. It made her eyes sparkle.

Or maybe that was just the beer swimming inside his body.

He raised one eyebrow. "You think you can deal with me?"

"Most assuredly."

"Lady, you don't know me that well."

Her eyes narrowed further. Maybe the sparkle was enhanced by the artfully applied eye shadow and eyeliner. That had to be the explanation.

"I might not have known you long, Clarke, but I know your kind."

"*My* kind?"

"And I know your reputation."

"Oh my." He splayed one hand on his t-shirt, which tellingly had *Stud for Hire – Cheap,* emblazoned on it. "I'm famous."

She opened her mouth but before a word could leave it, a voice purred huskily over his shoulder, "Where's your girlfriend, Tim?"

Shit. It was Sassy. Tim glanced at her over his shoulder to find her looking at him triumphantly. She knew perfectly well he didn't have a girlfriend here. This could turn messy. He didn't like messy, and this promised to get messy.

His gaze fell on Cindy, who was watching the woman behind him with amusement in her eyes. Oh yeah, she just had to be happy with this outcome. She -

Oh yeah. *Oh yeah!*

"Oh, no," groaned Rick. "Tim-"

In one smooth move, Tim hooked an arm around Cindy's waist and pulled her between his thighs. Giving her a smacking kiss on her lips, which had partially opened in surprise, he said, "She's right here!"

And her lips tasted like strawberries. *What the hell...?* His gaze dropped to those luscious lips and the shine on them had him realizing that she was wearing flavoured lip gloss. Rather yummy, really.

Cindy was staring at him as though he had a screw loose, one of her hands braced against his chest and the other on his thigh just above his knee. The rings she wore on nearly every finger sparkled in the light.

"*This* is your girlfriend?" Sassy asked in disbelief.

"Cindy is my girlfriend," Tim affirmed.

"I most assuredly am-" Cindy began hotly, only to be stopped by Tim leaning in quickly to give her another quick kiss and whisper, "Back me up and I'll owe you."

She looked from him to Sassy peering over his shoulder, and what she saw in the brunette's eyes must have made her change her mind, for she relaxed suddenly, melting into Tim, her luscious curves pressed against him, her soft stomach nestling between his thighs.

Whoa, and didn't that just produce the most interesting sensations?

"Cindy," she almost cooed, putting her arm around Tim's side under his own arm so she could shake the slack-jawed Sassy's hand.

Her breasts pressed against his chest and Tim almost swallowed his tongue when he glanced down to see those plump pillows pushing against the low neckline of her top.

Sassy shook her hand with obvious distaste.

Tim raised his gaze to see Rick's amused expression.

"*You're* his girlfriend?" Sassy asked disbelievingly.

"I know, isn't it a shock?" Cindy smiled widely as she picked up Tim's glass and sipped from it. "I'm not his usual type, I know, but I guess there's just so much more of me to love." Placing the tip of her nose against his, she rubbed it gently. "Right, Timmy?"

"Right." Two could play at this game. Tim lowered his hand and settled it firmly on her rounded bottom. "Just so much more to love." He squeezed one buttock.

He was rewarded with a flash of her eyes and a slight stiffening of her lush body, but his smirk was lost when her fingers above his knee dug in to the nerves. Mouth open in a silent yell, he couldn't miss the hilarity on Rick's face over Cindy's shoulder. He could only thank God that Sassy was sitting behind him and couldn't see his expression.

Pressing closer, Cindy rested one arm on his other side and settled her chin on his shoulder so that she could see Sassy. "So," she said to Sassy, "Where did Tim try to pick you up?"

What the hell...? Tim stiffened.

"He's such a wanderer," Cindy continued happily. "I've considered having him neutered to mend his ways."

Sassy actually laughed. Cindy patted his back fondly and Rick had to turn his head away.

"Without his Lassie," Cindy continued, "Timmy would get into a lot of trouble. Wouldn't you, Tim?" Pushing back, she lovingly looked up into his face and patted his cheek harder than needed.

Boy, she was really pushing it. "What are you doing?" he mouthed silently to her.

"Yes sir, he needs a lot of help." She beamed at him. "Take this slogan on his shirt, for example." She patted his chest. "*'Stud for Hire – Cheap'*. My goodness me, never has a slogan been truer!"

"Okay." Tim finally found his voice. "Let's not bore Sassy."

"I'm not bored." Sassy laughed.

"Oh honey." All fake concern, Cindy patted his cheek again. "Did I embarrass you? Poor baby." She settled her chin comfortably on his shoulder again and nestled really close, her hand sliding up his thigh.

Tim could feel every warm, lush curve of her, and his body was sputtering to life as surely as his temper. Both for different reasons.

"So anyway," she continued happily, "His wandering has been a problem, but after we got him treated for his last STD-"

Rick choked on his Coke.

"Okay!" Grabbing her by the shoulders, Tim pushed her back to stand on her own feet. "Enough of that now, *honey*. We don't want to go into medical conditions, do we?"

"We don't?" She looked at him in innocent bewilderment before her eyes widened. "Oh, I am sorry." She switched her gaze to Sassy who, no doubt, was watching avidly and more than willing to spread whatever gossip she could around. "He's a little sensitive about his wiener." Cindy simpered, actually *simpered*. "Or, as we like to call it, Big Hammer."

Oh God! "Time to go, sweetie." Tim slid off the stool and wrapped his arm firmly around her waist, forcing her to move with him. "Nice meeting you, Sassy. Rick, I'll see you later. You." He bared his teeth at Cindy in more of a snarl than a grin.

"Yes?" She batted her lashes at him.

"Home."

"Of course."

Thank God for small mercies. She came willingly, but then she stopped and neatly slid out of his arm, turned and hurried back to the bar. Tim almost ran after her but then he saw that she spoke to Rick in low tones and wrote something down before returning to Tim's side, tucking the piece of paper into her tiny beaded purse.

"Ready when you are, lover." She slid up against him and he sucked in a breath when her hand slapped his backside heartily.

With a tight smile on his face, Tim wrapped his arm firmly around her and almost dragged her through the crowded club. Once outside, he yanked her to the side and snarled, "What the hell was that about?"

"Hey, just playing the part, Tim. I did enjoy it."

There was no doubt about that, her eyes sparkled and laughter lurked in the blue depths.

It didn't ease his annoyance. "You do know that everything you said will get back to my mother, don't you?"

"Well, maybe you should have thought of that before you pulled me into your crazy scheme." Pulling a mobile phone from her purse, she pressed speed dial.

"Who are you calling? The cops?"

"No, the loony bin. For you." She raised one brow. "Why would I call the cops?"

"Because I'm about to kill you?"

She laughed.

Tim took a deep breath. "I asked for help, not for you to spread nasty gossip."

"Oh, you mean about Big Hammer and your STDs?" She put the phone to her ear.

"I don't have an STD and never have had, if you must know." He glared at her. "Damn it, couldn't you just lie a little like a normal girl? Couldn't you-" He stopped when she held up one finger.

"I'm at the Vic pub on Spencer Street," Cindy said cheerfully into the phone. "If you could send a taxi to pick me up and take me to 17 Bella Way, I'd be grateful. You can? Great. Yes, it's Cindy. I'll be waiting near the sign."

"Finished?" Tim asked sardonically as she clicked the bejewelled phone shut.

"Well, I think so." Cindy waved the phone under his nose. "I've only been using this for particular brand for two months, so I might not have completely got it right yet."

Disgusted, he folded his arms.

"So." She smiled widely. "You were saying about Big Hammer...?"

"I was saying nothing about Big Hammer. I – Damn it, I don't call my penis anything, understand?"

Dropping the phone into her purse, she nodded. "Dick with no name. Got it."

God, she was infuriating. "Thanks for nothing."

"Hey, you begged for my help and I gave it."

"You call what you did 'help'?"

"Sure. What do you call it?"

"How about aggravating?"

"No. Really?" And she laughed merrily.

Oh no, Cindy couldn't laugh delicately, she had a full-bodied, happy peal that drew all eyes and a few smiles from passers-by. Even her giggles were merry. He'd have found it smile-inducing himself except that the hilarity was at his expense.

"Remind me never to ask you for help again."

"Oh now, don't be like that." She patted his arm. "I *did* save your hide, after all."

"Thanks for nothing."

Placing one hand on her ample bosom, her eyes sparkling, she replied happily, "Your heart-felt thanks is received and will be treasured for life."

"You're drunk." With that biting retort, Tim started to walk away, but a sudden thought popped into his head making him stop and turn back to her. Maybe hilarity wasn't the only thing making her eyes sparkle.

"Seriously, *are* you drunk?" He leaned a little closer and eyed her closely. Okay, she might be an irritating bit of goods, but in all good faith he couldn't just walk away and leave her until her taxi arrived. She was Maddy's best friend, and Mike was Maddy's husband, and Mike was one of Tim's best friends, and that meant…crap, he felt a bit of responsibility for Cindy.

Damn his little shred of chivalry. That was definitely from his father's side.

"Me?" She looked genuinely surprised.

"Yes. You." He took a sniff and was able to smell some of his beer on her breath and her perfume.

Nice perfume. Suited her. Full-bodied and yummy.

Yummy? Hell, maybe he was drunk, even though he never got drunk anymore.

Placing the tip of one purple-nailed fingertip on his chest, she pushed him back slightly. "Down, Fido."

Straightening, he frowned.

"Sniffing isn't polite. Next thing you know, you'll be sniffing people's crotches instead of shaking hands." Taking a step back, she eyed him just as warily as he was suddenly eyeing her. "What's your problem?"

You. "Nothing." He tucked his hands into his pockets and rocked back on his heels. "I'll wait until your taxi comes."

"Why?"

He shrugged. "Good manners?"

"I doubt it." One fine brow arched. "I'm not drunk, you know."

"Okay."

"So you don't need to wait."

"Okay." Where was the damned taxi?

She stared at him before suddenly nodding her head. "Ah."

Refusing to ask, he feigned disinterest in her reply by watching the people passing them as they came and left the pub.

"You're worried that Sassy will come out and find you here alone. Why don't you just run along to your car and make your getaway before it's too late?"

He glanced at her.

"Or maybe you're worried that I'll get hit on the head while waiting for my taxi and Mike will clobber you for leaving me alone?"

He glanced away.

"Huh. Okay."

What she meant by that, he didn't want to know. Where was that damned taxi?

"You should run while you can," she said.

"I'm not running."

"You'll wish that you had." Laughter lurked under her tone.

Taking a deep breath, he watched as a taxi pulled to a stop and a giggling group of people got out. About to hail it for Cindy, he froze when a familiar husky voice sounded behind him.

"I'd have thought you'd have a car waiting for you, Tim."

Taking a deep breath, Tim turned slowly and managed a smile at Sassy, who was glancing inquiringly between him and Cindy. "Never drink and drive."

"You can afford a chauffer. Like your mother."

"I'm not my mother." *Thank God.*

Taking a tiny step back, her gaze slid to Cindy.

Cindy gave her a little one-finger wave. "He's very responsible."

"So I see." Sassy looked again at Tim. "You didn't mention that your friend was married."

"Who?" He looked blankly at her.

"Rick."

"Rick? Oh, Rick! Yes, yes, he's married." Tim gathered his unusually scattered wits as Cindy gave a gurgle of amusement beside him. "I gather he's left?"

"To pick up his wife from the hospital where she works." Sassy's eyes held more than a hint of frost.

Knowing that his friend was utterly devoted to his one-true love, Tim had no doubt he'd given Sassy the truth fast and sure as soon as she'd turned her gold-digging attention to him.

"He was killing time with me." Tim added belatedly, "And with Cindy, of course."

"Of course," Cindy echoed. "Oh look, here's my taxi. Bye, honey, love you!" And with that, she kissed him on the cheek, turned, and opened the door to the taxi that had pulled up to the curb behind her.

Sassy's eyes narrowed.

"Oh yes," Tim said, "*Our* taxi. Bye, Sassy." And he dived in after Cindy, unceremoniously shoving her across the seat as he slammed the door after him.

He didn't look at her as he buckled his seat belt and sank back against the backrest.

Cindy gave the startled taxi driver a cheerful wave. "Hey, Bernie."

"Hey, Cindy." Bernie looked at Tim warily in the rear view mirror. "He's with you?"

"Apparently. For now, anyway." Cindy laughed, long and loud.

Tim scowled.

"Oh, come on honey, don't be such a grouch." She hit him lightly on the arm with the little beaded purse.

"You enjoy watching me sweat, don't you?" Folding his arms across his chest, Tim scowled at her.

"I have to get my entertainment where I can."

He shook his head. "And you're Maddy's best friend. I just don't get it."

"Hey, you're Mike's best friend and I don't get that, either." She winked. "Guess it's true what they say, huh?"

"I know I'm going to regret this but - what?"

"Opposites attract."

"Is that the best you can do?"

A guffaw came from the front seat.

"Bernie thinks it's good."

"Sweetheart." Bernie chuckled. "Most things you say are good."

Personally, Tim thought that was greatly exaggerated, but he shrugged and turned his gaze out to the night to stare unseeingly at the traffic and buildings as they flashed past.

Idly he listened to Bernie and Cindy chatting. Her voice was light, a hint of gaiety underlying the tones as though she found most things amusing. He much preferred husky tones on women, the hint of sexuality and decadence.

Light and fluffy just wasn't his style. Nor was light and sly, as he was starting to think Cindy just might be. She certainly had a mischievous side to her that liked to watch him squirm.

A sudden realisation popped into his head. He had squirmed back at the pub. He'd been so caught up in Cindy's lies that he'd actually dived into the taxi after her rather than bid her a cool goodnight, given Sassy a careless wave, and gone on to find his own taxi.

Cripes, when had that happened? Why had it happened? He never squirmed, and certainly not where women were concerned. He was the one who loved them and left them, who shook the fragments of their tattered hearts from his shoes and walked off without looking back. He coolly avoided any and all who tried to cling to him or get their claws into him, and he'd never - *never* - run from a woman before…before Cindy came along and tied him up in bloody knots.

Broodingly, he stared out into the night. It was downright embarrassing. The sooner he got rid of her, the better. And tomorrow he was going to ask Mike about his beloved Maddy's sanity in having the bubble-headed blonde as her best friend. He just had to know what the attraction was, because he sure as hell couldn't even begin to guess.

The taxi rolled through the night and finally turned into a tree-lined driveway, going through high gates and up a winding road. Rounding a curve, Bernie drove the taxi right up to the front of a really big house. Or a small mansion. It actually teetered between being one or the other, falling into neither category. Not many lights lit the front, so Tim couldn't get a good look at the grounds. The only light was that above the door that stood at the top of four wide, stone steps. A big veranda swept above the door and disappeared around each side of the house.

"Thanks for a great evening." Opening the door, Cindy swung one leg out.

The split in her skirt enabled Tim to see a quite a lot of thigh, the silk of her stockings holding a shimmer that made it appear as though her whole leg shimmered with colour. And now he could see that tiny butterflies dotted the stocking, lacy wings spread in perpetual flight. Good grief.

Avoiding the sudden urge to reach out and test for himself just how silky that leg was, he muttered, "Glad I could be of amusement."

"Oh, you have no idea." Amused, she got out of the car, shut the door and went to Bernie's window.

Tim saw Bernie's eyes go straight to Cindy's ample cleavage as she bent to peer into the window. "Thanks, Bernie. Here's extra to take my unexpected, non-existent boyfriend home. Be kind to him, he's had a rough night."

Bernie laughed, got another good eyeful of that mouth-watering cleavage, bid Cindy what seemed to Tim to be a totally unnecessarily affectionate 'goodnight', gunned the engine in a bid to prove his manly presence, and then drove off down the drive in a careful manoeuvre that had Tim rolling his eyes.

He couldn't resist one last glance backward through the rear window to see Cindy's lush body outlined briefly in the light of the doorway before the door closed and cut her off from sight.

It had to be the luckiest thing to happen to him tonight.

With a sigh, Tim leaned back in the seat and gave his address to Bernie. As the taxi glided along, the soothing sounds of the tyres on the road and the passing traffic relaxed Tim slowly and his annoyance slipped gradually away. Now he was able to think of the evening with a little more clarity and he knew part of his annoyance was at Sassy's brazen attempt to get her claws into him. The other part of his annoyance was due to Cindy's dig at his non-existent STD, and the fact that she'd played him up to teach him a lesson.

His lips quirked in reluctant amusement. Yeah, the blondie had had the last laugh, all right. He was just glad that he didn't see her very much. The odd time he'd caught sight of her at Mike's house, but it had been fleeting meetings. Frankly, that was more than enough for him.

Chapter Two

Sitting in the window seat and enjoying the cool breeze that blew through the open window, Cindy gazed out towards the city lights and thought about Tim Clarke, Veterinarian and son of one of the wealthiest people in Western Australia, the prestigious paediatrician, Dr. Margaret Clarke.

Many sons would be basking in the glory of old money and working for the family business. However, Tim worked as a vet and that, she knew, galled his mother. It was what she described as a working class position and not befitting a Clarke.

Personally, Cindy admired Tim's chosen profession. Animals didn't get half the help they needed.

Maybe she should look into doing something with animals. She loved them but since her old cat, Bast, had passed away four months previously, she had no pets. Maybe it was time she got another cat. She missed not having a fur-ball romping and sleeping around the house. A house just wasn't a home without some cat hair.

She wondered if Tim had a pet. Somehow she doubted it. He seemed to be out most times picking up dubious women, loving and leaving them in his typical cavalier way. From her understanding, and what she'd seen of him in the distance at clubs, pubs and more upper crust parties, the women he chose were hard in nature and no strangers to climbing the ranks of the rich by sleeping and clawing their way there. It was just that none had managed to capture Tim in a web of marriage, which seemed to be his main aim.

So why the hell he hung around with them, she'd never understand. She'd certainly never had much to do with him apart from a nod of recognition at parties, and once or twice a couple of words when she met him while visiting Maddy. That was more than enough for her.

Shaking her head, Cindy rubbed the cocoa butter into her arms. There were more things to think about than that ass. Such as her cousin's wedding and the fact that she had no one with which to go.

Well, she could take her housemaid/cook, but even her mother, as sweet as she was, would shake her head and empathically declare "No!"

Darn it.

Yawning, she walked across to the dresser and sat down, reaching for the face moisturiser and massaging it into her cheeks. The scent was lovely and she made a mental note to buy Maddy some for her birthday. Plaiting her hair into a long braid, she went to bed.

~*~

Stumbling into the kitchen the next morning, she squinted at the bowl of diced fresh fruit topped with a dessert spoon of cream. "Wow, fruit and dairy, two of the main food groups."

Sam, her very crotchety housemaid/cook, glared at her from where he stood at the kitchen sink. "Fruit is good for you."

"Never said it wasn't." She sat down and picked up the cup of tea. Taking a mouthful, she almost gagged. "What the hell…?"

"Green tea. Lengthens our lifespan." Sam placed one gnarled hand on a scrawny hip. "Got a complaint about it?"

"Yeah, I have. I want my regular tea."

"Can't. All I bought is green."

"Geez." Cindy placed the tea cup back on the dainty saucer and stood up. "I'll have orange juice."

With a grunt of disgust, Sam crossed to the table, picked up the tea cup and swallowed the contents in several gulps. "There. Now I'll live longer than you."

"I doubt that." Cindy poured the orange juice into a tall glass. "You're seventy years old already. I'm less than half your age." She saluted him with the glass and a grin. "So I guess I win."

Grumbling to himself, Sam took the cup and saucer to the sink and commenced washing it with renewed vigour.

The door opened and the tall, thin, angular body of Ruth, Cindy's gardener and wife of Sam, entered.

"Take those boots off!" Sam barked out. "My floor is clean."

Ruth sourly toed off her boots on the mat.

Cindy continued eating, not really taking notice of the morning ritual in her home. It was played out on Ruth and Sam's three work days a week.

Padding across the floor, Ruth sat down at the opposite end of the table in front of the bowl of fruit her husband placed in front of her. Sam put a generous dollop of cream atop it and returned the cream pot to the 'fridge. "Want a cup of tea, Ruth?"

Ruth looked across the table at Cindy, who shook her head. Taking the hint, she replied in her slow drawl, "No thanks. I'll have orange juice."

"Humph." Sam gave Cindy a narrow-eyed look as he poured out the juice.

Cindy grinned back at him.

"I planted those roses," Ruth stated. "The red ones."

That sobered Cindy. "You don't need to be doing that digging, Ruth. We can hire someone-"

"I'm the gardener here." Ruth spooned up some fruit. "I'm not too old, Miss Cindy. I may be old in years, but I'm strong."

Taking in the pull of wiry muscle in the lean arms, Cindy had no doubt about it. It was also an old argument, so she shrugged. "Okay."

Sam glanced over at her and nodded. There was no doubt that if it got too much for his wife, he'd let Cindy know, but the older couple were so healthy and strong that she had no doubt they'd be going for many years yet.

Ruth commenced to fill her in on what she had planned for the garden that day, just as she did every work morning. Cindy nodded, commented and made a few suggestions, and by the time Ruth started on her bacon and eggs, she was a happy gardener. Well, as happy as she'd ever display, her gaunt face and placid expression showing only a slight smile of approval and contentment.

"So what are you doing today?" Sam whisked the empty bowl off the table.

"I'm going to pick up a present for Maddy's birthday and drop it off to her," Cindy replied. "Then I might call in and see Mum and Dad. How about you?"

"Mop the floors."

"Exciting day for us both."

Sam eyed her sourly. "Maybe you need to get a hobby."

"I've got one. It's paying you to insult me."

"Har-de-har."

"Anything you want me to pick up at the shops?"

"Like I'd trust you to do the shopping? You'd come back with pavlova for tea and chocolate cake for dessert."

"I suppose you want something like brussel sprouts for tea and carrot cake for dessert."

"You'd suppose correct."

"You know I wouldn't touch a brussel sprout with a ten foot pole."

"Precisely why I don't waste them on you."

"But you won't give me pavlova for tea, either."

"I have to amuse myself in my own way."

Laughing, Cindy left the kitchen. Running up the stairs, she went to her bedroom and took off the dressing gown and nightie. A quick shower later, she stood in her lacy pink panties and bra in the walk-in wardrobe to contemplate the clothes hanging neatly on the racks. Finally she chose a pale blue sun dress that swirled lightly above her knees. Once dressed, she applied lipstick and mascara - her two main staples of make-up on what she considered a 'light make-up day' - pulled her hair into a jaunty pony-tail high on the back of her head, tied it with a big, wide, blue bow, slipped a pair of dangling earrings on, and slid her feet into a pair of silver stilettos with just a wide strap across her toes.

Pivoting in front of the mirror, she surveyed herself in satisfaction, gave a happy nod, picked up a dainty, pale blue shoulder bag and tripped down the stairs into the wide entry.

"I'm going, Sam!" she shouted.

"Okay." His voice drifted back from somewhere towards the back of the house.

Going through into the kitchen, she went through a side door and into the garage. Climbing into her little Hyundai, she lovingly ran her hands over the steering wheel. Man, she loved her car. Pressing the control where it was attached to the dashboard, she waited until the garage door had opened fully before backing out into the sunshine.

Pulling out into the drive, she waved at Ruth who was standing with a row of roses in pots behind her. Ruth waved back before returning to her beloved gardening.

Turning up the radio, Cindy drove into the city and to one of her favourite shopping centres. Pulling into the car park, she hopped out and went to the ticket machine. Humming to herself, she paid for her ticket, then, spotting a harassed-looking mother towing a crying child behind her and pushing a pram, she slid more coins into the slot and pressed the ticket button before leaving. As she neared her car, she glanced over her shoulder and saw the bewildered mother holding the ticket in her hand, and she smiled.

As her mother always said, spread the cheer.

Once inside the coolness of the shopping centre, Cindy made her way to The Body Shop and browsed among the goodies, finding the lotions she wanted quickly. While having them gift-wrapped, she watched a dispirited-looking man sit down at a nearby coffee table. In his hands he held the employment page. He glanced once at the menu board with the names and prices of the food and drink on sale, and with a small sigh, he started pursuing the paper with pen in hand.

After paying for the present, Cindy ambled over to the coffee counter, ordered a hot coffee and salad roll and paid for it, and pointed to the man at the coffee table who still had his head down as he circled employment options. The waitress, Maryanne, knew Cindy, and she grinned and nodded.

Yep, nothing like spreading the cheer, Cindy thought as she left the coffee shop. A glance over her shoulder showed first bewilderment, then pleasure on the man's face as he looked up at Maryanne. She was pleading ignorance of who paid for his meal, and when she left the food at the man's table, the smile on her face was genuine delight.

Yep, that bit of cheer had touched two people.

With a bounce in her step, Cindy returned to the car.

Her next stop was Maddy's home. As she pulled into the driveway, she hooted her musical horn. Immediately she spotted Chaz in the window, his big Siamese head pushing up the curtains as he peered out at her. Beside him a much smaller head reared up, and little grey-furred Yamaha stared at her before being side-tracked by a butterfly that flitted past the window.

Cindy couldn't resist running her finger along the glass, laughing as Chaz tried to remain dignified in front of Yamaha, but finally he succumbed to the lure of fake prey and slammed his seal paws against the glass, chasing her movements.

"Teasing cats now?"

Surprised, Cindy froze for several seconds before straightening to face Tim. His car was parked behind hers, a low-slung, two-seater with 'playboy' practically screaming from the black leather interior.

"Well, hello, Timmy," she said cheerfully. "Loving the shirt, sunshine. Suits you."

Tim ran his hand across his chest. His shirt proudly proclaimed *I'm a nut who needs screwing.* "Glad I don't disappoint you."

"Never."

His gaze skimmed across her, taking in everything from the jaunty bow in her hair to the tips of her silver stilettos. "Going to a party?"

"Not today." She held up the gaily wrapped present. "Maddy's birthday."

"Ah." He rocked back on his heels.

Cindy studied him. Dressed in t-shirt, battered jeans and sneakers, with his dark hair carelessly - or maybe artfully - tousled, he looked boyishly handsome...if one didn't notice the sharp intelligence in his brown eyes. His face was lean, his jaw strong, his lips a little too full for a man, but saved from being too girlish by their firmness.

Yeah, it would be easy to dismiss Tim Clarke as a boyishly handsome, charming man. Luckily she knew him to be a real hound dog with women, or she could just as easily be suckered.

"You two coming in?" Mike's voice rumbled from the doorway. "Or are you just going to stand there, eyeballing each other?"

Cindy smiled brightly up at him, genuinely glad to see him. Mike was a bear of a man, but he loved her best friend unconditionally and that made him almost perfect in her eyes.

"Hello, Mike." She didn't miss the way he watched almost warily as she hurried up the stairs, finding it immensely amusing that men kept waiting for her to fall flat on her face due her high heels.

"Cindy," he greeted her, standing aside so that she could walk right past him. "Tim."

"Got the tools ready?"

"Yeah. Let's start on it."

Obviously the men were going to be tinkering with a car engine or something, and that suited her just fine. Hurrying into the kitchen, she saw Maddy straightening up from where she was crouched checking something cooking in the oven.

"Mads!" Cindy flung herself at her best friend and hugged her tight. "Happy birthday!"

"Thanks." Maddy laughed as Cindy gave her a resounding kiss on the cheek, taking the present that she pressed into her hands. "Oh, Cindy, you shouldn't have."

"Of course I shouldn't have." Cindy dropped into a chair and stretched her legs out, crossing her ankles and placing her hands behind her head. "Open it!"

She waited impatiently as Maddy peeled the sticky tape off and neatly unwrapped the lotions. The delight on her friend's face just tickled her pink.

"Oh, Cindy, thank you!" Maddy moved across the kitchen and gave her a hug. "It's beautiful."

"Trust me, Mike will get one whiff of the scent of that moisturiser on your skin and he'll eat you right up." Cindy winked. "In every way."

Maddy laughed. "He does that now."

"Really?" Cindy arched a brow. "Do tell."

"Not on your nelly." Maddy opened the 'fridge. "Diet Coke?"

"Absolutely. I'm parched." Cindy watched her friend open the cans and place them on the table as she sat down. "So what did Mike get you?"

A slight blush of pleasure tinged Maddy's cheeks. Pulling the chain out from around her neck, she showed the elegantly set, small amethyst that exactly matched her ring. "This."

Leaning forward, Cindy fingered it carefully. "It's beautiful."

"He's taking me out to dinner as well."

"And so he should." Cindy took a sip of Diet Coke. "Where are you going?"

"Well, if the car gets fixed, the Steak House. If it doesn't, then its pizza delivery, because I refuse to ride that monstrosity of a motorbike he's so fond of."

"Your car is broken down? Why don't you get a mechanic out to look at it?"

"Because Mike reckons he and Tim can fix it." Maddy smiled wryly.

"Don't you need it for work?"

"I've got a week of holidays, so that's not a problem." Getting up, Maddy crossed to the stove and opened the door. Sticking a thin, wooden stick into the cake, she nodded approval as it came out dry and clean.

Cindy chewed her bottom lip as she considered how to make an offer without offending her friend.

Guessing correctly, Maddy said as she placed the cake tin on the wire rack, "We can afford a mechanic, don't worry."

"Then this is just a man thing?"

"This is just a man thing."

"Promise?"

Maddy levelled a look at her.

"Fine." Cindy held up both hands, palms outwards. "Peace, sister. I'll keep my nasty old money."

Maddy grinned. "You do that." Placing a plate on the counter, she opened a container of home-made muffins.

"Oh, man." Cindy's mouth watered. "Chuck one of those here, please!"

Without missing a beat, Maddy tossed a muffin through the air and Cindy caught it unerringly. Taking a bite, she moaned. "Yummy."

"I thought I'd take some out to the blokes." Maddy carefully placed four muffins on the plate and added some biscuits before deftly covering the plate in gladwrap. "Could you grab some iced coffees out of the 'fridge?"

"I have to pay for the muffin by being your servant?"

"Nothing is for free."

"Why don't you just call the blokes in?" Cindy retrieved two cartons of iced coffee.

"Because once Mike starts something, he's loathe to stop." Maddy picked up the plate and walked out into the hall.

Following her through into the lounge and the newly made archway that entered into what was once Mike's half of the duplex, Cindy glanced around. "What are you going to do with all the furniture?"

"We're still deciding."

"You could always buy new."

"Nah. Mike's a big man, his furniture is pretty tough. We'll probably keep his lounge suite."

"What are you going to do with the extra rooms? Still making one into a library?"

"We'll probably make this the library, a nice quiet room to sit and read."

"Don't you mean a place you can escape to when he's watching car racing?" Cindy asked dryly.

"That too." Maddy laughed and led the way out of the door and onto the veranda.

Now they were on the side that was once Mike's, and going by the sounds coming from his garage this was where the repairs were happening.

"I told him he could mess his garage up," Maddy informed Cindy, "But he's to leave mine nice and clean."

"Laying down the law. I like it."

"Laying down the law to a cop like Mike?" Maddy laughed louder. "Are you kidding me?"

"Mike's putty in your hands."

"He can be stubborn when he wants to be, trust me."

"You like it."

Maddy's grin grew wider.

They rounded the corner and came to a stop in front of the open garage door. Inside it the two men were bent over each side of the open bonnet while tinkering with the mysterious innards of engine pieces. They straightened at the same time and looked from the engine to each other, discussing the problem.

Cindy glanced at Maddy and saw the softening of her face, her rounded cheeks flushing slightly as Mike glanced around at her. Mike's eyes softened as well, but the glow that lit them held a lot of desire.

Yeah, Mike loved Maddy, loved every bit of her lush curves and voluptuous body, as he termed it just to make her blush and laugh. But there was no joke about the desire that burned in his eyes every time he looked at his fiancé. The desire and the love, the total acceptance.

Cindy wondered if anyone would ever look at her own overly generous hour-glass curves like that, but somehow doubted it. Oh well, it was something that she never allowed herself to dwell on if she could help it. She'd made her decision a long time ago to enjoy life and live it to its fullest, and not worry about what other people thought. Most times she managed it. Life was too short.

Definitely too short not to appreciate Tim's body as he stood side-on, then slowly pivoted around to face them.

Yeah, the man was lean of build all right, tall and almost lanky, but there was surprising strength in that lean body. His pectorals were defined, as surprisingly was the hint of a six pack stomach. Wow, who could have guessed that?

Cindy actually blinked in surprise and, yes, appreciation. Those jeans hung low on lean hips, and his biceps and triceps bunched as he wiped his hands on a rag he'd pulled from a back pocket in his jeans.

A light smattering of dark hair went from his pectorals down to a thin line on his stomach to disappear in a tantalising trail into the waistband of his jeans. No doubt an arrow to Big Hammer, she thought with a grin.

"Like what you see?" Tim drawled.

Her gaze snapped back up to meet his, but not a blush rose in her cheeks as her grin widened. "Not bad. Not bad at all, sunshine."

"I think that falls under the context of sexual harassment." Shoving the rag in his back pocket again, Tim walked forward in that long, lanky, easy stride he had that was so natural.

"Hey, you don't want me to look, don't flaunt it."

"Definitely sexual harassment." Stopping right before her, so close she could feel the heat from his body, Tim reached out and plucked a carton of iced coffee from her hand.

Rather than move politely back, he stayed right where he was, his gaze steady on her face, studying her with deliberate leisure. A gleam of amusement was more than evident in his brown eyes as he dropped his gaze to her lips, then her throat and lower. Deliberately lower in a movement she just knew was an attempt to unnerve her.

Good thing she wasn't the kind of girl who got unnerved. She'd just have to ignore the little coil of something unmentionable that slithered through the lower - very lower - regions of her stomach. The cream she'd had that morning must have been bordering on sour.

Placing one hand on her ample hip, she took a deep breath, pleased when Tim's pupils dilated a little as her breasts swelled against the low neckline of her bodice.

"Like what you see?" she retorted brazenly.

His gaze lifted and the heat in them was almost a shock. "Show me more sometime and I'll let you know."

Good grief. "Is that an invitation?" No way was she backing down.

"Unless you want to -"

"Right." Mike stepped in-between them, grabbing the last iced coffee from her hand while shoving Tim back unceremoniously. "Thanks for the coffee, Maddy. It's a bit hot out here-"

"In more ways than one," Tim interjected from behind Mike.

"And I think Cindy needs to go indoors." Mike frowned down at her. "Now."

Cindy's mouth dropped open in surprise. "But I don't feel hot."

"Maddy."

Just that one word from Mike had her friend placing a hand at her back and steering her back the way they'd come. "It is a little warm. Hope you get the car fixed, boys."

"I'd like to fix something," Tim said. "But I don't think it's the car- *oof!*"

"Get back in your box," Mike growled, and he didn't sound happy.

Cindy glanced back over her shoulder to see Tim watching her while rubbing his abdomen. Or rather, watching the sway of her ample bottom. His gaze lifted to meet hers and the corner of his mouth quirked a little.

The bastard must have found the sight of her ample bottom humorous. That heat she'd imagined was just that, imagined.

Maddy practically shoved her through the door and her hand at Cindy's waist just kept pushing until they were both in the kitchen.

"What the hell was that?" Maddy demanded.

"What?" Cindy took refuge in picking up the can of Diet Coke.

"Sticking your boobs in Tim's face?"

"Hey, he asked for it."

"To be sexually harassed?"

"Come on, he sexually harasses everyone with his shirts." Cindy laughed.

"This is no joke," Maddy said sternly. "Playing with a man like Tim is out of your league."

Cindy sobered. "As in a man like Tim Clarke wouldn't find me attractive?"

"That's not what I meant."

"Then what do you mean?"

"Tim isn't a man to mess with. His kind of women are...hard."

"He dates cold-hearted bitches with figures that could slip down a drain if they stood on it sideways, I get it. No plus-sized chicks like me." Annoyed, Cindy plopped inelegantly down into the chair at the table and crossed her legs. "As if I wanted to attract him, anyway. As if he could be attracted to anyone like me."

Maddy frowned. "Don't get snooty. Even a blind man could have seen the heat in his eyes when he looked at you. Or rather..." She gestured towards Cindy's chest. "Your bosom."

"It's just been awhile since he last saw a pair the size of mine." Not wanting to fight with her best friend, Cindy leaned back in the chair and blew out a sigh. "Look, Mads, Tim isn't interested in girls like me. I don't fit his profile. It was just a harmless bit of teasing."

"I don't want you hurt."

"No chance of it." Cindy took another sip of Diet Coke.

Quietly, Maddy studied her.

"What?" Cindy finally asked.

"I've never seen you so blatantly flaunt yourself like that before."

A little uncomfortable now that she thought back to it, Cindy shrugged. "Spur of the moment thing."

"Yeah." There was a hint of foreboding in Maddy's voice.

"Look, when someone *blatantly* sets out to embarrass me-"

"I think he was just teasing. At first."

"Tease, whatever, I give it back. It wouldn't have gone any further."

The expression on Maddy's face wasn't so sure.

"Look, don't worry about it," Cindy said. "Tim and I don't often meet, and when I see him at any pubs, clubs or dinners, I promise not to give him a look at the girls, okay?"

"The girls?"

"These." Cindy palmed her breasts. "The twins, fantastic as they are."

Maddy rolled her eyes.

Laughing, Cindy circled the base of the drink can on the table. "So what are your plans for the week?"

Taking the hint, Maddy changed the conversation.

~*~

"What the hell are you playing at?" Mike demanded.

"What?" Tim took a mouthful of iced coffee, his mind still on Cindy's impressive bosom - and that luscious behind that swayed with every step she took in those sexy stilettos.

"You damned well know what."

"Cindy?"

"Yes, Cindy. My Maddy's best friend. Jesus, I thought you were going to rip her clothes off and take her here on the garage floor!"

"Really?" Tim arched a brow. It didn't sound half bad. "It'd be a change."

"Cindy is a lady."

"Even when she pushed her delectable - you know." He cupped his hands in front of his chest and moved them a fair way forward. "At me?"

Mike's nostrils flared. Uh-oh.

"Kidding." Tim walked back to the car and stuck his head under the bonnet. "So, we should get this sorted out pretty quick. It's straightforward now we know the problem."

When silence met his words, Tim glanced up to find Mike staring at him, his pale- eyed gaze holding a threat. And hulking Mike with muscles like boulders in a threatening mode was a little scary. Good thing Tim was his best friend, though that wouldn't save him from a blood nose if Mike thought he was going to hurt Cindy.

"I won't touch her," he assured Mike.

"Not just touching."

"I wouldn't hurt her."

"Not physically, no, but emotionally."

"Seriously? We're discussing emotions? Two blokes? Oh wait, I forgot." Tim slapped his forehead. "This is Mike I'm talking to. The man who loves to talk out his feelings. Shall we go inside and have a chat while painting our toenails?"

"How about we have a chat over my fists?"

"How about we don't? Maddy wouldn't like blood on her bonnet."

Mike stabbed a forefinger in his direction. "Don't play with Cindy."

Personally, the very words conjured up all kinds of interesting images. Weird. Tim shook his head.

Mistaking the gesture for agreement, Mike grunted and turned his attention back to the car.

Personally, Tim had no intention of playing anything with Cindy. The woman was off limits as far as he was concerned. Not only was she Maddy's friend, but she wasn't the kind of woman around whom he hung. She might be brazen, but she wasn't hard, and hard were the only kinds he played with, then he didn't have to worry about hurting anyone's feelings.

Nope, Cindy definitely wasn't on his play list.

It didn't stop him thinking of her bountiful bosom, however, nor that swaying walk. She had a generous backside and he'd found it more than a little fascinating, especially after having a good eyeful of her cleavage. Nothing wrong with a little fantasizing - as long as Mike never found out.

Not to worry, unlike him, Tim never found it necessary to share his feelings. In fact, he shelved them and took them out later when he was alone to examine. Or fantasize about.

Grinning, he glanced up to catch Mike's narrow gaze and he gave his friend the thumbs up.

"I'm watching you," Mike growled. "Don't forget it."

"I didn't know you cared." Tim placed his fingertips coyly over his nipples. "I think I'm getting a little self-conscious."

Mike gave him a last glower before returning to the work at hand.

Grinning, Tim followed suit.

The time passed companionably and by the time they had the car going it was late afternoon. Leaving the garage, Tim pulled his t-shirt back on and walked out into the sunshine. Cindy's car was no longer parked in Maddy's driveway and he wondered when she'd left.

Maddy came down off the veranda. "Thanks for helping, Tim."

"No worries." He bent and kissed her cheek. "Thanks for the muffins. When you come to your senses and leave Mike, my door is always open."

"Shame you'll be dead inside the house." Mike came up behind Maddy to slide his arms around her waist and pull her back against him.

She tilted her head back to smile up at him, and the love was plain on both their faces.

"I feel ill," said Tim.

"Then don't look." Mike placed a kiss on the tip of Maddy's nose and straightened, still keeping her hugged against him. "Thanks for your help, Tim."

"No worries. Now you can take Maddy out for her birthday dinner. Though you could have gotten a taxi, you tight-arse."

"Me?" Mike was indignant. "I mentioned it and Maddy was against it."

"We need the money to finish the renovations," she reminded him. "We're not wasting it on taxis."

Tim frowned a little. "I could help out."

Mike and Maddy levelled their gazes at him.

"Or not. Definitely not." Tim crossed to his car, pulling the keys from his pocket. Just before he slid inside, he looked seriously at his friends. "I know you won't accept help, but if anything ever really bad happened, you'd come to me, right? There would never be strings attached, you know that, right?"

Mike looked down at Maddy, and she slid out of his hold and walked across to Tim. Placing her hands each side of his face, she tugged gently and he bent down. Giving him a kiss on the cheek, she whispered, "We know."

He glanced up at Mike, who nodded.

And that was all that needed to be said and done.

Feeling a lot more cheerful, Tim got into his car and drove home. Pulling into his garage, he closed the door remotely behind him and got out. Entering the house through a side door, he listened to the silence. Everything smelled clean, a hint of lemon in the air. His housekeeper had been and gone, and everything was in its place. He could even smell the remnants of his cooked meal.

Going into the kitchen, he picked up the notebook that he and Janet, his housekeeper, used to leave each other messages, and read it.

'Dinner is in the 'fridge, just put it in the oven and heat at 180 for half an hour. Dessert is trifle, and it's in the 'fridge as well. Janet.'

Straight and to the point. Dropping his wallet and car keys onto the counter, he stretched and yawned while making his way upstairs to his bedroom. Kicking off his sneakers, he yanked off his socks and walked into the big, marble bathroom. The twin shower heads were a bit of a waste of time, as far as he was concerned. He only ever used one. The shower was made for two people but he'd never brought any woman home with him. His home was his personal oasis and no one was going to crash it. It was the one place he could relax and forget about the outside world for awhile.

After a brisk shower, he dried himself and debated what he was going to do for the evening. The options were to go out and see if he could get lucky with a hot chick, or stay indoors, eat the dinner his housekeeper had cooked for him, and watch TV.

Towel low on his hips, he regarded his reflection in the mirror. He knew he was good looking without being obnoxious about it. It wasn't just his money that attracted women, though it certainly helped. He suddenly found himself wondering what Cindy thought as she'd looked at him. There had certainly been interest in her eyes, appreciation even, and he wondered if she'd felt even a smidgen of interest that bordered on sexual attraction.

Then he laughed at himself. Women like Cindy didn't go for men like him, not when they knew how callous he could be with the so-called fairer sex. He steered clear of the good girls, and even though Cindy was brazen, she was a good-type girl. There hadn't been a hint of scandal attached to her name, and if there had of been, he'd have been one of the first to hear of it. Her family was rich, she was rich, and scandal always had a way of reaching far and wide when it involved the rich.

Nope, Cindy was a good girl and out of his reach. If he'd wanted to reach for her, which he didn't. Good God, no. Not Cindy. Not luscious, full-blown, curvaceous Cindy.

Maybe he needed to go out and get laid.

The thought of finding a woman in a nightclub, no matter how exotic or upper class it was, was suddenly unappealing.

Okay, a night in with the giggle-box was the go. Pulling on a pair of boxers, he strode barefoot down the stairs and put his dinner in the oven. Yum, home-made lasagne.

Going through the dining room and into the luxurious lounge, he threw himself down into his comfortable armchair and tilted it up, resting his heels on the footrest that rose up as he leaned back. Grabbing the TV remote that lay on the little table beside his chair, he flicked it on. The news flashed across the screen and he watched it with lazy interest.

In the quiet of the house, the grandfather clock in the foyer bonged the hour. Everything was quiet apart from the low drone of the TV. Leaning back in the armchair, Tim wondered why he didn't do this more often.

Maybe it was time to bring home a dog, one of the strays brought in to be euthanised at the vet clinic. Yeah, a dog would be company. Or a cat, God knew there were a lot of them coming in over the summer period, homeless, un-sterilized and abandoned.

Eventually the oven chime rang out and he got out of his chair and padded back into the kitchen. The delicious smell of lasagne filled the big room as he took it out of the oven and set it on the wooden block on the bench.

He had just cut into it when the phone rang. Choosing to ignore it, he carefully ladled the big chunk of lasagne onto a plate and listened as the answering machine kicked in. The voice he heard had him jerking his head up.

"Tim?" There was a definite wobbly tone to the normally happy voice. "This is Cindy. I hope you're there. Can you pick up? I don't know who else to call. I-"

Tim practically leaped at the phone and snatched it up. "Cindy? It's me."

"Oh, thank goodness." Relief was evident in her voice.

"What's wrong?" Tomato sauce dripped onto the counter.

"We found a kitten. Two, actually."

"Kittens?" Tim relaxed a little.

"They're really tiny, their eyes are shut. One is crying a lot, the other one isn't making much noise."

"Okay." His mind was already falling into vet mode. "Bill's on call tonight-"

"I tried your clinic but there's only an answering service, he's out of range somewhere."

Obviously on a call-out in the country or in the middle of an emergency. "Right." He was already putting the spoon down.

"I'm sorry." She sounded desperate and definitely unhappy. "I'll call another clinic-"

"No." He glanced up at the clock on the wall. "I'll meet you at the clinic in twenty minutes."

There was a slight pause. "Are you sure?"

"I'm sure. Twenty minutes." He hung up the phone, put the lasagne back in the oven and ran up the stairs.

Fifteen minutes later he was pulling up outside the vet clinic. Unlocking the door, he deactivated the alarm and heard a car pull up just as he was about to walk around the reception desk. Glancing outside, he saw that it was Cindy's Hyundai under the light, and as he watched, she got out of the car and hurried around to the passenger door, opening it and leaning inside, coming back out with a shoe box.

Turning, she rushed across the parking lot, and he half expected her to go arse over tit in her high heels, but she missed nary a beat as she hurried to the door.

Tim held it open as she entered. "Follow me."

She did as bidden and he flicked the light on as they entered a consult room. Moving to the other side of the bench, he watched as she placed the box down on the surface. As she lifted her face towards his, he could see the sheen of tears in her eyes.

"Are you all right?" He pulled the box towards him.

"Yes. Just worried. One of them..." She swallowed and cleared her throat. "I don't think it's made it."

Gently, Tim took out one of the kittens, a tabby, and it lifted its tiny head and meowed weakly. He looked at the other one, a little tortoiseshell, but it lay unmoving and he couldn't see it breathing. Passing the meowing kitten to Cindy, he took out the tiny, unmoving kitten. It was cool to touch and he knew without even having to listen that it had died. Nevertheless, he took the stethoscope and gently laid it under the kitten, listening for a heartbeat he knew he wouldn't hear. There was nothing. He turned it gently, checking its skin and looking in its mouth and, as he suspected, it was dehydrated. Going by the umbilical cord still attached, it was only a day or two old.

"I'm sorry, Cindy." He gently laid it aside and held out his hand to her. "Let's have a look at this other little scrap and see what we can do for it."

Silently she handed the kitten to him, and he placed the stethoscope in position and listened. The little heart gamely beat and the kitten cried weakly and struggled. A check of the skin proved dehydration.

The stomach was quite distended, and he checked the kitten's mouth. It seemed healthy enough and there were no sores or signs of problems with the umbilical cord.

Taking a gauze packet, he broke it open and took out a square of gauze. Wetting it under the tap, he squeezed out the excess water and wiped the kitten's bottom. Immediately he felt the warm trickle of urine.

"What are you doing?" Cindy queried.

He glanced at her, taking in the wet tear track on her cheek and the way her hand rested protectively on the still body of the kitten on the bench. And his heart clenched a little.

Reassuringly, Tim smiled at her. "Kittens can't pee on their own. Their mothers stimulate them by licking, so I'm mimicking it with wet gauze. A wet cloth will do the same thing. Going by the amount of pee, it's been awhile since this little scrap was last attended."

"Will it live?"

"I think it stands a chance. I'll get some milk into it and get it warm and we'll see."

"So it's not a guarantee."

"No, it's not." Seriously, he regarded her. "But I'll do my best, I promise you."

She nodded.

"I'm going to get a bottle ready with special formula, and we'll see what it does. Okay?"

She nodded again.

Tim went out the back and made the formula, ensuring it was warm, and poured it into a small bottle with a little kitten teat. Carrying a clean towel, he returned to the consult room and saw that the kitten was cuddled up to Cindy's cheek. As he watched, she turned her head and nuzzled the kitten's cheek, and it meowed.

As soon as Cindy saw him, she handed the kitten into his waiting hands. Placing it down on the towel, he bent over the tiny animal and carefully opened its mouth to put the teat inside.

The kitten tried to turn away, but he persevered, managing to squeeze a drop of milk from the teat into its mouth. Still it tried to turn away from the strange taste of the teat.

"Is it going to work?" Cindy was bent over the other side of the bench, her head close to his as she watched anxiously.

The scent of cashmere powder drifted to his senses. He couldn't help but notice that her other hand remained firmly over the dead kitten.

She cared so much and he glanced up to find himself close to her face, the blue of her eyes almost startling in their clarity. Her long lashes were still damp. How he wanted to see her smile again.

"We'll get there," he assured her.

The kitten tugged on the bottle, drawing his attention down, and he saw that it had latched onto the teat and was sucking.

"Success." He grinned, feeling the familiar sensation of satisfaction when something was going right with a patient.

"It's sucking?" Hope filled her voice.

"Yep."

"So it's going to live?" Reaching out a finger, she gently touched the little head.

"It's not out of the woods yet." He didn't want to build false hope. "But it's got a chance. I'll take it home and see how it goes tonight."

"You'll take it home?"

Tim glanced up at her. "We're not open at night, Cindy. Trust me, every vet and nurse here has taken animals and other things home that need attention."

"But what about the animals here?"

"Either the vet or the nurse on call comes in and attends to them, depending on what is needed."

She was silent for a few seconds, watching the kitten drink, before she said softly, "I'm sorry I got you out on your night off."

"It's not a problem." The kitten pulled its head back and he let the teat slip free. "I'm glad you called me."

"You are?" Again there was surprise in her voice.

"Yes." Picking the kitten up, he cradled it in his hands and looked at her. Really looked at her. Her mascara was a little runny around her eyes where she'd wiped tears away and her nose a little red from crying. She looked so soft and concerned and uncertain that it made his heart warm.

It had been a long time since anyone had made his heart warm.

"Yes," he said again. "I really am glad you called me." And he really meant it.

She smiled a little, a soft curve of her plump lips, and he felt something inside his chest shift.

Dropping her gaze, she reached out and ran her fingertip along the kitten's tiny head. "This kitten…"

"Yes?" He looked down, watching how carefully she touched it.

"If it's okay…if it makes the night…" Her voice grew a little wobbly again and she cleared her throat. "If it's okay, I want it."

"You do?" This time it was his turn to be surprised.

"Yes. My old cat died a few months ago and I've been thinking about getting another cat." She glanced up at him and smiled. "Why not this one?"

"Why not indeed," he echoed, and then regarded her seriously. "Bottle feeding a kitten so young can be very time consuming and tiring."

"I guess so."

"In the case of this little scrap, maybe every hour, depending on how dehydrated it is."

"I've got an alarm clock."

"Speaking of clocks, hourly to two hourly feeds *around* the clock."

"I can do that."

He studied her closely.

"I can do it," she stated firmly.

"Okay." He nodded slowly. "I'll see how this scrap goes overnight and if all is okay, I'll call you."

She reached out and touched his arm. "Let me know either way."

He felt the warmth of her fingers clear through to his bones. "Okay."

"Can you ring me in the morning?"

"Sure. I come in at seven thirty, so I'll give you a call." He stepped back and she took her hand away. "Let me put this kitten on a warming pad and I'll be back to get your details."

By the time he had the kitten snuggled on a warming pad and covered with a fluffy sheet, and returned to the consult room, he found it empty. Poking his head out, he saw that Cindy was waiting patiently by the reception desk.

Coming out, he went behind the desk and revved up the computer. While it warmed up, he looked curiously at her, realizing how little he actually knew about her but how much he wanted to know. Now how to ask without sounding nosey?

Ahhhh… "So, what's your work number?"

She looked blankly at him.

"To ring you tomorrow." He held up a pen.

"I'll give you my mobile."

Damn. "Okay."

She rattled off the number and he wrote it down along with her address, which he already knew.

"For now we'll enter the kitten as just 'kitten' on your records until we know if he's going to make it." Tim continued to jot down notes. "You can name him when you take him."

"Him?"

"Yeah, I had a quick look. Your stray is a boy."

Genuine pleasure was reflected in her smile. "I'll think of a nice name."

"Cindy…" He hesitated uncharacteristically.

"Yes?"

"I just want you to understand that the kitten has a tough fight ahead of him, okay?"

"I know. I understand." She looked gravely at him. "He's in the best care, right?"

"Right."

Taking a deep breath, she stepped back from the counter and now he noticed that she held the shoebox in her hands. Inside was the unmoving body of the dead kitten. He felt a little twinge of sadness at such a young life cut off so callously.

"I'm taking it home to bury it." There was a sudden sheen of tears in her eyes. "It deserves that much."

That just tore his heart in two. Moving around the counter, he laid one hand on her shoulder. "Are you sure?"

"Yeah." She glanced down at the kitten. "I'm not going to desert it."

"I'll follow you home and bury it."

"No." She smiled up at him reassuringly. "I buried Bast myself; I can do this little darling as well. It can rest beside Bast under the lilac tree."

"Are you sure? I don't mind doing it."

"No. You take of the living, and I'll take care of this one."

He nodded. "It's a girl, by the way."

"A girl?" She gently stroked the little body and he didn't miss the tear that slid down her cheek. "I'll remember. She'll have a nice name, too."

Jesus, his heart was going to break. He followed her out to the car and waited while she got in and locked the door. When she looked up at him through the open window, he couldn't stop himself from leaning down, reaching in, and wiping the tear away with his thumb. "It'll be okay."

She nodded. "I know." She started the car.

"Call me when you get home," he said abruptly.

"I'll be fine."

"Please."

"Okay."

Nodding, he straightened and stepped back. He watched until her rear lights vanished in the traffic. Only then did he return to the clinic and enter all the details of the consult into the computer before going out the back and getting the kitten. After packing him, the warmer, the bottle and formula into a cat carrier, he turned off the lights except for the reception, reset the alarm and locked the door. Placing the cat carrier in the passenger seat, he heard a faint meow from the kitten and smiled.

This was one little scrap he wouldn't have to euthanase due to being unwanted. Now all he had to do was keep it alive. If it didn't make it, he had a feeling that Cindy's tears just might kill him.

Once home, he checked his answering machine but there was no message light glowing. Maybe Cindy was going to bury the kitten first. He still felt wrong leaving her to do it, but he understood her need.

Placing the carrier on the kitchen bench, he turned the oven on to rewarm his food and plugged in the kettle.

The phone rang about twenty minutes later and he grabbed it off the counter. "Hello?"

"Tim?"

Relief coursed through Tim and he relaxed on the stool at the kitchen counter. "Cindy. Everything okay?"

"Yes. I buried Princess beside Bast."

He waited several heartbeats before saying, "Princess, huh?"

"She was a little princess, Tim."

"Yeah, she was." He took a breath. "You okay?"

"I'm fine. How's the boy?"

Reaching into the carrier, Tim carefully lifted a corner of the fluffy sheet. "Fast asleep."

"He's okay?"

"Doing well under the circumstances."

"Good. That's great. Give him a kiss goodnight for me."

He blinked. "Sure."

There was silence for several seconds before she said quietly, "Thanks, Tim. Really, I mean it."

"No need, sugar."

"No, there is. Thank you."

He smiled. "I'll call you in the morning."

"I'll be waiting." She rang off.

Tim slowly lowered the mobile to the counter and turned to face the cat carrier. "She'll be waiting for my call but I've no illusions, kitten. It's you she's interested in."

Why that would make him feel a little put out, he had no idea. Or at least, not one he wanted to scrutinize too closely. Nor did he want to scrutinize the fact that he rather looked forward to the phone call in morning.

Chapter Three

Troubling thoughts of the kittens plagued Cindy all night, and she felt incredibly sad that one of the kittens had died before she could get it - her - help. But she prayed so hard that the little boy kitten would live.

Five thirty found her in the kitchen sipping on coffee and gazing unseeingly out the window to the beautiful gardens beyond. Birds flittered through the branches of the huge Poinciana tree, and several of the birds were splashing in the bird bath beneath. The sun was just clearing the horizon.

It promised to be another overly warm day and she screwed her nose up. Summer wasn't her favourite season.

Looking at the phone on the wall, she wished heartily that it was time for Tim to call. Surely if the kitten had died during the night, he would have let her know?

No, he'd wait until the appropriate time, which was probably after seven thirty.

With a sigh, Cindy took the cup to the sink and rinsed it out. Now would be a good time to go for a walk, try to get her mind on other things and enjoy the cool of the day before the heat set in too much.

Walking around the gardens was lovely, but she found herself passing the lilac tree and seeing the little patch of raised dirt that marked the grave of Princess. Beside it was the more settled earth where Bast lay.

Lengthening her stride, she walked down the driveway and out onto the road. The footpath went past several stately homes, and she admired the gardens while privately thinking that Ruth's magic fingers definitely made hers look the best in the neighbourhood.

By the time she returned home, Ruth was out checking the plants for pests. She watched Cindy approach and come to a stop. "You're up early."

"Couldn't sleep."

"Late night?"

"Not really." Cindy rocked back and forward on her heels. "We're getting a kitten."

"Oh?" Ruth inspected a thin branch.

"If he survived the night."

"I see."

"I found him. Or rather, Marty and I did."

"Uh-huh."

Ruth, lady of few words. Cindy smiled a little. "You're so curious."

"I figure you'll tell me what you want to." There was a small crinkle of amusement at the corners of Ruth's eyes.

"Think Sam'll mind?"

"Would it make a difference?"

"No."

"There you go." Ruth glanced up at the sky. "Going to be hot today."

"Yeah." Cindy checked her watch. Six thirty. "Think I'll have a shower to freshen up and get some breaky."

Ruth nodded and resumed checking the bushes.

Cindy had just finished drying off when the phone rang. Heart thumping, she wrapped the towel around herself and ran into the bedroom. She nearly fell over the kitten-heeled slippers she'd left beside the bed, stumbled against the set of drawers beside the bed, and snatched up the phone as she managed to right herself before hitting the floor. "Yes?"

There was complete silence on the other end for several seconds before a male voice asked cautiously, "Cindy?"

"Oh. It's you." She sat down on the bed.

"Glad you're pleased."

"Sorry. Didn't mean it like that. I'm just waiting for an important call."

"At this time of the morning?" Her brother was surprised, then suspicious. "Who is the bloke? Anyone I need to know about?"

"Marty, it's the vet."

"You're shagging a vet?"

"What? No! I mean, he's going to call me this morning about the kitten."

"Okay." She could clearly hear him take a slurp of coffee before he spoke again. "So, you all right after last night?"

"Fine."

"Dad gave me heaps for not coming with you to the vet."

"Dad worries too much. I was fine."

"I know that. He knows that. Hell, we all know that."

"You should do. I got four separate calls last night after I got back. Scratch that, three of them were on my answering machine."

"Don't you just feel the love?"

Cindy laughed.

"You're just lucky Dad and Mum didn't come over to check on you personally. Alex was going to but I talked him out of it. You owe me, sis."

"Put it on my tab."

"Already there. You owe me big time."

She lay back on the bed and stared at the ceiling. "You rang me at this hour to ask about the kitten?"

"Sure. I knew you wouldn't be asleep."

"But there's something else, too, right?"

"Well…"

"Out with it."

"You know our cousin's wedding?"

"Don't remind me."

"I broke up with Christy."

"I am so surprised. Gosh." Cindy rolled her eyes. "The shock of it."

"Sarcasm. Why am *I* not surprised?" Marty grumped. "Would it hurt you to fake a bit of sympathy?"

"Not at all. Not if I knew that Christy had actually meant anything to you." Lifting up one leg, Cindy studied her toenails. They needed redoing. Maybe she'd go hot pink this time. "So I'm guessing no Christy and the cousin's wedding equals one thing."

"Give it a shot," Marty replied. "I'm sure you'll get it if you try really hard. Just don't pull a muscle."

"Marty, are you asking me to be your date?" Cindy cooed. "Oh, Marty! I am…I am so…oh wow!" She panted into the phone. "Yes! Yes! I thought you'd never ask!"

"You are so sick," her brother returned in disgust. "I've got you on speaker phone, you know."

"Liar."

"Everyone in the office can hear you."

"If you were in the office. Which you're not."

"How do you know?"

"At seven in the morning? Even you're not that dedicated."

"Never mind that." He blew out a sigh. "Look, you haven't got anyone to bring, I haven't got anyone to bring, let's just bring each other, okay? Save a lot of hassles."

"Ellen will go nuts with the seating arrangements."

"Ellen can kiss my skinny arse."

"Can I put that in writing and you sign it before we post it to her?"

"Sure, why not?"

Cindy laughed. "Fine, let's go together."

"Dumb idea to have 'Marty and Partner' on the invite anyway."

"Trust me, Ellen put that on there because she knows you change women as often as your underwear. You've already gone through three girlfriends since the invites were sent out."

"Yeah, well, right now I'm too busy to be canvassing the joint for a female. It's settled, then." She could hear the grin in his voice. "I'll tell Ellen."

"Be my guest." Cindy could just imagine the screech of frustration her cousin would give. "And this is one less thing I owe you, so you can take that off my tab."

"You wish." He rang off.

Pushing herself into a sitting position, Cindy placed the phone onto the hook and smiled. At least she'd be sitting with someone fun. Marty was irreverent to the point of embarrassing sometimes, but he could be counted on to keep her entertained. Knowing Ellen - or more precisely, her knowing Marty so well - she'd stick both he and Cindy at the back of the hall behind a potted plant. That suited Cindy, she could bring a book.

Thinking it wasn't such a bad idea, she reached for the phone when it rang again. "Hello?"

"Cindy?"

"Tim?" All hilarity fled her and she bit her lip anxiously. "The kitten?"

"He's fine. Kept me up most of the night, so out of the two of us, he's the better looking one right now." Humour seeped through the phone.

Her shoulders slumped in relief. "I'm so glad."

"Do you still want him?"

"Of course! Can I get him now?"

"We're not officially open until eight, but I'll be here. I'm here now, actually, if you want to come straight away."

"Great! I'll just replace this towel with some clothes and be right there."

There was silence for a split second, then, "A towel?"

"I took a walk and showered."

The silence was broken only by what sounded like a heavy breath being taken.

"Tim?" Concerned, she tightened her hold on the receiver. "Are you okay?"

"Sure." There was a definite trace of irony in the reply. "By the time you get here, anyway."

She frowned. "What's wrong?"

"Just a little clothing adjustment needing to be made."

"Huh?"

"Never mind. See you when you get here." He hung up.

Rubbing her forehead under her fringe, Cindy eyed the phone. The man was stranger than the shirts he wore, and that was a fact.

Excitement bubbled through her at the thought of finally picking up the kitten. Racing into the walk-in robe, she grabbed a pair of figure-hugging, tiny-flowered pants that stopped just below the knee in a little frill. Wriggling into it, she snapped the button closed and nodded in satisfaction. Yep, fitted like a glove. *Eat your hearts out, you voluptuous-babe-loving men!* A low-necked, plain white blouse with frilly cap sleeves topped it, and she finished with a pair of white wedges. In deference to the heat, she pulled her hair up into a loose knot on top of her head and fastened it with a dainty clip. Little tendrils bounced around her ears.

White button earrings, a tiny-beaded white necklace that hugged her throat, a swipe of lipstick, a smear of eye shadow, a buff of the cheeks, a dollop of mascara, and she was good to go.

Grabbing a little, tiny-flower printed purse, she tossed her mobile phone inside, grabbed her car keys and ran down the stairs, almost colliding with Sam at the bottom.

He frowned at her. "It's only seven thirty in the morning. What are you doing up?"

"Things to do!" She yelled gaily as she ran through the kitchen.

Sam followed a little more slowly on her heels. "What mischief are you up to?"

"You'll find out." She slammed the car door shut, flicked on the air conditioner and pressed the remote for the garage door.

When she pulled out, Ruth was approaching for breakfast. She nodded to Cindy in her usual stoic way and continued on into the house.

By ten to eight she was pulling to a stop in front of the vet clinic. One of the vet nurses must have been watching for her, because she was holding the door open by the time Cindy was out of her car.

"You must be Cindy." The vet nurse smiled.

"I am." Cindy stepped through the door into the waiting room.

The vet nurse led her to a different consult room to the one she'd been in the previous night. "Just wait here and Tim will be in to see you with your kitten."

Your kitten. Cindy couldn't help the smile that curved her lips. It felt so good. *My kitten.* Yes, the little scrap was all hers, and it was up to her to see that he lived.

The door in the back of the consult room opened and Tim came in carrying the cat carrier basket in one hand and a small bag in the other. "'Morning, Cindy." His gaze went from the top of her head and swept downwards, a small smile crinkling the corners of his eyes.

Cindy smiled back at him. "You look a little tired."

"Tough Stuff here kept waking me up." Tim placed the basket on the examination table. "He drinks like there's no tomorrow."

"Thirsty?" Eagerly she watched as he opened the lid and reached in under the blanket, withdrawing his hand with a squalling kitten gently, but firmly, held in his grasp.

Handing it to her, Tim smiled as she snuggled it against her cheek and the kitten turned and bunted its little nose along her skin. "He's a hungry boy. But you need to be careful not to over feed him or he could end up with diarrhoea."

Nuzzling the top of the kitten's head, she looked at Tim. "How often do I feed him, and how much?"

Reaching into the bag, Tim drew out a small glass bottle and a teat. "I've marked on the side of the bottle for you. If there's any left, you can pop it into the 'fridge and warm it up for his next feed. For now,

I've been feeding him every hour, but I reckon by tomorrow you can stretch that to two hourly."

"Last night you mentioned making him pee?"

"Yep. You'll need a warm, damp, soft cloth." He showed her what to do and the kitten rewarded him by squalling, stretching out his little legs and producing a warm trickle.

Cindy couldn't help but laugh.

"Trust me," Tim said dryly, "At three in the morning, this stops being a laughing matter."

"I'm sure." Cindy took the bottle that Tim handed to her once he'd finished toileting the kitten.

"Hold this to his mouth," Tim instructed.

Within seconds the kitten was blissfully sucking on the bottle, little paws stretched straight out in front of him.

Taking a deep breath, Cindy inhaled the scent of milk, kitten, and Tim's cologne. It was such a nice mix.

"Now," he continued. "The warming pad is electric, so just plug it into the power at home. It can't burn him, it's not set high enough, but it will keep him warm. Don't put him in direct line of air conditioning, and just check him now and again to ensure he's warm."

"How will I tell if something is wrong?"

"He'll go very quiet, he'll stop drinking or moving. If he's unable to urinate, bring him in and one of us will see him straight away."

Looking after this little boy was going to be a bit more involved than she'd first thought.

"Cindy?" Tim studied her. "Are you sure you want to do this?"

"Absolutely," she replied, and meant it. "He's going to take a bit of work, but it's going to be…I can't think how to describe it."

"Basically, you're going to be his mother."

"Thank God the poor little scrap doesn't take after me!"

"Oh, I don't know. You're pretty easy on the eyes."

Surprised, Cindy glanced up to find Tim gazing directly at her, but as soon as she met his gaze he dropped it to the kitten as he reached out once more and gave it a little rub on the head. "Well, that's about it for now." He was all business suddenly, straightening and taking the kitten from her to settle him in the carrier. "The formula is in the bag, as is the instructions on how to make it up. Any queries, don't hesitate to phone."

"Okay." She picked up the carrier.

"Oh. I forgot. Who are you doing?"

Cindy went blank. "What?"

"I mean, who is doing you?"

"*Doing* me?" What the heck was he asking?

Thrusting a hand through his hair, Tim took a deep breath. "Sorry. Got a bit tongue-tied there. I mean, who was doing - looking after - your cat before? Your old cat?"

"Oh." Cripes, the man was actually a little red-cheeked. Surely Tim Clarke, the playboy vet, wasn't embarrassed? "I was going to Bellacross Vet."

"Right. Did you want to take him there?"

"The kitten?"

"Yes."

Cindy thought for a few seconds, her gaze sweeping over Tim, remembering his gentleness with the kitten, how he'd actually said he was pleased she'd phoned him. In fact, phoning her own vet hadn't even crossed her mind when she and Marty had found the kittens. The first thing she'd done was phone the clinic where Tim worked, and when there was only an answering service, she'd rung Tim. He'd come through for her, so that pretty much answered the question as far as she was concerned. That and the fact that he seemed genuinely fond of the kitten and had helped it live through the night.

"Actually," she replied quietly, "I'll bring him here, if that's okay."

Was it her imagination, or did his eyes soften just a little?

"Good." Tim nodded. "Glad to have you on board."

"Glad to be here, Cap'n." She saluted him briskly.

Grinning in amusement, Tim came around the table, picked up the cat carrier and placed his hand in the small of her back. "Time to pull up anchor, mate. I have pirates filling the deck."

"Oh, I'm so sorry." Remembering the time, Cindy picked up the bag containing the bottle, teat, formula and instructions. "I've taken up too much of your time and-"

"Cindy, taking care of orphans and injured or sick animals is never taking up valuable time." Tim looked down at her. "I'm here if you need me."

His brown eyes were warm and his hand in the small of her back flexed slightly. His cologne, faint and clean, tantalized her nostrils, and his nearness made her acutely conscious of just how close they were standing.

Feeling her knees go just a little weak, she had to sternly remind herself that this was the playboy vet, the charmer, the man who chased and boinked women as though it was his personal hobby.

Hell, maybe it was his personal hobby, what did she know?

However, she wasn't on his hobby list, this was her new kitten's vet, and she had no business imagining things or going weak at the knees at a little show of caring on his part.

Reaching for the door, Cindy swung it open and smiled up at him. "Thank you, Tim, I'll remember that." She walked ahead of him into the waiting room.

"I hope so," he muttered.

"Pardon?" She turned to look up at him.

"Hmm? Oh, just thinking aloud." He handed her the carrier. "Let me know how everything goes, and remember, I'm here for you." He tacked on hurriedly, "*We're* here for you."

Just what was going through his mind? Not sure what to think, she went up to the reception desk and looked at the vet nurse. "How much do I owe?"

"Nothing." The vet nurse smiled. "We don't charge the first consult to people who take on orphaned animals."

"Really?" Cindy was surprised. "But what about the call-out last night?"

The vet nurse shook her head. "Nope. Call-outs for abandoned animals, hurt or too young to fend for themselves, aren't charged."

"But the milk and stuff?"

"We're not a charity, but we respect people who try to do the right thing." The vet nurse smiled at the cat carrier in Cindy's hand. "Just enjoy your baby. Will we see you again?"

"Not unless something goes wrong." Cindy bit her lip at the thought.

"Well, that too, but I meant for vaccinations and things?"

"Oh, of course. This is our vet now."

"Great. Welcome aboard." The nurse plucked out a toy mouse from the container at the counter, a business card from the plastic holder, and popped both into the bag Cindy held. "I'm Lara, one of the nurses here. If you go to our website, you can check out the rest of the staff, our hours, and the services we provide."

"You have a website?"

"Sign of the times, Ms Lawson. Everything is technology."

"Please, call me Cindy."

"Cindy it is."

Seeing more people coming through the door, Cindy bid Lara farewell and took the kitten out to the car. After making sure the cat carrier was secure on the passenger seat, she clipped on her seatbelt and started the car.

For several seconds she sat there, studying the vet clinic in her rear-view mirror, a small smile crossing her lips. The clinic felt homely, the staff seemed caring, and Tim had looked after her furry baby. Somehow, she just knew she'd made the right decision in choosing Tim.

She blinked at the thought and amended quickly, "I mean choosing the *clinic*." She nodded decisively. "Yes, definitely, I chose the right *clinic*."

Glancing around quickly to make sure no one had noticed her talking to herself, she checked for traffic and pulled out of the parking bay, taking her kitten home.

~*~

One brisk knock at the door and Tim rocked back and forwards on his heels, hands thrust into his pockets. When there was no answer straight away, he knocked once more.

Where was Rick? His car was here, Cherry's car was here, why didn't they- uh oh. A sudden thought struck him and he stopped rocking on his heels. Maybe Rick was having a little early evening delight. A roll with his honey.

Oops. Taking a step back, Tim eyed the door. That had to be the only explanation for it. He'd better return later. He should have phoned first.

He'd just taken another step back when the door opened and his friend stood there with flour on his nose.

"Sorry," Rick said. "I was in the middle of making a cake."

"Making a cake?" Tim stared at him.

"Well, Cherry promised me chocolate cake, but she's tired from a hard day at the hospital, so I volunteered to do it." Rick grinned. "I had to finish beating the mix." Turning around, he added, "Come in."

Tim followed him down the hallway and into the kitchen. The bowl of cake batter stood on the bench and he stuck his finger in to taste the mix. Sucking the rich concoction off his finger, he nodded admiringly. "Martha, you have done a good job."

Rick rapped him smartly on the knuckles with a wooden spoon. "Get your germy paws out of my cake mix."

"Is that a nasty reference to my vocation?"

"No nastier than the t-shirts you insist on parading around."

Tim smoothed his hand over his shirt. "It happens to be a very suave quote."

"*Not Neutered - The Two That Got Away*'. Oh yes, very suave. Has the ladies panting after you, does it?"

"Let's them know I'm in good working order, ready to pleasure myself."

In the act of pouring the batter into a cake tin, Rick stopped and stared at him.

Tim quickly amended, "I mean to use *them* for *my* pleasure."

"Okaaaaay."

"I've been getting my words mixed up lately." Reaching for the now empty bowl and a spoon, Tim proceeded to scrape the batter off the sides and eat it.

"Yeah, you'd want to be careful what you say to people."

"Especially when you ask a lady who she's doing."

"You did that?" Rick slid the cake tin into the pre-heated oven.

"Then when I tried to correct myself, I asked her who was doing her."

"I bet that went down well."

Tim licked the spoon and smacked his lips. "I only meant to ask what vet did she go to."

"Did you get an answer or a slap in the lug?"

"I got a stunned expression."

"Answer enough."

Tim watched Rick wash the beaters, measuring cup and weighing bowl. "She finally told me, though."

"Who was doing her? Or who she was doing?" Rick gave a snort of laughter.

"Har-de-har. Who her vet was, smart-arse."

"Maybe she saw your shirt and got scared."

"For your information, she decided to continue coming to me."

"You?" Rick took the bowl and spoon from Tim.

"I mean, our clinic."

"Boy, you've got it bad."

"I haven't got anything bad." Tim looked closely at Rick. "What have I got bad?"

"Being tongue-tied around a lady. That's not like you."

Tim frowned.

Rick swung back from the sink to stare at him in glee. "That's why you've come here!"

"What?"

"To *talk*!" Rick grinned widely. "To have a chat - and cake in the oven, no less. Stay put, I'll make us a nice cuppa and we can *chat*!"

"You are such an arse." Tim glared at him. "I didn't come to chat about Cindy."

"Cindy?" Rick's mouth fell open. "Maddy's best friend, Cindy?"

"Uh…" Tim silently cursed himself. Cripes, he hadn't meant to blurt out her name.

"You got tongue-tied around Cindy?" Throwing the dish towel on the sink, Rick pulled a Coke from the 'fridge and popped the tab. "Tell me all about it."

"Nothing to tell." Scowling at the Coke that Rick placed before him, Tim picked it up and walked to the kitchen table. Dropping down into a chair, he took a deep swallow.

"Sure there is." Popping the tab of another can of Coke, Rick took the opposite chair and sat on it facing backwards, leaning his forearms on the top of the back rest and dangling the Coke can from the fingers of one hand. "Tell me what's troubling you sweetheart."

That was usually his sarcastic line, damn it. "I don't know why the hell Cherry married you."

"Don't change the subject."

Tim shook his head. "Nothing to tell."

"Oh, come on. I shared the problems of my love life with you."

"That's the difference. I don't have a love life."

"Says you."

63

"Says me, because I know." Tim placed the can squarely on the table. "You and Mike are regular old gossips, you know that? I can just see you both in your twilight years, sitting on the porch, sharing cake and coffee and chatting about your wrinkles and what you can do to fix your sagging arses."

"Men don't get saggy arses. We get saggy bellies."

"Is that the official medical verdict?"

"You're right. Can you imagine Mike with a saggy belly?"

"He'll be pumping iron all the way to the grave. Probably bench press his coffin."

They both snickered.

"Rick?" A sleepy voice came from the doorway and Tim turned around to see Cherry standing there, rubbing her eyes and looking all soft and sleep-mussed, her hair half out of a ponytail and her dressing gown skimming her knees.

A plus-sized armful of sweetness that Rick just adored. In fact, his friend was already walking towards her with a sappy look on his face. Bending down, he kissed her tenderly on her lips, one hand brushing her hair back over her shoulders before slipping behind to gently tug the elastic band from her hair.

Brushing the flour off his nose, Cherry smiled up at him. "You've been baking. You should have woken me and I'd have made it."

"Honey, you were so tired that I didn't have the heart to." Sliding his arm around her waist, Rick walked her to the kitchen table.

"Hey, Tim." She smiled easily, but he didn't miss the blush on her round cheeks nor the way she brushed her hand down the front of her dressing gown to ensure that every button was neatly in its slot.

Yeah, Cherry might be at ease in her husband's presence, but she'd never gotten over her self-consciousness when around other men. But under Rick's care she was improving, for she didn't immediately go and get dressed, instead staying at the table and accepting the glass of iced chocolate her husband handed to her before he sat down, tugging his chair up beside hers and looping his arm around the back of her chair.

"Tim was just telling me how Cindy has him tongue-tied," Rick said cheerfully.

"Cindy?" Cherry looked curiously at him.

"Your husband is so starved for gossip he'll make up anything," Tim said. "Don't you have any juicy gossip at the hospital to tell him? Hot nurses, randy patients, handy doctors for that matter? Anything at all?"

"Our hospital isn't exactly a cess pool of rampant, torrid affairs."

"Then it needs to be."

Smiling, she took a sip of the iced chocolate.

"So, what do you think caused the tongue-tie?" Interest shone in Rick's eyes.

"I don't think it's polite to ask," Cherry said.

"Hey, he came here to chat." Rick twirled a lock of her hair around one finger, his gaze steadily - and laughingly - fixed on Tim. But there was also a touch of curiosity.

Uh-oh, that never boded well. Once his friend had the bit between his teeth, he wouldn't let go easily.

"I called around to say g'day," Tim informed Cherry. "I happened to mention being tongue-tied and Cindy in the same conversation and Rick started obsessing. Me." He placed a hand on his chest. "I'm fine as ever. In fact, I'm heading to the Bevan Club to see if I can score tonight."

"Yeah, you looked dressed for it." Rick grinned. "Don't lie to me, old son."

"Look, Dad, I was just on my way home to change, all right? Seriously, you need to get out more."

"Nah. I have everything I need right here." Rick squeezed Cherry, making her blush as he kissed her ear.

His friend had never spoken a truer word and it showed in his manner. He was the very picture of a contented, married man, more than happy with the path his life had taken.

Which was all very well for him, but Tim wasn't a marrying man and women were for flings, not ever afters.

Well, some women, not all, and he made sure he only hung around with the fling chicks, not the ever afters. Okay, he amended silently, he hung around a little with Cherry and Maddy, because they were both a part of his best friends' lives, but that was it. Well, apart from his vet nurses but that was work only, and Nancy, his sixty year old neighbour whom he took on dates to his mother's parties to annoy the shit out of her, but that was it. Oh, and clients were off limits, too.

Geez, he was getting a headache just thinking about it.

Shaking his head, he drained the last of the Coke and stood up. "Well, gotta get going."

"Do you want to stay for tea?" Cherry asked.

"Thanks, but no. I'm off for some fun." He looked at Rick. "Any final words of advice, Dad?"

"Pack your condoms."

Cherry took refuge in her drink.

"Be safe," Rick continued, straight-faced. "Don't drink too much. Take a taxi home. Call me when you get in."

"The first four I'll do, the last is in your dreams."

Bidding them farewell, Tim got in his car and drove home. The house was quiet as normal and Janet's usual note was ready. His dinner was in the 'fridge to warm up.

Tim looked around. His bachelor home was neat as a pin and as quiet as the grave. The only sounds were the soft hum of the 'fridge. It was around this time the night before when Cindy had phoned and he'd gone to her rescue.

What a romantic, absolutely stupid thought. He'd gone and done his job.

The phone rang and he picked it up, glancing at the caller ID and losing heart almost immediately. Clicking the phone on, he put it to his ear and said politely, "Mother."

"I'm just checking to ensure that you're still coming to my party on Saturday night."

"I'm actually thinking of skipping it."

"You're going to skip your own Aunt's birthday? The woman who took a chance on you?"

Jesus. "I'll send her a birthday card."

"Oh, I'm sure she'll be touched. She's been telling everyone that her favourite nephew is coming. Now she can tell them he sent her a card instead." The frosty disapproval was overlaid with tart expectance.

"Shit. Fine. Yes, I'm still going."

"You've got a date, I trust."

"Well, the demand was torched with the words 'Tim and Date.' I rather thought the summons from Hell was pretty straight forward."

"Don't be dramatic, Timothy."

Goddamn it, his mother had the knack of making him feel like a naughty ten year old. As usual.

"I'm sorry, Mother. I'm standing here with a hard-on while my current chick is waiting half dressed for me. In the lounge." He waited a heartbeat. "On the floor."

"I don't expect any better."

"Then you won't be disappointed. Glad I made you proud yet again." Tim hung up the phone.

Shit. Moodily, he contemplated his kitchen. Now he had to find a date. Time to visit Nancy.

Striding out of the kitchen and down the hallway, he went out the front door. Standing on the stoop, he looked over at his neighbour's house. Yep, her light was on. She was probably in there watching porn while smoking her cigars.

Walking up to her door, he rapped smartly and waited.

It didn't take long before it swung wide open and Nancy stood there in all her glory and looking older than her sixty years. The mini-skirt she wore showed wrinkly legs and her high heels made her totter even as she stood on one spot. Tonight her short, curly hair was dyed white with a wide black streak running down the middle of it. A lipsticked mouth so red it almost burned his eyeballs out just looking at her turned up into a wide smile, revealing her dentures. The fake front right tooth had a minute gold rose stuck to it.

Nancy was one classy chick. He grinned.

"Timmo!" Nancy grabbed his hand.

"Are you watching porn?"

"Oh honey, am I ever." She giggled.

Her giggle wasn't anything like Cindy's. Actually, Tim had the brief thought that maybe this would be Cindy in about forty years time, in tight clothes, high heels and outrageous - everything.

That made him wonder if she watched porn. He'd have to ask her.

No, he wouldn't! Jesus!

Shaking the thought away, as tantalizing as it was, Tim shook his head. "And you didn't invite me over to watch it with you? I'm so disappointed."

Nancy winked brazenly at him. "I was afraid you'd get carried away and have your dirty, dirty way with me."

"Exactly. And you'd ruin me for all the other women out there wanting a piece of me."

"Probably a good thing I didn't invite you." Nancy jerked her thumb over her shoulder. "My friend Bert is visiting."

Tim's brows rose, though he wasn't really that surprised. "Your friend? You're watching porn with your friend?"

"We class it as educational." She winked, her hand fluttering to land on her large bosom. "Let's just say, we're getting some pointers." Her laugh this time was downright bawdy. "Or, should I say, Bert's getting a pointer!"

"Seriously, I don't think I should be hearing this." He could barely maintain his stern façade.

"Says the stud of the neighbourhood - oh hell, the stud of the city!" She nudged him with her elbow.

"Hey! Nancy!" The rough-hewn voice bellowed from the depths of the house. "This film is on hold, but I'm old! I can't be on hold for much longer! I forgot my Viagra, you know!"

"Oops!" Nancy waved to Tim. "Catch you later, sugar."

"Wait." Tim held up one hand. "I need a date Saturday night."

"Your Mum's party?"

"Yeah. You in?"

"Will she have those dishy waiters again?"

"Probably new ones. She wasn't impressed when you hit on that young bloke who turned out to be gay." Tim grinned. "Now he's bi, thanks to you."

"My lucky day. Who knew he was into older women? That surprised us both." She cackled. "Honey, I am so there."

"Nancy!" Bert bellowed. "We gotta hurry, woman, I'm starting to deflate!"

Just the image was enough to make Tim inwardly shudder.

"Ta-ta, Timmo!" Nancy shut the door in his face.

Shaking his head, Tim returned to his house. He really needed to get laid and forget about Cindy, Nancy, Bert, his mother and everyone else.

A half hour later he was dancing in the club, watching the slim nymphette shimmying in front of him, her sparkling dress low cut to reveal a tantalizing glimpse of her breasts.

They weren't very big, which shouldn't have mattered because he rather preferred a moderate handful, which was exactly what this nymphette had - a nice, moderate handful. Certainly not an ample bosom that threatened to explode out of a tight top.

Seriously, he really needed to get laid.

Grabbing her hand, he towed her back to the bar and sat her down, swinging easily up onto the stool beside her. "So, Sharon, how about we ditch this club and go somewhere private?" He smoothed his hand down her trim thigh.

"Sure." Grabbing her glass, she tipped back her head and swallowed the last of the vodka, her elegant throat working as the liquid slid down. Replacing the glass on the bar, she smiled sultrily. "Your place?"

"How about yours?" He smoothed his hand a little higher up her thigh, working his fingertips under the hem of her skirt. "Mine is being repainted." No way did he take women back to his home. That was his sanctuary, not for his flings.

"Okay." Smiling, she took his hand and started to lead him from the club.

Not a good sign. *He* led the women, *they* didn't lead him. In a firm move, he turned their hands so that his was above hers, holding her in an undeniable dominant gesture, and he stepped ahead of her so that she followed him.

Outside, he hailed a taxi and opened the door to let her in first.

"Wow, a true gentleman." Sliding in, she gave him a good eyeful of thigh as she moved across the seat to allow him to get in beside her.

"Where to?" The taxi driver glanced at them in the mirror.

Sharon gave her address and the taxi moved out into the traffic.

"So, Tim." She smiled at him. "You're having your home painted?"

"That's right." Settling back in the seat, he gazed out at the passing lights.

"New house, is it?"

And there it was, the snooping. "Not really."

"You've had it awhile, then?"

"It's old." Turning to her, he gave her his full attention, secretly amused when she blushed just a little. Had to be a bloody good actress to blush like that. "So, Sharon." He almost purred her name.

"Tim."

And just like that he fell easily into his smooth line of talk, asking her general things while appearing to be deeply interested. Actually, he was studying her. Out of the noisy club and spinning lights, he could get a good idea of her looks and attitude. Or some of it. The main thing was that she was female, beautiful, slim and, most of all, mercenary. Just the kind of woman with whom he could have sex and walk away from without a backward look or thought. Gratification, that was the plan, and he knew it would be gratification for them both.

Only he intended to end it right after he walked out her door, whereas she was no doubt planning to get her hooks into him. *Not gonna happen, baby.*

Her home was a typical up-and-coming career woman with some money. Neat, feminine, with a touch of class. The air was fragrant with artificial scent that was expelled from a spray can high up on a shelf in the hallway and on her bookcase as well, he saw as he started to enter her lounge.

Walking ahead to a well-stocked bar in the corner, Sharon dropped her lacy, black, barely-there cardigan on a bar stool and reached for a bottle of wine. "Drink?"

"Sure." Crossing to the bookshelf, Tim studied the tomes. Law books, almost every one. The few novels there were autobiographies.

Turning slowly, hands in his pockets, Tim's gaze dropped to the low coffee table. Several magazines, big and glossy, were spread artfully on the top. Class practically screamed at him.

Crossing the room, Sharon handed him a glass of wine. "Like what you see?" She took a slow slip from the glass she held.

"Nice." He couldn't help but add, "Classy."

"Thank you." Taking another sip, she reached out and splayed her hand on the front of his shirt. "So, Tim…"

Reaching out, Tim took her glass and placed it with his glass on the bookshelf before resting his hands on her waist. "So, Sharon…"

One sway forwards and she was in his arms.

The woman practically attacked him. Her mouth slanted beneath his, her hands were beneath his shirt, and long nails scratched lightly across his abdomen. She tugged at the waist of his pants and pulled him towards her, taking a step back as she did so.

This woman wanted to be in charge and Tim was having none of it. He took a step back, pulling her with him, taking over the kiss.

After a surprised gasp, Sharon practically wilted in his arms. A practiced woman in the arts of seduction she might be, but he was a master, and damned if it was going to change.

The phone rang and when she would have reached blindly for it, he caught her fingers and entwined them with his own. "Leave it," he breathed into her mouth before taking possession of it once again.

He had cause to regret it when Cindy's voice said clearly, "Sharon, you randy hag. Bet you've got some poor sucker trapped against your book shelf while you pretend to be all submissive!"

Lifting his head, Tim looked down into Sharon's eyes, shocked to hear Cindy's voice, shocked that she knew exactly what they were up against, and even more stunned to see the guilt in Sharon's eyes.

"Just calling to tell you that I've a new baby here if you want to pop around tomorrow and see him on your way home. Now I'll let you get back to your shagging. Bye!"

Every bit of desire fled as Cindy spoke and by the time she'd rung off, Tim felt…well, Jesus, he felt dirty. As though he'd been sprung cheating. Bloody hell!

Grabbing Sharon, he yanked her back into his arms and started kissing her again.

More than willing to take up where they'd left off, she pressed herself to him while tugging the shirt tails from his pants and sliding her hands right down the back of his trousers.

Taking control again.

Not going to happen.

Grabbing her hands, he tried to continue kissing, but damn if the moment wasn't gone. His lust had vanished. He tried to get it back, tried to arise, as it were, to the occasion, but it was a no go. His desire for a beautiful woman, for some hot sex, was gone.

Before he knew what was happening, he'd pulled her hands completely off him and was pushing her back.

"Tim?" Puzzled, Sharon looked at him.

"Uh - sorry." Shoving a hand through his hair, he started to move towards the doorway. "Look, this isn't working out-"

"What?"

"I'm sorry. I don't feel-"

"You were as hard as jack hammer a second ago." Sharon's eyes flashed angrily.

He sure as hell wasn't now. "Look, let's take a rain check on this, okay?" Giving her a winning smile over his shoulder, he added blithely, as he'd done countless times before, "It's not you, sugar, it's me."

"It for sure is!" Striding furiously past him, she whipped open the door. "You men who blow hot and cold make me sick! Think you can string us along and have all the power, and then leave us standing while bleating that it's not us, but you! Out, you jerk!" The door slammed behind him.

It was the first time Tim had ever been kicked out of a woman's house. Standing on the sidewalk, he looked up at the closed door. Normally he snuck out while they slept, or promised them he'd call and, of course, he never did, because after all, he'd end up being hooked.

Shit, he'd never been kicked out of a woman's house before in his entire, sex-driven, playboy life! He'd sure as hell never lost his libido while starting to make out with a woman while hell bent on getting himself inside her, but what do you know, it was a night of firsts.

And he knew just who to thank for this first very unwelcome development. Cindy bloody Lawson.

Scowling, he took his mobile phone from his pocket, hit speed dial and ordered a taxi to take him home.

He'd had enough of women for one night.

Chapter Four

Cindy was developing a new respect and understanding of mothers with newborn babies. Standing in the kitchen at two in the morning, heating up Al's bottle, she yawned widely.

Al squealed as she toileted him and then bumped his little nose against the corner of her mouth, just as he'd have done if she'd been his real mother. Well, heck, to Al she *was* his mother. Cindy fed him, toileted him, cuddled him, and kept him warm, loved and safe.

At two in the morning, three days after she'd acquired him, Cindy still loved him. She was just very tired. Really tired. Every hour on the hour was wearing her down, but good ol' Sam had volunteered his care of Al and let her have a couple of hours sleep during the day while he babysat. Her mother came over and babysat a couple of times, utterly delighting in her 'grandson' as she laughingly called him.

The good thing about working for her family and being rich, was that Cindy could take off all the time she needed and still get paid. That allowed her time to rest and it didn't matter that she had bags under her eyes big enough to rival the biggest suitcases in the world.

She wouldn't have traded those bags in for anything. She loved Al, and though she was so tired she could just about fall to her knees, she wouldn't have traded the last three days for the world.

Placing him down in his carrier, she listened to him squeal his indignation and hunger with a smile while she took the bottle from the microwave and checked the temperature. Becoming an expert by now, she nodded her satisfaction, picked Al up in one hand and held the bottle to his mouth with the other.

Al latched on to the bottle, tiny paws clawing at the mouth of the bottle before he settled to sucking, stretching his little arms out ahead of him.

He was so cute. His little eyes shut tight, his little snub nose just so snubby. Cindy sighed in contentment. This little fellow was just what she'd needed, someone to love and care about, and someone with whom to share her life. Until he'd come along, she hadn't known just how much she missed having company at night. How much she missed having her old cat.

Okay, maybe it wasn't the kind of company she knew her mother wanted her to have at night, but it didn't matter. Al was hers to love and cherish, he was non-judgemental, and he just wanted to be loved and cherished in return.

He was also very demanding in his own little way.

"Just like a man," she murmured, giggling a little and giving him a kiss on top of his little head.

By the time she'd fed and settled him again and set the alarm, she was almost asleep herself. It seemed as though she'd just shut her eyes when the alarm sounded again.

Peeking wearily over the edge of the bed, she saw that Al was sleeping peacefully in his warm carrier. Remembering what Tim had said about lengthening the time to two hourly feeds as Al improved, she decided to set the alarm for another hour. Settling back, she only dozed, partly awake and listening for Al to cry.

When the alarm went off for the second time, Al was stirring. Going through the whole regime of feeding, toileting, cuddling and settling down, she set the alarm for another two hours time and Al slept right up until the alarm went off again.

Feeling a little brighter, Cindy kept the feeding regime to two hourly during the day, and seeing that Al was suffering no ill effects and was still content, she punched her fist in the air and did a silent jig of joy. Yes! Her baby was sleeping for two hours at a time, and so could she!

"Ah, the joys of motherhood," Sam said dryly, coming through the door to peek into the carrier on the kitchen bench.

"Sam, he's sleeping for two hours at a time." Grabbing an orange, Cindy sat down at the table and peeled it.

"What have I told you about putting the cat carrier on my bench?"

"Don't do it."

"So why is it on my bench?"

"Because I did it." Breaking the orange into pieces, she offered Sam a piece.

"You still look tired." He bit into it.

"I've gone from hourly to two hourly sleeps. It's a breakthrough."

"Huh. You could benefit from some more, though." Sam peeked into the basket, just able to see Al's tail sticking out from under the fluffy sheet. "Want me to baby sit this thing so you can get some more sleep?"

"Aw, you're so good to me." Cindy grinned, knowing full well he was fond of the kitten. "Don't you have stuff to do today?"

"I have stuff to do everyday. I can do it while keeping an eye on Al."

Hopping up, Cindy gave him a kiss on the cheek. "Thanks, Sam. You're the best."

"And don't you forget it."

"His bottles are soaking, there's a clean one in the cupboard along with a clean teat and his formula, and-"

"I know, I know." Sam flapped his hand at her. "Just go and get some sleep. You're looking scary with those dark circles under your eyes."

"Call me if there's a problem." Cindy took a last look at Al before leaving the kitchen.

Oh yeah, she was tired all right. Flopping face down on the bed, she fell asleep almost instantly and slept dreamlessly. When she finally awoke, it was six hours later and she rolled off the bed sluggishly.

"Sam?" she called down the stairs.

He stuck his head around the corner of the kitchen door. "What?"

"I've slept for ages."

"Really? I hadn't noticed."

"Ha ha. How's Al?"

"Your Mum came and took a shift with him and I tell you, she can't stop nursing the damned thing. Ruth fed him the second time, all cooing and clucking and being altogether soppy. Good thing I'm here to stop him being spoiled. I fed him the third time, no nonsense, and he settled down right away afterwards. He's still asleep and not due for a feed for another twenty minutes."

"Goodo. I've time for a shower then. Thanks Sam."

Taking her time in the shower, Cindy washed her hair and leaned against the wall, letting the water slip over her shoulders and down, washing away the fragrant soap suds.

She couldn't believe how content she felt knowing she was bringing up the orphaned kitten. Okay, it might be small and a lot of people did it, but it gave her a sense of fulfilment. Of purpose. Goodness knew, she hadn't had a real sense of purpose for a long time. Apart from working for the family business, of course.

By the time she'd dressed in a plain white t-shirt and a flowing skirt that reached her calves and had a split up each side to above her knees, she felt a lot more awake than she had for awhile. Almost bright-eyed and bushy-tailed, in fact.

Slipping on a pair of white, high-heeled sandals and a last spritz of perfume, she left her hair hanging loose and went down the stairs. By the time she got to the bottom, she heard Al meowing.

Sam was warming his bottle as she entered the kitchen.

"His Highness is awake," Sam told her needlessly.

"So I hear." Opening the top of the carrier, Cindy scooped Al out. "Hello, baby."

He bunted along her chin eagerly.

"As long as you don't start licking him, I can take the 'baby' crap." Sam handed her a warm, damp cloth.

Cindy laughed and started wiping Al. By the time she was ready to feed him, Sam was picking up his car keys and Ruth was waiting at the door.

"We'll see you tomorrow morning," Ruth said, her face softening slightly as she glanced at Al.

"No worries." Cindy smiled at them both. "Thank you for babysitting Al."

"No worries." Sam echoed her words as he went out the door and shut it behind him.

Within seconds she was alone with Al. When he finished his bottle, she picked up his carrier and took it into the lounge. Sitting in an armchair, she laid Al on her lap and gently rubbed his back with one finger and wiped him carefully with a clean, warm, damp cloth. Finished cleaning him, she picked him up and nuzzled him, delighting in the tiny, sputtering purr that came from his tiny body.

It wasn't long before Al started to fall asleep, and she carefully placed him back in his carrier on the fluffy sheet that lay over the heat pad, and covered him up a little with a piece of the sheet. With Al unable to sleep in a kitty pile for warmth, she had to ensure he stayed warm.

Placing him on the coffee table, she went back out into the kitchen, flicking on the radio as she did so. Finding nothing but sports on it, she slid in a CD and turned it up a little as the first song rocked out. It had her toes tapping. She did miss going out and dancing, but not as much as she'd have missed caring for Al. After all, she could dance as easily here as she could in a club.

Pouring a glass of berry juice, she did a few steps on the spot, then with a grin she spun on the spot and started to dance, pausing only now and then to sip from the glass.

With no one around to see her, she could do as she liked.

The song ended and another up-beat song started. Grabbing the broom in the corner, she held onto it as she shimmied and spun, using the broom as a substitute partner. It wasn't much, but who cared? She was having fun.

Downing the last of the juice, she spun, placed the glass on the sink and spun around again, only to shriek in shock as she found herself face to face with Tim.

He plucked the broom from her hand, slid one arm around her waist, took her other hand in his and pulled her in close. Arching his brow, he asked, "May I cut in?"

"Tim?" Her heart beat fast. "What are you doing here? How did you get in?"

"I knocked on the front door and when there was no answer, I came around the back." His eyes twinkled. "And what did I see? A luscious babe dancing all by herself. That's a crime."

The warmth of his body seeped through her t-shirt and she smiled up at him in amusement. "My hero, come to rescue poor little lonely me."

"A hero, that's me." And with that, Tim swept her into a fast moving dance that had her laughing.

He spun her around, snatched her close, spun her out again and danced with a dexterity to match her own. They moved fast to the beat, finding a natural rhythm in each other's movements that had them both breathless and laughing out loud.

Around the kitchen they went, moving close and apart, grabbing a hand, then releasing it, going through two more upbeat songs before a slow song started playing.

Tim drew her into his arms and she leaned against him as they both laughed and panted, catching their breaths even as they continued to move slowly around the kitchen.

"Great dancer," Cindy said.

"Great partner," he replied.

"Great music."

"Great day."

"It's not bad," she agreed, resting her cheek on his shoulder as they moved lazily around in circles. "Where did you learn to dance?"

"Let's just say mother didn't want me to embarrass her in front of her friends at parties."

"She isn't into boogying."

"Nope."

Closing her eyes, she relaxed against him.

They moved slowly and as her breathing evened out, she felt a slight change in the atmosphere, a sudden awareness of the man holding her, a realisation of whom she was resting against, and there was a definite hardening against her belly that made her eyes open.

That erection wasn't anything to do with her anatomy.

Lifting her head, she looked up to find Tim gazing down at her with hot intensity, the light brown of his eyes darkening with desire.

He stopped moving and her skirt swayed against their legs before growing still as they looked at each other.

"Tim," she began a little tremulously, unsure of what she was seeing, not quite able to believe that Tim Clarke, playboy vet, was actually attracted to her.

She just wasn't the sort of woman he pursued.

At least, that's what she'd thought before he started looking at her with desire in his eyes and absolute proof pressed against her belly.

A nervous lick of her lips had his gaze zeroing in on her mouth, and he lowered his head.

All Cindy could do was stare up at him as he came closer…and closer…and then he was there, his lashes sweeping down to cover the heat of his eyes, but there was no doubting the heat of his kiss.

He took her, plain and simple, his lips on hers, his tongue tracing the seam of her lips in an undeniable demand to allow him entrance.

All she could do was open to him, and immediately he dominated her, his tongue sweeping in to plunder the depths, his hands at her waist and shoulders holding her so close that they were pressed together from chest to knees.

And then just when she thought he couldn't be any more masterful, his hand at her shoulder tangled in her hair and he angled her head expertly, smoothly, firmly without hurting her, positioning her so he could take total advantage of her mouth.

He plundered her mouth like a pirate of old, taking over, complete control.

Making her knees so damned weak all she could do was grab onto his shirt and hold on.

Sweet God have mercy, she'd never been kissed like this before, and she'd had quite a few kisses in the past. But no man had ever taken such total control while ensuring she had as much pleasure as he was taking.

Tim did like kissing and he did it expertly, tasting her, licking deep, taking her essence without mercy and leaving her gasping for more.

She wasn't even aware that he'd backed her across the room until her bottom hit the table behind her. It partly brought her to her senses, but before she could get a grasp on her swimming senses, one of his hands was on her bottom, his palm spanning one buttock, and in several skilled moves, he had her skirt up around her waist and his palm sliding under the waistband of her panties. The calloused skin on his palm was flat against her derriere, and all she could do was press closer as his hand print seemed to burn into her suddenly highly sensitized flesh.

Her nipples pebbled, pressing against his chest, and she couldn't help but hook one leg around his, tilting her pelvis so that she could feel his hard thigh slide between her softer, rounder ones.

"Oh yeah, luscious babe," he murmured, rubbing his thigh against her intimate heat. "You feel so good."

Her blood seemed to bubble with erotic heat, burning through her and spreading a tingle from his palm on her bottom through to her feminine secrets. She could feel herself getting damp, invisible strings plucking deep inside her as his other hand released her hair and came around to cup her throat, his thumb under her chin tilting her head back as he released her mouth so that he could look down into her eyes.

Pure, unbridled passion darkened his cheeks, making his eyes glitter almost hedonistically, and in that second he had the stamp of a man determined to have the object of his desire.

Her.

Panting a little, she could only close her eyes in anticipation as he lowered his head again, his lips feathering lightly against the corner of her mouth, but when she turned her head, blindly seeking his mouth and its hot, damp secrets, he chuckled darkly and evaded her.

No sooner had she opened her eyes to moan her disappointment than she could only bite her lip as his mouth, that dark, magic, wicked mouth, found her pulse and pressed a kiss there before he laved it roughly with his tongue, working the skin, pressing the flat of his tongue against the pulse and whirling the roughness against her skin.

And then he fastened his mouth on her and sucked, shooting flames of liquid heat to the apex of her thighs.

With his mouth at her throat and his hard thigh pressed against her, all hardness against sensitivity, she could only press closer, trying to wriggle, and then she nearly exploded when his other hand slid beneath the waistband of her panties, unerringly gliding through the curls that protected her secrets and beyond, over her mound and down, those long, skilled fingers trailing a burning path between her sheltering labia and downward, ever downward, wickedly brushing her clitoris, pushing against it and making her arch up and whimper before they moved onward relentlessly, slipping through damp folds and further, further, and then he was there, one finger pushing at the entrance to her body before sliding unerringly into her sheath.

She nearly fell apart then and there. Her blood rushed through her, roaring in her ears, tingling with fire that licked through her body as he played her.

Dimly she felt him leave her throat and then his mouth claimed hers again. He took her mouth as his finger thrust deep and withdrew before pushing deep again. And then he turned his hand, hooking his finger and dragging backwards, and she almost exploded then and there.

Caught up in prurience, she dimly felt his finger leave her, and even as she whimpered her desperation she felt his hands at her waist, heard his voice hot at her ear giving instructions she couldn't remember but obeyed.

A little hop on her part, his hands at her waist lifting at the same time, and then she was sitting on the edge of the table. She didn't know where her panties had gone, all she knew was that Tim was between her spread thighs, his eyes hot as he looked down at her, and her arms were wrapped around his neck.

Taking something from his back pocket and tossing it onto the table beside her, he unzipped his jeans and pushed them down, his boxers following to bunch at his knees. Moving forward, he caught her mouth while taking her arms from his neck and positioning them back on the table, bending over her, crowding her backwards so that she rested on her elbows.

He pushed her t-shirt up, exposing her bra, and without pause he flicked the clasp open, pushing the white lace aside so that her breasts were freed. Without hesitation he moved downward, taking one nipple in deep and sucking firmly, making her tip her head back and gasp for air as that delicious heat surged through her again.

She couldn't think, couldn't manage anything except to feel him, his clean, male scent teasing her senses with every ragged breath she took, the calluses on his hands scraping languidly along her sides as he feasted on her breasts.

And sweet mercy, his hard thighs between her own, spreading her legs further apart, his hardness pressed between them.

Restlessly, caught up in carnal heat, she lifted her legs, rubbing her thighs against the outside of his, pressing herself unashamedly against him.

His mouth was on her stomach, his tongue dipping into her belly button, and she shuddered, flying higher.

As though sensing how close to the edge she was, Tim lifted his head, looking up the length of her body with hot eyes, and then he straightened, keeping one hand low on her belly as he did so. Reaching to the side, he picked up the object he'd tossed there earlier and brought it to his mouth, catching the edge of it between strong, white teeth and ripping it open. Taking the condom out, he rolled it over his shaft, and now she could see how thick he was, how long, and she wanted him in her - now.

"Stay there," he commanded huskily. "Right there." One hand on her belly, one encircling his shaft, guiding him as he looked down to watch.

Watched her as his shaft caressed her curls, saw her secrets as the thick head of his shaft parted her labia, pushing between the sensitive flesh to probe deeper. His cheeks were flushed with sexual heat, his eyes glittering as he looked up at her at the exact moment his shaft notched itself at the entrance to her body.

He caught her gaze, held it, demanded she look at him as she lounged wantonly back on her elbows, her body spread for his pleasure, waiting for him to bring her to the heights of ecstasy she had no doubt he would do.

"Cindy." Her name was a throaty growl in the air.

His hips flexed, drew back and then thrust forward, seating himself deep inside her, so deep that his groin was pressed against hers. He was so thick he had to push inside, and that made her shudder more as the muscles in her sheath spasmed and clamped tight around the invading shaft.

His groan was low and blissful, and he bowed down over her, pushing and pushing, his hands on the table at her sides before he shifted, pulling out and pushing back in, his movements hard and demanding.

It wasn't enough and she wriggled, wanting more, wanting it fast, wanting it hard, wanting him. "Tim," she moaned huskily, "Please."

Strong hands clamped onto her hips, fingers holding her tightly as he adjusted his stance, the movement with him still inside her making electric sparks shoot through her sheath and up into her lower abdomen.

Tim started to move, his hips thrusting powerfully, the muscles in his arms flexing as he gripped her, holding her for his pleasure and hers, working inside her in a single-minded determination to reach ecstasy.

Never having been taken in such a manner before, dominated, in fact, Cindy revelled in what he gave her, tremors inside her bubbling up to burst into erotic little volcanoes, sending her blood firing through her body, her very being straining upwards.

Lifting her legs, she gripped his hips with her thighs, and his pleasure was there to see plainly on his face, his eyes glittering, and then he moved suddenly, releasing her hips to come over her, his hands sliding beneath her back to lift her up into a sitting position.

He would have slid out of her with the sudden position change if he hadn't manoeuvred her so expertly, sliding her even closer so that they were belly to belly, his shaft able to thrust deep as she balanced on the edge of the table, having to rely solely on his strength to keep her in place.

The new position allowed him to take her mouth, and she couldn't help it, sinking back onto one hand and having him follow her, his growl of displeasure only heightening her own senses, especially when he nipped her throat in punishment, only to lave it roughly with his tongue seconds lately.

His hips pounded harder, deeper, dragging against her inner muscles which spasmed, seeking to hold on to him as he invaded her, plundering her body deeply and giving her such erotic pleasure she thought she'd surely explode with the concupiscence of it.

One hand at her bottom clutching her tightly, the other in her hair as he kissed her hard, both hands holding her to his satisfaction as he fed their combined desire, the strength in his lean body more than she'd realised, the feel of his muscles flexing against her only adding to the eroticism of the moment.

The desire welled up between them; she felt the tension coiling inside Tim's body as he thrust harder, pounding into her faster, hips moving powerfully. Her body responded, her inner muscles clamping down, trying to milk him as he pushed her higher up the pinnacle, and then he shifted the angle of his body, his shaft rubbing over something deep inside her, and she shattered almost immediately.

Every sensation she had welled up and burst forth, tossing her away in a splintering of fiery eroticism before rolling her under and back, only to throw her back out in another wild, fiery tide.

The last thing she heard before sweet, blessed, delicious oblivion took her, was her name shouted out and Tim's hips slamming against her, his stiffening, and the bite of his fingers on her bottom as he climaxed.

Floating down in euphoria, Cindy smiled against Tim's chest, her cheek pillowed on a surprisingly hard, yet comfortable pectoral muscle. She felt it flex under her cheek as he moved slightly.

Mmmm, well, this had been a day for surprises.

He shifted again and she felt his lips against her hair, nuzzling contentedly. Long fingers spread out on her bottom, the fingers of one hand grazing her bottom cleft.

Oh shit. Her eyes popped open. She was half naked, in Tim's arms, and he - what the hell had just happened?

Her relaxed stance of leaning against him with her arms looped loosely around his neck changed as she stiffened, her arms sliding down.

Oh shit. Oh shit shit *shit!* Oh, God, it had been - damned wonderful, in fact. More than that. He'd totally rocked her world.

Probably rocked her kitchen table, too. She couldn't stifle the sudden giggle that broke free.

In response, Tim shifted and the nuzzling in her hair stopped. Abruptly he straightened, his hand disappearing from her bottom like lightening.

He stepped back so fast that she almost fell off the table, mainly because it was only his body holding her balanced on it. Immediately he stepped forward again, cushioning her as she tipped over so that she landed hard against him. Only this time his arms didn't lovingly curve around her, instead, he gripped her upper arms firmly.

But definitely not a loving grip. Or a sexual one.

Looking up, she met his shuttered gaze, but his bemusement was plain to observe.

"Well." She finally broke the silence that grew between them. "If this is your idea of a house call, I must say, I'm impressed."

He pulled her off the table so fast her head swam. Grabbing the table behind her to steady herself, she watched as he pulled the used condom off and yanked his boxers and jeans back into place.

Pulling the zipper up, Tim glanced at her. "I'm sorry."

"What for?" She tugged her skirt down and it swirled around her knees.

"This." He gestured to the table behind her.

"Don't be." She smiled. "I'd be a hypocrite if I said I didn't enjoy it. And you didn't force me."

His gaze flicked over her, from the top of her mussed blonde hair, over her breasts which she was in the act of trying to get into her bra cups, down over her belly and lower, barely skimming her thighs before rising up again to study her face. "You're not the kind of girl I have sex with."

The words made her flinch, but she wasn't sure if he meant her type or girls her weight. "In what way do I not meet with your approval?"

Stepping back, Tim sighed and flicked his fingers at her. "It's not that, it's just…you. You're not the usual kind I have…intimate relations with."

"Intimate relations? That's rather cold."

"Sex is meant to be just physical gratification."

"I didn't gratify you?" A little angry now, not to mention hurt and, yes, a growing sense of embarrassment, Cindy snapped her bra closed and pulled her t-shirt down.

"Sure you did. It was…nice."

"Nice."

"Different. Yes, a different experience."

"Because I'm not the usual skinny girl you date."

"Yes."

Her eyes narrowed.

His widened a little as her meaning hit home. "I mean no!"

"Yes or no? Though I rather think the second answer might be closer to the truth."

"I mean…" She could just see the wheels turning frantically inside his head. "I mean, no, it's not because I date skinny girls. Slim girls. It's just I don't date your kind."

"That hole is getting deeper, arsehole. Keep digging and I'll cover it up with you in it."

Obviously trying to regain control of the situation, Tim placed his hands on his lean hips and stood straighter. "You're reading this the wrong way."

"Am I?" Placing her own hands on her ample hips, she glared at him.

"Definitely."

"Have you ever dated a big girl, Tim?"

His jaw worked a little. "Um…"

"Don't lie to me."

"Okay, no."

"So your normal type is slim."

"Don't forget rich and grasping."

"I'm rich."

"You're not grasping."

"So wouldn't that make me perfect for a quick shag?"

"No."

"Why not?"

Tim floundered for words, she could see his mind practically swelling under the strain of it. "You're a nice girl."

"You think?"

"I don't have sex with nice girls."

"Apparently you just did. But I was a mistake."

"That's right." He shut his eyes and pinched the bridge of his nose between thumb and forefinger. "I - Goddamn it, Cindy, stop twisting my words!"

"I'm a mistake, I'm a different experience, and I'm not your normal type, which happens to be rich, grasping and slim. Let's not forget the slim part." Marching across to the door, she swung it open. "Get out."

"Now, Cindy-"

"Don't make me grab your ear, Clarke, because I swear if I have to use it to drag you from my house, I will."

"Are you kidding?"

"My foot is about three seconds from launching with your arse as the mark. Want to know how much I'm kidding, wait around and find out." She could see the indecision on his face. "Or I'll call the cops."

Tim frowned.

"Your choice."

"Cindy, let's talk about this."

"Oh right, because you wouldn't talk about it with your *usual* type, would you? Take a hike, Clarke. *Now.*" When he hesitated, she marched across the room and picked up the phone, her finger hovering above the buttons. "I have the cops on speed dial."

Damn if he didn't call her bluff.

Stalking across the room, he grabbed the phone from her hand and placed it down on the hook with admirable restraint. Looking down at her, his eyes sparkling with fury, Tim opened his mouth to say something before thinking better of it and spinning around to stalk to the open door.

Standing there a moment, he was obviously thinking, but before he could say anything or turn back, she was right behind him. Placing a hand on his back, she gave one hard shove and pushed him out the door, slamming it behind him and flicking the lock.

Immediately he knocked on the door. "Cindy, open up."

She ignored him.

"This is ridiculous."

He had that right.

She stood by the door and waited. When silence greeted her, she looked out the window and saw no sign of him. Hurrying through into the lounge, she peeked through the curtains to see him getting into his car. Watching him drive away, she sagged in relief.

Relief and embarrassment. Stepping back from the curtain, she hugged her arms around herself. It had been a long time since she'd last allowed herself to feel embarrassed about her weight. Okay, she wasn't the ideal weight by society's standards, but she was healthy and happy, and she was a good person.

It seemed she didn't meet Tim's expectations, either. Okay, fair enough, she wasn't his usual type, but to class her as a different experience, that was too close to an old wound from an affair that had long ago healed. But his words threatened to rip a new hole in it.

Feeling that spiral of despair tugging at her, she sat down slowly in the armchair.

She'd only had sex a couple of times since that ill-fated affair, and that was when she went to Italy and a man she met there liked ladies both large and slim. He became a good friend and a casual lover, but she hadn't bothered to see him the last time she'd gone back to Italy for a holiday. Somehow, casual sex just didn't seem worth it.

Unlike Marty, who had to have sex at least four times a week or his dick, he said, would fall off from disuse. Personally, she thought it would fall off from an STD, but he laughed her remarks away.

This latest episode with Tim just went to show that casual sex, whether planned or unplanned, just wasn't worth it. Hell, she decided then and there that she wasn't having sex again unless it was with that one special man. Bugger these useless jerks and their egos.

At that moment Al woke up, his little meows filling the air as he lifted his head and sniffed for her, his little head turning to either side as he stretched up on his two little front legs.

Smiling, she opened the lid of the carrier and scooped him up. Bring him to the side of her face, she nuzzled him and was rewarded in turn with his little nose bunting along her cheek, his little purr sputtering to life.

"Forget that jerk," she told herself. "He's not worth it. If he can't see past my weight or imperfections, that's his loss, right Al?" A tiny paw tapped her cheek and she laughed. "Yeah, I don't need him. I've got you, and you're all the man I need in my life."

Getting up, she carried Al into the kitchen and started his feeding and toileting regime.

Yeah, she thought to herself. She'd long ago gotten over the embarrassment of her weight, life was too short to worry about the jerks that dotted the horizon. Not all men were like Tim, Rick and Mike were testament to that. Maybe one day a man like that would come into her life, but meanwhile she had a great life, good friends, a wonderful family, the good fortune to do pretty much as she pleased, and a good attitude. And Al.

That was all that mattered.

And she'd just had great sex. The day wasn't all bad.

She couldn't help but giggle at that last thought, but it wasn't her usual happy giggle. Okay, it was going to take a more than a few minutes to get over Tim's words, but get over it she would.

Damn it, she was worth it.

And really, did she want a relationship with an emotional retard like Tim? Not bloody likely. And why she'd even thought of Tim and a relationship in the first place was just weird.

Which just went to prove that sex messed with the brain cells.

~*~

That was the second time he'd been kicked out of a woman's house. Tim brooded as he drove to the clinic to check on the animals for the night. Unbelievable. Even more unbelievable, he'd had sex with Cindy Lawson.

Hot sex.

Hard sex.

Mind numbing sex.

Bloody shock to his system. How could he have made love - had sex - with Cindy Lawson? Worse, he'd gotten all tongue-tied when he'd realised what he'd done, she'd gotten defensive, things had gone to hell in a hand basket, and if Mike found out he'd nail Tim's nuts to the wall.

And he'd deserve it, too.

Jesus, making love to Cindy Lawson. Of all the wrong type of women to have unplanned sex with, it had to be her. A nice girl, sweet, a little odd at times, annoying at others, but a nice girl. Not to mention her big bosom, ample hips, long blonde hair, lush lips, soft thighs, a voluptuous bottom, sweet scent, and blue eyes that darkened with passion. Just the memory was enough to make his loins tighten.

But in true Tim fashion, he continued to torture himself with visions of making love with Cindy Lawson.

God, the woman had been *hot*. So responsive, so uninhibited it made him want to turn the car around and go right back for another bout of mind-blowing sex.

No, it didn't. Tim hit the steering wheel in frustration. It was a one-off. A mistake. He winced at that particular thought. So not a cool thing to say to a woman after you'd been inside- deep inside - her body. Her voluptuous, delicious body.

Not cool when he had the used condom mashed up in his pocket. Ick. But how could he possibly have disposed of it in a cool manner when she'd tossed him out? Where was the unshakeable, suave Tim Clarke, playboy vet, when she nearly had hysterics?

Turning into the parking bay, he stopped the car.

Okay, she hadn't been hysterical. She'd been mad. Furious, in fact, those lush lips pressed together, those blue eyes flashing with fury, that mouth-watering bosom rising up and down in righteous indignation.

Oh God, Cindy Lawson was hot.

Rubbing his forehead, Tim closed his eyes and took a deep breath. Cindy Lawson was off limits. *Stop thinking about her.*

Getting out of the car, he locked it and set the alarm, went into the clinic, turned the alarm off, fed, medicated and checked on patients, then went into the office. Grabbing an iced coffee from the' fridge, he sat down and swung his sneakered feet up onto a corner of the desk. Opening the carton, he drank half of it in several deep, long swallows.

He wondered if Cindy did oral sex. He wondered if she swallowed.

Choking at the thought, he coughed iced coffee all down the front of his t-shirt. Seriously, even when she wasn't around he got a hard-on and in trouble. Became a regular bloody butter-fingers.

Wiping his hands on the front of his t-shirt, he scowled. What he needed was to get a hard-hearted woman and boink her brains out.

However, just the thought of being intimate right after sharing that special, unplanned time with Cindy, seemed…disgusting. As disgusting as the used condom in his pocket.

With a shudder, he removed it, wrapped it in tissues and went out the back to throw it into the big bin. It slid out of sight beneath an assortment of paper and other paraphernalia.

Just as easily as he'd slid into Cindy's tight heat.

No no no! No more Cindy Lawson!

Storming inside, he scrubbed his hands, did a last check of the animals, set the alarm and locked up before going to his car. He was so frustrated that he accidentally set off his own car alarm when he tried to unlock and open it without turning off the alarm first.

Fumbling with the keys, he dropped them and watched them go under the car. Cursing beneath his breath, he dropped onto hands and knees and fished under the car. A press of the button and the annoyingly loud alarm peal was silenced. He heard another car pull up behind him and thinking it was a client, he straightened and tried to wipe the scowl off his face.

He obviously hadn't totally succeeded, because when he turned around it was to find a cop car right behind him and Mike regrading him steadily from the window. Alan, his partner, waved cheerfully from his seat beside him.

"Having a little trouble?" Mike rumbled.

"Not a good day."

"Going by your face, I'd guess not." Those cop eyes felt like they were drilling holes into his forehead. "Want to talk about it?"

"Seriously, what is with you and Rick and friggin' talking?"

Those pale blue eyes became even more intent. "What'd you do?"

"Me? What did *I* do?" Tim threw his hands out to the sides. "What makes you think I did anything?"

"I've known you a long time. You're rattled about something."

"I just want to go home and forget today ever happened. And no." Tim stabbed his finger towards Mike. "I don't want you to drop around and have a little heart-to-heart with me."

"Chick problems," Alan observed cheerfully. "I can tell."

"Yeah?" Mike's gaze never left Tim's face.

"Yeah. Only a chick can stir a man up like that." Alan nodded sagely. "Must be some chick."

"Jesus," said Tim.

"You will need His help if you continue like that."

"Thank you Dr Freud."

"Ooohhh, sexual reference." Alan nudged Mike. "Told you. Chick problems."

Shaking his head, Tim moved the key towards the lock.

"Uh-huh." Mike continued to study Tim. "Seen Cindy lately?"

A jerk of his hand and Tim missed the lock altogether, wincing as his key gouged a line in the metallic paint of his door. "Damn it!" What, did Mike have x-ray vision? See visions, in fact? See the past?

See the guilt stamped all over Tim's face?

Probably. Which was why Tim didn't turn to face his friend until he'd managed to don a blank façade.

Mike took one look at that façade and pointed at him. "We're having a talk later."

"What?" Tim watched as the cop car pulled away. "What for?"

Mike just looked back at him once and drove off.

Yeah, Tim's nuts were going to be nailed to the wall.

Unlocking the door, he dropped into his car, rammed the key into the ignition and started the engine. The powerful roar of the sports car didn't soothe his feelings and he'd have been tempted to irresponsibly burn a bit of rubber going out of the car park to relieve some of his tension, but Mike, damn his shrewd hide, had his cop car parked right at the entrance and was standing there with the radar gun aimed right at Tim.

Friends. Couldn't live with them, but sometimes he was damned sure he could live without them.

Having enough of everyone, Tim drove straight home. Entering his home, he took a deep breath of lemon-scented air and felt the peace settle into his very bones. Tension seeped from him and he relaxed.

Ahhhh, nothing like home sweet home.

Putting his dinner in the oven to heat up, he went upstairs and showered, donned clean boxers and padded downstairs again in bare feet.

Dishing up a heaping bowl of casserole, he went into the lounge and settled into his armchair. Flipping on the TV, he rested back into the chair and ate every delicious bite of food.

Now, this was the life. No damned women, no damned friends, no damned anything. Just him, the giggle box, food and an iced coffee.

This was just sad. This was what life had become, and there was one person to blame - Cindy Lawson, that voluptuous babe.

Sighing, Tim concentrated on the TV and ruthlessly pushed the irritating woman to the back of his mind. Within an hour he was asleep. An hour later he awoke with a hard-on and the memory of those luscious curves beneath his hands.

He had a bad feeling that dismissing Cindy wasn't going to be as easy as he'd determined.

That's what happened when you had sex with the nice girls. It messed with the brain cells.

~*~

The next morning, Tim buried himself in work. If there was one thing that could take his mind of any problems, it was the care of animals. He tended to the animals and the sometimes neurotic owners as well.

He was just coming around the corridor corner when he heard Cindy's name. It was spoken in a man's voice, and curiously he stopped and peered around the corner.

The blonde-haired man at the reception desk just had to be related to her. No one could miss the similarities - blonde hair, blue eyes, only his features were definitely masculine. Didn't Cindy have a couple of brothers? He'd heard about them at a party, and he was sure he'd seen this one with a giggling woman hanging off his arm. Two, in fact, one off each arm. The man was a regular lothario.

Today he was alone but he was doing a good job of chatting up the smiling vet nurse. Seriously, he actually made normally straight-laced Lara giggle and simper like some vapid miss of old. Tim supposed some women would find the Lawson man handsome.

Lara turned to take a receipt from the printer and saw him. "Tim, this is Marty, Cindy's brother."

Marty lothario Lawson.

Pasting a smile on his face, Tim came forward and offered his hand in a handshake. "I'm Tim, Cindy's vet." Wow, that rolled off his tongue so easily.

Marty took his hand and gave it a real man-to-man handshake. "Good to meet you, man. Cindy's told us a lot about you."

Uh-oh.

"She was so impressed with what you did for Al."

"Al?"

"Her kitten. That screaming little shit machine she's fallen in love with. I'm telling you, it's taken over her life. It's taking over everyone's life. Cindy hardly goes out, Mum's besotted with it, hell, even Dad was over there today baby-sitting it."

"Really?" Tim relaxed a little. Somehow he just knew that if Marty knew he'd had sex with his sister on her kitchen table and then upset her, he wouldn't have been so friendly. From what he remembered hearing, Cindy's family was close. If one family remember got hurt, the rest would come looking for whoever did it.

Handy to remember and a great help in his decision to stay well away from Cindy.

"Yeah. It's just what she needed, though."

"She told me her cat died."

"Man, she loved that old flea bag. Cried for a week when it died. Al is good for her." Marty reached out and picked up the kitten formula.

Tim couldn't fail to notice the rather dreamy smile Lara bestowed on Marty as she handed him the receipt. "Picking up the baby formula, huh?"

"Cindy asked me to. I thought she'd love to come in and give you all an update on her pride and joy, but I guess she's probably a little tired from feeding it night and day." Marty winked at Lara. "New baby and all."

Lara laughed.

"Anyway." Marty waved the can of formula at them. "Thanks for this. I'll let her know I met you, Tim. She'll be pleased."

Tim somehow doubted it, but he nodded and smiled and watched Marty leave the clinic. Going to the window, he saw him get into a fancy four wheel drive - looked like a Jeep or Land Rover or something - and talk to someone waiting in the passenger seat.

Tim's heart stuttered just a little. Was Cindy in the passenger seat? He waited with bated breath as the Jeep-Land Rover-whatever - backed out and turned, and he saw it was a cute little redhead who was chatting animatedly to Marty.

Tim sighed.

Lara sighed.

They both looked at each other.

"What are you sighing about?" Tim queried.

"I know what I'm sighing about, but I'm a little worried about what *you're* sighing at," she returned.

"Ha ha. I do not bat for the opposite team."

"Good. I don't need the competition."

"You don't have enough work to do."

"Says the man hanging out the window with me."

Shaking his head, Tim went back out to the treatment room to check on the surgical cases that had been operated on already.

The day passed busily and when knock-off time came, he was relieved to finally be on his way home.

He half expected Mike to be waiting for him but then realised that he was probably working a late shift again. His nuts were his own for another day, hallelujah.

Not feeling in the mood to go out, he showered and padded around in his usual dress of boxers and nothing else. Sitting down in his armchair, he thought he was getting to be a regular stay-at-home-old-fart. Sericusly, he had to start going out again. Being in every night just wasn't the thing to do.

Thank goodness tomorrow was Saturday and he had the whole day off. He could sleep in and later go out to the pub and see what women were on the prowl that might suit him for a - Tim groaned. *Saturday*. His Aunt's birthday at his mother's house. No clubbing, no pubbing, no boinking unless he picked up a shagger's delight at his Mother's party.

Oh joy. Way to spoil what should have been a perfectly good day.

The thought called for a beer.

Chapter Five

"Mads!" Cindy bounded up the steps. "I'm here!"

Opening the door, Maddy smiled. "No kidding?"

"Too true." Hearing the low music in the background, Cindy easily picked up the beat and danced past her best friend and into the house. "Good tune. Dance with me."

"I'm not a good dancer, you know that - oh!" Maddy gave a shriek as Cindy grabbed her hands and whirled her around.

It didn't take long for them to both bogey up the short corridor to the kitchen.

"I am so glad Mike didn't see that." Maddy laughed.

"He ought to take you dancing." Cindy tickled a wide-eyed Chaz under the chin, laughing as the big Siamese went all dreamy-eyed.

"Mike and dancing don't mix. The only dancing he likes is…" Maddy blushed.

"The horizontal tango?" Cindy winked. "Mads, you cheeky chit, you."

"Let's just say that he - let's just say nothing." Crossing to the sink, she filled the kettle. "How's the new baby?"

"Al is gorgeous. When are you coming to see him?"

"How about tomorrow afternoon? I can call in on my way home."

"Sounds like a plan."

Plugging in the kettle, Maddy glanced at her. "I hear Tim is your new vet."

"He did so well in getting Al through the first night, so as far as I'm concerned I'm happy to have him do me." Cindy blanched as Maddy's eyes widened. "I mean do Al. Look after Al."

Good grief. Cindy mentally rolled her eyes. Tim had already done her and look how that had turned out.

Taking a tin from an overhead cupboard, Maddy withdrew some home made biscuits and placed them on a small plate. "Don't you feel a little disloyal to your old vet?"

"I haven't thought about it." Leaning her chin on her hand, Cindy watched Yamaha, the grey kitten, come running through the door and skid to a halt just before she banged into Chaz. "Do you ever think about changing to Tim's clinic, him being Mike's best friend?"

"Nope. My vet has looked after Chaz since he was a kitten and I'm happy with her." Maddy placed the plate in the middle of the table.

"Huh."

"What?"

"I guess I just thought that Tim and Mike being best friends would influence your decision." Cindy nibbled thoughtfully on a biscuit.

Maddy shook her head. "Nope. Mike knew Tim long before I did, and I knew my vet long before I knew Tim."

Cindy nodded. "Fair enough." She watched Maddy get a pot of tea ready. "So, where's Mike? Working?"

"Yep, late shift."

"Good thing you understand shift work."

"Trust me, after working in a hospital as a nurse, shift work becomes a part of your life."

"Glad you're not doing it anymore?"

Maddy smiled. "I like working for the Gold Link Nursing Association. Attending to people in their homes gives you a whole new understanding of them."

"Probably why you can handle Mike." Cindy grinned.

"And probably why I can handle being around you." Maddy poured the tea.

"Uncalled for. We met in primary school."

"Even then, I was able to handle the weird ones."

"That's just lovely." Cindy accepted the cup of tea. "Touches my heart, that does."

"The tea?"

"No, you dork. You calling me weird."

Maddy looked pointedly at the tube top Cindy wore.

"This is classy." Cindy preened.

"In what universe?"

"Mine."

"It must be nice in your own little universe."

"It's great, you should try it sometime."

Maddy laughed, then sobered. "Seriously, you are so at ease with who you are. I used to envy you that when we were teenagers."

"Maddy," Cindy replied seriously, "You chose early on in life to do what you wanted as well."

"Yeah, but I was never as free as you."

"Hey, in what way?" Cindy winked. "Sex?"

"Please, if you're going to start telling me about that Italian bloke who thought you were God's gift to men, I don't want to hear about it."

"Oh, come on. You're just jealous."

"Me?" Maddy's eyes softened. "I have Mike."

And there it was, Cindy thought, observing her friend. Maddy, so self-assured, yet she'd just blossomed completely under Mike's love. The only time she'd known her friend to retreat into her weight worries was after her wretched family had thrown a spanner in the works, but Mike had ripped that spanner right out and now her best friend was the happiest she'd ever been in her life.

"If you're going to start sharing tales of Mike's prowess in the bed-"

Maddy's eyes twinkled. "Who said it was just in the bed?"

Cindy perked up. "Really? Do tell."

"Don't tell." Maddy's round cheeks were flushed. "That's between me and Mike."

"Oh, come on. I'm your best friend. Besides, you can't just throw out that tid-bit and expect me stay quiet."

"Cindy, I bet you've had sex in other places apart from a bed."

Most recently, on the kitchen table. "We're not talking about me."

"And I'm not talking about my sex life."

"Huh." Picking up the cup of tea, Cindy blew lightly upon the hot surface. "Spoilsport."

Smiling, Maddy nibbled on a biscuit. "So, Al. Cute name. Bet he's going to be a right little scrapper with a name like that."

"It's been awesome looking after him." Cindy yawned. "Tiring, but awesome."

"Oh, poor little mummy." Reaching over, Maddy patted her hand. "But you have such a glow!"

"Shut up." Cindy laughed.

"Seriously." Maddy settled back in the chair. "You're normally so outgoing, out to parties and clubs, yet here you are, all content to stay at home and care for this furry orphan. I'd never have thought it of you."

"He depends on me." Cindy shrugged. "What can I say? Once he's older, I'll be able to go out again. Meanwhile, I'm a stay-at-home mum."

"Cute."

Thoughtfully, Cindy took a sip of tea. "I've been thinking-"

"Oh geez."

Cindy kicked out at her friend lightly under the table but Maddy, knowing her too well, already had her shins out of range.

"As I was saying," Cindy said a little haughtily, "Before you so rudely interrupted..."

"Sorry. Do go on."

"As I was saying, I've been thinking..." Cindy gave her friend a hard stare, only to get an innocent look back. "I have a big home, plenty of room outside, and there are a lot of orphan animals out there. Maybe I'll consider becoming a foster carer."

"What?" Maddy blinked in surprise. "Really? You?"

"Sure. Why not me?"

"Well, you love to travel and party and things. Having orphaned animals to look after can take a lot of time up."

"I won't have orphaned animals all the time. Kittens tend to be seasonal."

"You're only looking at fostering kittens?"

"And cats. Mads, I love all animals, you know that, but cats are my thing, and so many kittens and cats get euthanased every year. If I could foster some now and again, it would give them a chance."

"You're building a cattery?" Maddy's eyes were wide.

"No, you wally. To foster them, I'd have them in the home. They need to be used to living indoors amongst people, handled regularly, shown love. That way, when they go to their new homes, they're used to all of that. And, of course, the kittens might need to be hand-reared."

"So where are these orphans and strays coming from?"

"The vets. They get them in almost every day during kitten season."

"Wow, that's a lot of work."

"Sure. But I'm not silly. I'm not taking in ten cats and kittens at a time. Just a litter of kittens if needed, and their Mum if she's with them, or a couple of adult cats here and there. I can't risk becoming over-run with them and not able to get homes, I'll only take what I can handle, and won't take on more until what I have are re-homed."

Maddy looked at her admiringly. "You've really thought about this."

"I did some research on-line, as well as visited the RSPCA shelter and animal havens. There's a real need for foster homes and education. I'm not too good at talking to people, but you know, looking after Al has made me realise just how much I love it. Caring for something."

"You're going to re-home Al later?"

"What? No! Al is mine."

"You've got a soft heart, Cindy. You'll cry when the kittens and cats you foster go to new homes," Maddy pointed out practically.

"Don't I know it. But if it gives a couple of our feline friends a chance, isn't it worth a few tears?"

"It is." Maddy shook her head. "Wow, Cindy the party-girl becomes Cindy the feline foster mum. Who would ever have guessed? But, honey, what about your work in the family?"

Cindy smiled. "Thanks to the wily minds of my Dad and Mum, all our monies are invested wisely. I already work for the family business mostly from home anyway. That's what computers are for."

"Well, yes but-"

"Mads, it's not like I'll never travel again, or never leave the house for a party or a few hours at a club. I can still have fun, still work, but I'm fortunate enough to be able to work around whatever needs the feline foster kids have." Cindy's smile widened. "I'll be doing something worthwhile, apart from helping fill the family coffers. Plus I know a lot people and contacts are a good thing to have when it comes to homeless animals."

Maddy nodded. "I know a lot of people from work, too, both workmates and clients. I can make some contacts for you and keep my ears open for anyone wanting a cat or kitten."

"You're a pal."

"What are friends for?" Maddy gently nudged Yamaha with her foot as she slid around Maddy's chair looking for a piece of biscuit. "After all, they're worth it."

"Yeah." Cindy looked down at Yamaha. "Still sleeping on Mike's pillow?"

"Yes, and we never discuss it."

"Of course not. Mike's such a big, tough man. He's not a push-over for an itty, bitty kitty."

They both laughed.

Leaving Maddy's house, Cindy felt a lot better than she had since her encounter with Tim, and she drove home to feed Al and spend some time with him before she got ready for the party that night.

Entering the kitchen through the door connected to the garage, she was amused to see Sam holding Al in one hand and cooing to him, while holding his bottle steady with the other hand. As soon as he saw Cindy, he frowned and stopped cooing.

"Spoiled," he announced. "This kitten is becoming spoiled."

"Really?" she returned dryly.

Ruth looked up from the stool she was perched on, a gardening magazine before her. She rolled her eyes before looking back down at the magazine.

"Ruth has been treating it like a human baby."

"There's not a whole lot of difference, you know. They both drink, poop, wee, cry and sleep."

"Humph. Anyway, I'm glad you're back to take over this thing."

She noticed that he kept hold of Al, cradling him against his chest while the kitten sucked on the bottle. "Anytime soon, you think?"

Ruth snickered.

Sam scowled at her before switching the same scowl to Cindy. "You can't just toss Al around from person to person while he's drinking. You'll give him gas."

"Then we can add farting to his repertoire as well." Grinning hugely, Cindy walked past him to sit at the counter opposite Ruth. "What are you going to do on your days off without Al?"

"Have a rest. My job description doesn't include cat-sitting." The way Sam's thumb gently rubbed Al's side as he spoke was a direct contradiction to his words.

Ruth winked at Cindy.

"I am forever in your debt for taking on such a horrendous chore," Cindy told him gravely.

"And don't you forget it." Sam looked down at Al as the kitten released the teat. When the kitten refused to take it anymore, he set

105

the bottle down on the counter and cradled the kitten in his big, work-roughed hand, one finger gently rubbing the tiny back.

"Burping him?" Cindy queried.

Sam cast her a narrow-eyed look.

"Or not." Cindy looked at Ruth. "How's the gardening going? Anything we need?"

Ruth closed the magazine. "I've sprayed the roses for aphids. This heat is burning the leaves, but I think they'll be fine. The rest of the garden is good."

"Okay." Knowing that Ruth was more than content to take care of the garden and tell her when they needed anything, Cindy was happy with the report. "Got plans for tomorrow?"

"Seeing the grandkids," Ruth replied. "They're coming over for lunch."

"Messy and noisy as usual," Sam grumped.

Knowing perfectly well how much he looked forward to the visits from his grandchildren, Cindy sighed. "It's a harsh life, Sam, gotta take the good with the bad."

"Yeah, well, someone's got to make sure those kids get brought up right."

Ruth rolled her eyes again.

Sam placed Al in his carrier and tucked him in, his sharp gaze switching to Cindy in warning.

Miming zipping her mouth closed, she locked the imaginary lock and tossed the imaginary key away.

Getting off the stool, Ruth rolled up the magazine and tucked it into the back pocket of her old work pants. Sam gathered his car keys and wallet from the drawer that he and Ruth used for themselves and after bidding Cindy and Al goodnight, they headed out to their car.

Smiling, Cindy picked up Al's carrier and took it upstairs with her, placing it on the floor beside the bed while she went to the shower.

Afterwards, clad only in bra, panties, and a thin pink dressing gown which reached mid-thigh and was almost transparent, Cindy slipped on the kitten-heeled slippers and went downstairs for a drink. Choosing a snack of biscuits and dip, she went back upstairs to sit in the deep armchair that stood in a small alcove off her bedroom. Switching on the TV before it, she leaned back and lifted her legs to rest on the footstool. Placing the saucer of biscuits on a little table beside the chair, she took a sip of the drink and sighed in contentment.

This was the life.

Everyone thought they knew her so well. Cindy the party girl. Cindy who lived fast, played hard, and was a good-time girl. She wondered what they'd think if they knew that sometimes, when she was supposedly out partying, she was actually tucked up here in her little alcove, enjoying some peace and quiet.

Yeah, she loved to party, loved to dance, but she loved time alone as well. Time to reflect on her life, her day, to just sit and enjoy some alone time.

It had been during this time alone, nursing Al, that she'd come up with the idea of being a foster home for cats and kittens. It was up here that she'd phoned her old vet clinic and had a word to the staff there, and then phoned Lara at Tim's clinic and spoken to her. Then she'd phoned up the RSPCA and the cat havens and spoken to them. There was a huge need for foster homes. Good, reliable foster homes.

Choosing to be a private foster home, doing it on her own initiative, Cindy had spoken again to Lara and her old vet and had decided that in a couple of weeks, when Al was old enough, she'd take in the next cat or kitten that needed fostering. Maybe later she'd extend to the RSPCA and the cat havens, but for now she'd start small.

Stretching luxuriously, Cindy glanced at the clock and sighed. Time to get ready. More than comfortable, she'd have been happy to stay in her little alcove, but she'd accepted the invitation awhile ago and one thing she did take seriously was keeping her word.

Besides, she hadn't been out for at least a week.

"Poor, deprived me," she informed a sleeping Al with a grin.

Dressing in a long, flowing, sleeveless, dark red gown with gold threads at the cleavage and shot through the skirt, she nodded her satisfaction. It framed her bosom, flowed inward at the waist and then draped over her hips to shimmer down to the floor.

To complement the gown, she slid on gold stilettos, fastened a gold chain with a ruby tear-drop on it around her throat, snapped on a matching cuff around her wrist studded with rubies, and picked up a gold clutch.

A last inspection of her hair, which she'd left loose, and she decided that she'd fasten back the side pieces after all. Several minuets later, she nodded in satisfaction and picked up Al's carrier.

Downstairs she got his bag ready, putting into it his clean bottle, teat, formula and a clean, soft cloth.

The doorbell played its merry tune and picking up the bag and carrier as well as her clutch, she strode through and opened the front door.

"Hey." Marty peered at the carrier. "Al's going to the party? Isn't he a little young to drink?"

"No. I can't trust him to hold his liquor," Cindy replied. "He's going to a baby-sitter."

Marty perked up. "Baby-sitter as in female baby-sitter?"

"Female as in Lara, the vet nurse."

"Lara." He pursed his lips, thinking, and then his eyes brightened. "Oh yeah, cute little vet nurse at that playboy vet's clinic."

Playboy vet was right. "That'd be the one."

"Tim. Met him there when I picked up Al's formula." Marty opened the taxi door for her and took the carrier while she sat inside. Handing it back to her, he added, "Lara is cute. Wonder if she's single?"

"I don't think she has a death wish, so it might pay you to stay away from her."

"Every woman likes a little danger in her life." Closing the door, he went around the other side and slid in. "And I'm that little bit of danger." He winked at her. "In fact, I'm a whole lotta danger, but I promise to just give her a taste. Maybe."

"That makes me feel so much better."

The taxi driver glanced at Marty in the rear-view mirror but kept his thoughts to himself.

Cindy gave him Lara's address and settled back in the seat.

Marty proceeded to fill her in on what he'd been discussing with their father for future plans for the Bellacross Restaurant they all held equal shares in, and they threw ideas back and forth, arguing and agreeing until the taxi drew to a stop in front of Lara's house.

Cindy speared her brother with a narrow-eyed look. "Stay."

"I'm hurt." Marty placed one hand on his chest. "What if you get attacked between the gate and her front door? How can I protect you?"

"You're the only danger around here, remember?"

"I'm hurt."

Getting out of the taxi, Cindy took the bag and Al's carrier up the garden path to the front door. Knocking on it, she waited.

It opened within seconds and Lara smiled out at her. "Hi, Cindy. Wow, you look great."

"Thanks. And thanks for agreeing to baby-sit Al." Cindy held out the carrier. "I'd have gotten Maddy to baby-sit him, but she has to get up early for work and my family are at this party."

"No problem." Lara took the carrier carefully as well as the bag. "He won't be the first kitten I've bottle-fed, and he won't be the last."

"I promise to be back by midnight." She looked wistfully at the carrier. "This is the first time Al has left home since I got him."

"He'll be fine," Lara assured her. "I'm staying up watching movies and he can snooze beside me on the sofa."

"Thanks again. If there's anything I can do in return, let me know."

"Hey, you're offering to help us with our abandoned kittens and cats, least I can do is help you out." Lara grinned. "Plus, I'm dying to see how much Al has grown."

Cindy took a step back. "You have my phone number."

"On the pad by the phone." Lara's eyes twinkled.

109

"If he needs me-"

"I'll ring straight away."

"If you think he looks a little peaky-"

"Don't worry, I have some training." Lara laughed and flapped her hand at Cindy. "Go. He'll be fine. I'll see you in about four hours."

Cripes, who'd have thought the little fur ball would have crawled so thoroughly into her heart already?

Cindy sat back down in the taxi and Martin looked at her as the taxi pulled out onto the road. "You all right?"

"Fine." She cleared her throat. "Lara's a vet nurse. Al is in good hands."

"That's right. Now, did you notice if she had a man in her house?"

"Marty, I was only at the front door."

"Did you look over her shoulder?"

"You are such a hound dog."

"Woof woof."

Cindy punched him in the arm.

"I'm telling Mum," he said.

"Tell-tale-tit."

He laughed.

Eventually the taxi pulled up in front of the mansion belonging to Dr Margaret Clarke. Marty held the door open for Cindy and she walked beside him up the marble steps.

Lights spilled from the windows and music filled the air. Sophisticated music, subtle orchestra. Men and women dressed in clothes that clearly cost a lot of money entered ahead and behind them.

"Wow. Dr Clarke still has her hooks into Martin Shaw, poor bastard." Marty looked across to where Dr Margaret Clarke stood greeting the guests with a neatly dressed man by her side.

"Maybe he's here for keeps?" Cindy smiled at a woman who passed nearby, her expensive perfume thick in the air. "Hi, Maryanne."

"Cindy." She beamed at them, and then her smile dimmed as she saw Marty. "Martin."

"Maryanne." Marty smiled widely. "Looking good, sweetheart."

Her gaze turned sour and she walked off.

"Oh, well done," Cindy said. "Another conquest of yours that bit the dust?"

"Her choice, not mine."

"Because you're such a hound dog. Did you cheat on her?"

"Nah. She was just too snooty for my tastes." Marty steered her over to where Dr Clarke stood. "You're looking hot, Dr Clarke, as always."

Margaret Clarke's cold gaze swept over him. "Martin."

"Thanks for inviting us." He held his hand out to Martin Shaw. "Same name as me, eh? Dr Clarke does love her Martins."

Martin Shaw shook his hand with polite amusement.

Dr Clarke looked at Cindy, her gaze assessing her clothes. "Cindy, glad you could come." There was a touch of frost to her tone, and a glint in her eyes that was a clear indication that she didn't think it was appropriate for Cindy to wear such a tight-fitted bodice that showed off her ample bosom.

Cindy smiled widely. "Dr Clarke, a pleasure to be here. Place looks lovely as always."

The almost-smile Dr Clarke bestowed upon her was as much approval as she'd ever show anyone.

"So, where's the birthday girl?" Marty inquired.

"Right here," a new voice replied.

Turning, Cindy saw Dr Clarke's sister-in-law, Hannah Harding, approach in a cloud of chiffon and perfume.

"Marty, Cindy, so glad you could both come." She enveloped them in a shared hug before gesturing to another door. "Eat, drink, and be merry."

"You may place your gift upon the table to the side of the room," Dr Clarke instructed.

"Nah," Marty replied. "We'd rather give it now." And so saying, he whipped a small wrapped box from his pocket and grabbed Hannah around the waist, dipped her into a laughing and shrieking bend backwards, gave her a smacking kiss on the lips and straightened her up again, steadying her with his hands until she got her balance.

Hannah giggled in delight, cheeks flushed as she patted her white hair and pulled her dress a little straighter.

Dr Clarke's eyes went a little colder and Cindy nudged her brother in the ribs with her elbow. "Come on, lover boy."

"Save a dance for me," Marty told Hannah before taking Cindy's elbow and hustling her through into the big ballroom. "Now where's the food? The drink? The tarty babes?"

"The decorum?"

"Where's the fun in that?"

"Trust me," said a deep voice behind them, "There's no fun if you upset your mother."

They both turned around to face the tall, thin, slightly stooped man standing behind them, his lined face kind, his brown eyes shrewd, and his short blonde hair liberally touched with grey.

"Hi, Dad." Cindy went up on tip toe to kiss him on the cheek.

"Sweetheart, you look amazing." Mr Lawson turned his gaze to his son. "And you look good, too."

"Thanks."

"But as wild as ever."

"I'm the picture of a sophisticated man."

"And I'm a dumb blonde."

"I don't dare answer that."

"Wise move." Taking Cindy's arm, Mr Lawson ushered her across the large ballroom. "Your mother is over here."

Marty obediently followed. All the Lawson siblings knew not to scatter and find their own amusement at parties until they'd greeted their parents.

Stopping just behind four women chatting to each other, Mr Lawson waited politely.

The tallest and plumpest of the women glanced up, her blue eyes brightening upon seeing Marty and Cindy. "Darlings!"

Immediately she enveloped them in smothering hugs, her impressive bosoms mashing against them. Expensive perfume filled the air and her many bracelets clinked together.

Holding Cindy's arms, she stepped back and looked her over. "Marvellous gown, darling. Loving the accessories. What do you think of these?" Lifting the skirt of her black gown, she showed trim ankles clad in outrageous platform sandals.

"Oh, very nice." Very girly, too, perhaps a little too girly for an older woman, but then again, who cared? Cindy grinned. "What about these?" Lifting the hem of her gown, she waved one gold-sandalled shoe at her mother.

"Adorable! I want some. Where did you get them?"

"Cabornas."

"I have to go there. Marty, dear boy, you look positively handsome."

"Thanks, Mum."

"Please try to control your lustful urges while here. I swear, one day you'll get us all tossed out on our ears."

"Not with our money." He leered at a young woman passing nearby, delighting in her flush and bright eyes. "Grease enough palms and we'll slide through anything." His glance slid around the room. "Where's Alex?"

"Your brother is somewhere over there." Mrs Lawson waved in the direction of the tables holding food. "Avoiding the women and wanting to go home. He only came because I nagged him."

Cindy sighed. "Mum, he only just got home on leave from his tour of duty in Afghanistan. Maybe he wanted to stay home."

"He needs to get out, forget about that wretched war for awhile and enjoy himself. See if you can talk some sense into him." Mrs Lawson stopped a passing waiter and placed her empty glass on the tray. "Could I have a glass of orange juice, please?"

The waiter gave her an almost shocked look.

"If I get tipsy, I also get a little handy." She traced one hand down her husband's arm and winked at the startled waiter. "If you know what I mean."

"We save the tipsy for when we get home," Mr Lawson added gravely.

The waiter nodded his head and took off.

Cindy couldn't blame him. "Ewww. Please."

"Honey, where do you think you came from?" Mrs Lawson purred.

"Let's not even go there."

Her parents laughed before Mrs Lawson looked down at Cindy from her impressive height. "And who is looking after my furry grandchild tonight?"

"Al's in good hands, Lara is a vet nurse." Cindy took a glass of champagne from a tray held out by a waiter. "Thank you." She couldn't resist winking at the straight-laced man and he actually blinked before grinning just a little.

"Well, there're lots of people we know here," Mrs Lawson continued. "Mingle and have fun, darlings."

One of the first things Cindy did was go in search of her other brother. Going around the room, she followed the wall until she came to the tables loaded down with delicious nibbles. He wasn't there but she did see a tall, familiar, blonde-haired figure leave the presence of a couple of eager women and disappear through a French door.

Yep. Alex.

Heaping up a plateful, she grabbed a tray off a waiter, loaded it with the plate and a couple of glasses of orange juice that another waiter had thoughtfully placed on the table, and skirted around the room until she came to the French doors.

Slipping out, she carefully closed it behind her and spoke to the still figure standing near the marble rail. "Want some company?"

"Cindy?"

"Well, it's not the model for Jenny Craig," she replied, placing the tray down on the little table to the side and kicking out a chair. "Rest your arse, soldier, and be at ease."

Alex laughed a little and sat. Eyeing the plate, he raised one brow. "For me?"

"*Us*, greedy guts. It's for us."

Plucking a prawn from the little pile, he dipped it in the tiny bowl of sauce and popped it into his mouth. "Mmm. Good."

"What, they don't give you this on the road?" she teased.

"No, so I'll probably get the shits for eating it now." Picking up the orange juice, he took a sip and grimaced. "What? No beer?"

"Hey, be grateful for what you get."

They ate in contended silence for several minutes. Cindy didn't ask questions, she didn't push, she just let things happen as they would. One thing she'd learned early on was that Alex was a thinker and when he wanted to talk, he'd talk. Until then, no amount of urging would get him to say a word about his experiences.

Not once did he mention Afghanistan or the war, and she let it go. After a few minutes, she chatted about Al and her plans for fostering.

"Nice," he said. "Good plan. You'll do well."

"Really?" She was surprised and pleased. "You think so?"

"Absolutely." In the light coming from between the curtains behind the closed doors, his face was serious. "I can see you with a gaggle of kittens hanging off your apron strings - mummy-cat."

"You dick." She launched a dinner roll at him, which he caught with a laugh that sounded a little lighter than earlier.

She bit into a piece of pastry. "I saw you dodging the women panting after you."

"Yeah. None of them…" Voice trailing away, he shrugged. "Not interested in them, I guess."

"Hmm. And to think you were once as girl-crazy as Marty."

"Untrue. Marty was always the wildest."

"The horniest," she corrected.

He grinned, his teeth a white flash in the darkness. "Not you?"

"Let's just say my experiences so far haven't been that great."

"How about that Italian bloke?"

"Nah. No magic there."

"Look at us, we'll end up two unmarried, bitter old siblings, sharing a house and screeching at each other to be heard through our hearing aids."

"Overrun with cats," she added.

"Could be worse," he said. Reaching over, he patted her hand. "Could be worse."

Catching a reflection of something in his eyes, Cindy's heart did a little flip. She just knew he was speaking about something else, but even as she ached to ask him what had happened in the war, she did what she knew would comfort him. Turning her hand over, she gave his a little squeeze of understanding and acceptance, and immediately he relaxed back in the chair.

"Thanks," he said softly.

"Don't mention it."

The French doors opened a few minutes later and Marty stuck his head out. "Good grief. Holed up out here in the dark. Come on, Alex, I've got someone I want you to meet."

"Do I have to?" Alex sounded pained.

"Of course. I've kept the very best for you, you ungrateful sod. Cindy, if you don't get your arse inside soon, Mum will come out here and drag you inside. Mingle, girl, mingle!"

"We should have locked the door." Alex stood.

"Duty calls." Cindy started to pick up the tray, only to straighten when Alex took it instead.

"Ever the gentleman," Marty observed.

"More than you'll ever be, anyway." Alex shouldered him aside.

Marty retaliated, shoving him back, and they both ended up in a shoving match that had them spilling into the ballroom, by some miracle Alex retaining his hold on the tray without tipping anything off, and Marty without falling to his knees.

Grinning, Cindy followed them inside, only to catch sight of both her parents giving the siblings the eagle eye from right across the room. Changing her tactics, Cindy shook her head sorrowfully and pointed at her brothers ahead of her.

"I know what you're doing," Alex informed her without turning his head.

"Don't."

"There's a mirror across the room."

"Be sure your evil deeds will find you out." Marty smirked.

"I can't give it to you in public, but inside my mind I'm flipping you both the bird," she retorted.

Alex laughed.

Marty steered him away and Cindy wandered around, greeting several people she knew and stopping to chat now and again. She was pleased when she spotted Sharon DeLamer, who saw her and waved gaily before swaying across the short distance separating them. Her gown clung to a figure that made many men's mouths water, including Marty, who, Cindy noticed, was in the act of heading for the other side of the room but did a u-turn and headed straight towards them.

"Danger coming," Cindy warned Sharon.

Sharon took a look over her shoulder and arched one brow. "That man will come undone one day."

"Marty has a death wish," Cindy agreed.

Marty arrived and proceeded to try and chat up Sharon, but having gone out with him once she firmly put him in his place and with a resigned sigh, Marty headed off to find more forgiving prey.

Sharon introduced her to several people that she knew, and Cindy chatted, drank a little champagne, and eventually found herself sitting on a bench near a potted plant with a middle-aged man who was making nice with conversation, but lustful with his gaze drifting down to her cleavage every couple of seconds.

No doubt he thought he had a chance with her. She finally gave him a firm 'no' to his advances, threatened to name and shame him to his wife and Dr Clarke, and watched in satisfaction as he left, his back stiff and his cheeks flushed.

"Done with style," drawled a well-known voice behind her, one that infused a shiver of warmth right down her spine. Taking a deep breath, she looked up as Tim stepped into view from behind the potted plant.

And immediately she burst out laughing.

He arched one brow inquiringly. "Care to share the joke?"

"Your shirt."

"Oh." Tim smoothed his hand down over the t-shirt he wore beneath an open dinner jacket. On it was written *Hot for sex? Come and get burned, baby, burned!* "You like it?"

"Better than your mother does, I'm sure."

"You should have seen her eyes when she saw it. She loved it, only she doesn't like to show it."

"Riiiight."

"So." Tim nodded in the direction in which Cindy's unwanted suitor had disappeared. "Not wanting lover boy?"

"Let's just say we had different plans for the evening."

"Oh?"

"Yep. He wanted a piece of me, I wanted a piece of anything else."

Amused, Tim grinned.

That grin, that roguish, yet understanding turn of his lips, made that warmth shiver through her again.

Ye gods, what was wrong with her? Just looking at him, tall and lean, knowing the strength hidden beneath that smart dinner jacket, it brought back the memory of that strength, those arms, those hands, that wicked mouth…that hedonistic knowledge that - She looked away, moistening her lips. *Stop it. You're not his type, remember? Act normal.*

Act normal while she still had his fingerprints embedded in her bottom cheeks, his grip had been that hard.

Tim made to move away and she breathed an inward sigh of relief, only to have him sigh in turn, only out loud. He surprised her by sitting down on the bench right beside her. There wasn't much room, so unless she wanted to pointedly get up and walk away, she could do nothing but sit right beside him and watch the dancers.

Dancers. Oh boy. That's how their intimate encounter had started. Dancing.

"Cindy," Tim began, then, "Shit."

"Oh, nice place to put my name, right beside that swear word." She concentrated on getting her pulse to slow down.

Since when had she had a heart problem? Since Tim, obviously, going by the pulse that continued to leap a little at his closeness. He smelled clean, his cologne subtle yet distinctly male, drifting through her senses…just like it had that day he'd taken her on the table.

"Sorry. I didn't mean to." Leaning his elbows on his knees, Tim linked his hands together and dangled them between his knees as he also kept his gaze on the dancers.

Searching for something - anything - to say, Cindy said, "I guess Hannah being your Aunt gives you automatic invite?"

"If you mean the summons from Hell, yes."

"Huh. I'd heard you didn't get along with your Mum." She slanted a sideways look at him, studying his profile. "Seen it too, in fact."

"From her other parties." Tim nodded. "I've seen you at them."

"From a distance."

"Yes."

"Because I'm not your type." Now why had she said *that*?

"Precisely." Turning his head, he looked her directly in the eyes. "I need to apologise for the other day."

"Because it worked so well then."

"I can be a klutz when it comes to words."

"Really? I heard you can be a charmer - to the right kind of girl." Holy heck, where were these words coming from?

"You're still mad."

"Whatever gave you that idea?"

"Your eyes are positively sparkling with fury." His gaze wandered over her face. "Your lips are also pressed tightly together."

Consciously, she sought to relax her features. "Better?"

"I'm not sure. You did that so skilfully, it's scary. Reminds me of my mother."

"Oh, because that sentence is going to make me forgive you."

His eyes narrowed a little as he continued to regard her steadily.

Cindy eyed him right back because, hell yes, she was still mad at him. She'd thought she'd dismissed him so easily and look at that, turned out she'd just pushed it underneath and now she was sitting beside him, that anger was just bubbling back up to the surface again.

Tim studied her before saying quietly, "Yeah, I want you to forgive me, and isn't that the joke of the day?"

Cindy blinked. "I beg your pardon?"

A couple went past, talking loudly, and he stood up. "Let's go find somewhere private to talk."

"Why?"

"Because we need to." He closed his eyes briefly. "Jesus, Rick and Mike all over again. I have to stop spending so much time with them."

"What? How much have you had to drink?"

"Obviously not enough." He held his hand out to her. "Please?"

A glance across the ballroom showed Marty standing beside a beautiful brunette, his gaze fastened on Cindy and Tim, and he didn't look happy. Probably because Cindy wasn't getting up happily, which meant she wasn't happy, which meant that Marty was going to come across any minute to find out why.

That was not something she wanted to happen.

Taking Tim's hand, she let him help her up before releasing his hold.

It didn't deter him. Cupping his arm under her elbow, he steered them around the edges of the ballroom and out onto one of the verandas, closing the French doors behind them. The light from the ballroom spilt between the curtains and he drew Cindy to the side into the shadows.

Turning to place her back against the marble rail, Cindy folded her arms and regarded Tim in the gloom.

Gaze flicking down to her bosom, he inhaled loudly and leaned back against the wall, his hands going into his pockets as he slouched comfortably back. But she wasn't fooled, for while he might have appeared calm, she could feel his tension.

"Okay." She broke the silence. "I came out here to save you from Marty causing a scene. This better be worth it."

"Your family is close."

"You could say that."

Tim was silent for so long that Cindy thought he'd changed his mind about talking, but when she impatiently made a move to leave, he stepped forward quickly, grabbing her arm and blocking her.

She felt that touch on her arm clear down to her soul, warm and tingling.

For several long seconds there were only the combined sounds of their breathing, the cool of the night, the music floating through the closed French doors, and the heat between their bodies.

Cindy couldn't help but suck in a deep breath. God, he smelled so *delicious*.

Abruptly, Tim jerked her towards him, to kiss her, she just knew by the way his head inclined downwards towards her, only he just as abruptly shoved her back again.

Boy, did that hurt, and not physically. She blinked, refusing to show it. "Wow, man of decision. Am I that abhorrent to you, Clarke?"

"No, I - *damn it*. Damn it, Cindy." He thrust one hand through his hair. "I'm sorry, okay?"

"You want forgiveness now for the non-kiss? I ought to kick your indecisive arse. I don't blow bloody hot and cold like you, you jerk." She made to push past him again, only to be stopped once more by Tim grabbing her shoulders and whirling her around to push her up against the wall.

Before she could step forward he leaned down, his face close to hers, and she could see the glitter of his eyes, the frustration and desire mixed in his darkened expression.

"You want the truth, Cindy? I was going to ask forgiveness for the other day but you know what? I'm not sorry. I'm not sorry that I took you on the table, I'm not sorry that I buried myself in your body, that I found more pleasure in your lush heat than I've ever known. You turn me on, Cindy." He nodded, a muscle flexing beside his mouth. "Yeah, you make my dick so hard that I've had more than one cold shower since that day. Was it only the other day? Hell, it feels like weeks ago, yet it feels like hours only all at the same freakin' time."

Mouth open, she could only stare up at him.

"You think your weight is a factor I don't like. News for you, baby. Your curves turn me on, your softness, your - your - *everything*." He sucked in a hard breath, his nostrils flaring slightly. "And your scent, Jesus, your scent haunts me. Listen to me, I sound like bloody Mike or Rick." His laugh was short and hard, almost bitter.

"So why-"she started, only to have him lay a finger against her lips and shake his head.

"I'm not into confessions, Cindy. I'm not into this talking out our feelings crap, so listen up, because I won't be saying this ever again. You're not my type of woman. I choose women who can take the love 'em and leave 'em that I do. I'm not into forever after. I know it doesn't last. I-"

"So what about Mike and Rick?" she interrupted, really wanting to know. "You don't believe their marriages will last?"

His eyes narrowed. "Yeah, they'll last. Maybe I should make it clearer. My relationships don't last, I don't want them to, I don't seek to make them work. You're an ever after kind of woman, Cindy, and I'm not an ever after kind of man. That's why I don't choose you as my type of woman. I want sex, the instant gratification, no strings attached. You're not that kind of woman." Closing his mouth tightly, he regarded her steadily.

Daringly.

Bloody man.

"So, you think I'm not your type, huh?" She retorted furiously. "You choose your type of woman. What the hell do you know about me, Tim? What? I'll tell you. Sweet bloody nothing. You think I have forever after on my mind. *You* think *I* need a man to make my life complete. Boy, are you barking up the wrong tree - hound dog." Stabbing a forefinger into his chest, she snarled. "Listen good, sunshine. *I* choose who *I* sleep with. Who *I* have sex with. And so far, my choices haven't been the forever after kind of bloke. Do you know why?"

Tim's nostrils were flaring and the heat wasn't just coming from his body, his eyes fairly burned with fire. "Do tell."

"Because I don't need a bloke to make my life complete. I make my own choices, and listen up sunshine, here's a bloody big tip for you. Tonight I'll have sex with whomever I please, just like you will, and I'll damned well like it because it's my choice. Raise a flag for the revolution, Tim, because a woman's world doesn't revolve around you!"

Chapter Six

One hard shove and she stalked past him, ripping open the French door with enough furious power to send it slamming into Tim as he came after her. The bang of him hitting the glass was balm to her ears, and his cursing followed her into the room. A yank of the curtains and she was inside, moving through the dancers with dexterity and speed, a smile on her face, head held high, and calmness in every step.

Inside, her temper roiled. Goddamn Tim for being such a bloody egotistical jerk. And damn her for wanting to cry about it. She was so mad she wanted to hit someone - preferably Tim.

Half expecting him to chase after her, she glanced back over her shoulder to find him bent over Nancy, his sixty year old, outrageous-mannered date he brought to all his mother's parties to annoy her.

Nancy was speaking seriously to him, smiling outwardly, but her gaze fastened on his face. Tim was listening, but his own gaze was on Cindy, his brown eyes sparking with temper and - *no, with temper only, don't think of anything else.*

"Cindy." Mr Lawson stepped into her path. "This is - are you all right?"

"Absolutely fine," she replied smoothly, smiling up at the man by his side.

Knowing the signs of his daughter in a temper, Mr Lawson looked at her with concern.

Cindy gave him a smile and a nod. "Were you going to introduce me to...?"

"Yes, of course." With a last hard look at her, Mr Lawson gestured to the man. "Robert Dunsbrough. We're in talks to buy his chain of home ware shops."

"Pleasure to meet you." Slipping smoothly into her role of dutiful daughter and cool assessor of the opposition, Cindy shook Robert's hand. "I'm Cindy."

Robert smiled and she didn't miss the cold glint in his eyes. She'd seen it many times since accompanying her father or brothers to meet new clients. One of her roles was to meet and greet, play the dutiful daughter, and assess the competition or potential seller of a business while doing so. Her insight into the seller or buyer was a boon to her family.

Cindy played her role well.

Satisfied that all was done according to their personal plans, Mr Lawson greeted someone else and left them alone on the excuse of needing to talk to an acquaintance.

"I didn't know the family had such a charming daughter." Robert held out his arm. "Dance?"

Like hell he didn't know. Smiling, Cindy accepted, and immediately he slid his arm around her waist and swung her onto the dance floor.

It didn't take Cindy long to find out what Robert was like. The man was a sleaze. He tried to charm her, flowering her with compliments, showering her family with compliments, practically eating her up in his efforts to win her over. After all, win over daddy's weighty little girl and he might be halfway to making a huge sale.

For her part, Cindy pretended to lap up his compliments, while asking leading questions, probing deeper, and without him even being aware of it, Robert spilled more than he meant to, right into her shrewd, listening ear.

It was a shame she couldn't ignore Tim's words as easily as she ignored Robert's, she thought, catching a glimpse of Tim swinging Nancy through a waltz. The man danced like an expert and she could just imagine how much fun it would be to dance in his arms instead of Robert's.

Forcing herself to concentrate, Cindy remained by Robert's side, just as he'd obviously planned, going by the way he tried to ply her with champagne and more verbal crap.

He was so confident, in fact, that by the time Cindy was ready to leave Robert had offered to take her home. About to refuse, she saw Tim watching her and with a glare in his direction, she turned and smiled up at Robert. "How sweet of you."

As he led her away, her hand on his forearm, Cindy passed her father. Stopping before him, she gave him a hug. "See you later, Dad." And right before she removed her arms, she whispered, "Don't touch his business with a ten foot pole."

That was enough for Mr Lawson and he gave her a fatherly smile and wink.

Robert had a driver and limousine, and whisked Cindy home in it. Expertly rebutting his self-invitation to come inside, Cindy begged a headache - oldest cliché in the book - and headed into the house, only to stop and swear as the door shut behind her because she'd forgotten about Al.

Fine mother she was! How could she forget about Al?

Peeking through the lounge room curtains, she saw the taillights of the limousine disappear down the drive. Even though she hadn't drunk much champagne and was sober as a church-mouse, Cindy rung for a taxi.

When the knock came at her door, it was to find Marty standing there with his hands in his pockets and lipstick on his cheek and askew collar.

"Not quite your shade," Cindy observed.

"Told you, the women like a little danger." The amusement left his eyes. "Damn it, Cindy, you know you don't go home with clients."

"I beg your pardon?" Her temper, simmering beneath the surface, kicked up a notch.

Realising what he'd said, Marty held up a hand. "Sorry. Let me rephrase that."

"It'd pay you."

"Was it wise to let that total sleaze take you home?"

"He's trying to make good with Dad, so he wouldn't try anything with me." Cindy pulled the door shut behind her. "Is that my taxi?"

"No, it's mine. We met yours at the gate and I paid him off." Marty grinned a little. "Forget someone, did you?"

"I'm a terrible mother."

"Aw, you're not that bad." Slinging his arm across her shoulders, he led her down the steps. "Come on, let's go get my nephew. Mind you, he's so young to have all that hair. Can't be from our side of the family."

Laughing, Cindy got into the taxi.

~*~

Standing in the shadows of a veranda pillar with his hands in his pockets, Tim watched Cindy get into the limousine with Robert. Jesus, didn't she have enough sense to know what a sleaze he was? He couldn't even fathom why any woman would get into close quarters with the man.

The limousine swung out into the drive and he watched the tail lights disappear towards the road.

"She's a good girl." The frosty tones of his mother sounded beside him.

"The stamp of approval?" he asked without looking at her.

"No. I'm just saying that she's a good girl."

"Ah. A warning, then."

"Cindy Lawson isn't stupid, she has good connections though lacks the social graces necessary for our circles, and she needs to lose weight."

"Wow, I am so impressed. Praise and the tearing down of confidence all in one shot." He raised his glass in her direction. "Way to go, Mother."

"Don't be tiresome, Timothy. I see you brought that ridiculous woman along as your date again."

"Nancy. She's wild in the sack, by the way."

"Your constant attempts to annoy me makes you juvenile."

"You make my heart bleed."

Dr Clarke sighed. "When will you get your life together?"

"I have a life. I'm a vet working in a good practice." He took a sip from the can of beer.

You work a low-paying job at a vet clinic owned by your father's sister."

"Yes, Aunt Hannah owns the clinic." Tim stared towards the road, only half listening to his mother's words.

"If you're going to lower the tone of our family name by working with animals, the least you can do is own your own clinic. Bigger and better than the others in this city, in fact. Make something of yourself. God knows your father wouldn't have done so without me pushing him."

"And now he's pushing up daisies. Good on you, Mother. You hounded him to death"

Her silence was so cold that he half expected frostbite to set into his extremities. When she spoke, her words were positively frigid. "At least marry according to our status. You can marry well and then play at being a vet."

Turning his head, he gave his mother a look full of loathing. "I don't play at being a vet. I am a vet, and a damned good one."

"Then make more of yourself. If you applied yourself, you could be a professor at the university, teaching others. That would be so much more suitable."

"I don't want to teach. I like working with animals, being hands on." He gave a very childish, but impressively loud, burp. "Oops. Sorry. That's what happens when you're a low-life and drink beer from a tin. Must be Dad's side of the family coming out in me."

Dr Clarke gave him one frosty stare, equally as loathing, before she swung away and walked indoors.

"Are you saying your Dad's side of the family is uncouth?" Aunt Hannah peered up from near the shrubs that lined the house.

"Oh damn. No, of course not. I'm sorry, Aunt Hannah." Groaning, Tim pinched the bridge of his nose. "And I beg your pardon for that very rude and un-gentlemanly expelling of air."

With a light laugh, Hannah leaned her arms on the rail of the steps. "I was impressed by it, actually." Reaching out, she took Tim's can and swallowed a good mouthful. She also swallowed some air, thought about it, concentrated and managed a teeny burp. "Rats."

Tim laughed. "You need some practice."

"Obviously." Resting her chin on her arms, she gazed up at him.

Tim took a couple of steps down and sat, putting him on eye level with her. "Why do I come here?" He sighed.

"Because you got the summons from Hell?"

"Why don't I just stop coming?"

"Why don't you?"

"I don't know. Sadomasochism, perhaps?"

"A family trait."

"Really?"

"Yes. On your mother's side."

They both snickered.

"Okay," Hannah finally said after a few minutes. "Time to be the responsible adult."

"Me?"

"No, me. Well, both of us, really. Your Mum is a bitch. I know it, you know it, the whole world knows it. But honey, it's time you moved on."

"I've never been good enough for her, Aunt Hannah." Heart heavy, Tim turned the tin around in his hands. "Never."

"Sweetie, you could do everything she asked and you'd never be good enough."

"That's comforting. Why did she have me, then?"

"You're the heir."

"Jesus, she couldn't manage the spare?"

"No, she didn't want to spoil her figure with any more kids."

"I'm surprised she didn't use a surrogate."

"God forbid, no. She had to make sure you came directly from her." Hannah shrugged. "She only needed one and she got one. You."

"You're not being very comforting."

"It's nothing you don't already know, Timmy." Reaching out, she brushed a stray lock of hair back from his forehead. "And what I'm going to tell you, you already know as well. You're a top vet, the best in the city. Probably in the whole damned state. Probably not the best in Australia, though."

He grinned crookedly at her.

"You mean the world to me. You're the son I never had."

"Thanks." His heart got a little lighter.

"You mean everything to your clients, to your patients, to your friends."

"To the women I date."

"No, not to them."

Tim looked at her.

Hannah shook her head. "You're nothing but a deep pocket to them. A money maker. The heir to the Clarke fortune."

"Thanks again." This time there was a bit of sarcasm in his words.

"Don't give me that tone, boy." She arched one fine brow. "You know as well as I do that you date those cold-hearted, money-grabbing bitches because you can dismiss them as easily as your mother dismisses you."

Blowing out a breath, he stared into the darkness. Behind him sounded music and laughter.

He definitely wasn't laughing.

"You've got a great life, Tim, if only you'd take control of it a little more."

Surprised, he stared at her. "What?"

"I'm talking about your dating habits."

"Look, that's my business-"

"Sure. And I'm tramping all over it." Completely unrepentant, she wagged her finger inches from his nose. "You'd have a perfect life if you addressed that part of it. That's the part that sucks. Let your issues with your mother go, let your resentment go, and get on with your life."

Anger started to simmer inside him. "When did this get to be my fault?"

"It's not your fault. Never was your fault. Your mother carries a lot of the blame, and your father, God rest his push-over soul, also carries part of the blame. He should have stuck up for you more often."

Tim glared at her. "He left me the money in a trust fund so that I could attend uni. He knew I wanted to be a vet."

"He was a fine man, but he didn't speak his mind often enough when Margaret kept hounding you. He should have spoken up more." Hannah looked him directly in the eyes.

Damn it, she spoke the truth. But he didn't like to think of his dad that way. His memories were always of his dad being warm and loving and just...Dad.

"Now, honey." Hannah rubbed his arm. "I have to go in. But you think about what I said."

"Every nasty word?"

"Keep that tone, boy, and I'll kick your hindquarters like they've never been kicked before."

Tim had the decency to flush. "Sorry, Aunt Hannah. I know you mean well."

"I do." Standing up, she walked around to the bottom of the steps and came up briskly, stopping to bend down and kiss the top of his head in a motherly fashion. "And I do it because I love you."

"That's what Mother always said." He attempted a grin, but it came off poorly.

"Your Mother loves in her fashion. It's just not of this world. More like Hell."

Tim couldn't stop the laugh that broke free, and Hannah smiled and patted his shoulder before heading indoors.

He stayed where he was, staring out into the darkness. Lost in thought, he jumped when a pair of shiny dress shoes landed squarely level with his backside on the stone step. Looking up, he found his gaze ensnared by Martin Lawson.

"Just a warning, Clarke," Marty growled. "You seem a sort-of okay bloke, but hurt Cindy and I'll slice and dice you."

"Jesus, it must be the night for warnings." Tim shook his head.

"Just keep it in the back of your mind the next time you look at my sister." Marty returned to the party.

Standing up, Tim shook his head again. It was time to find Nancy and go home. He'd had enough of everyone and their words of wisdom or warning.

Nancy, however, had found an admirer and was in no mood to stop partying.

"I'll drop the little lady home," said the portly, red-faced, elderly man with his arm looped around a giggling Nancy's waist.

"Are you sure?" Tim asked her.

"Of course. Arnold here assures me I'm in good hands." She winked. "If you know what I mean."

Arnold guffawed.

Tim grimaced. "I'd rather not think about it."

"Don't worry, old boy." Arnold clapped a hand on Tim's shoulder and breathed whiskey fumes in his face. "I'll take care of Nancy and bring her home safe and sound."

"Your mean your chauffer will, correct? Because I seriously date you can walk a straight line right now."

"Of course my chauffer! Your little Nancy will be right as rain." He winked again. "And happy as a lark."

Nancy waved Tim goodbye and they disappeared into the crowd.

Seriously, his old friend was going to get laid and he couldn't even find a woman to interest him. What were the odds?

Turning to leave, Tim was stopped by Nancy reappearing to grab his arm. Her face was serious, all laughter gone. "You all right, Timmo?"

"Fine." He smiled reassuringly.

"I don't have to go with Arnold. I came with you, you're my date."

"When has that ever stopped you?" He patted her hand. "Go and enjoy yourself."

"I'm worried about you."

"No need to be, I'm a big boy. I'm going to take one of the limousines mother has kindly put on standby for guests who didn't bring their own cars, go home and go to bed."

"Timmo-"

"Go." Turning her around, he gave her a gentle push. "Enjoy. Tell me about it all tomorrow."

He didn't bother to bid goodbye to his mother.

By the time he got home, his annoyance had grown. Yanking off his jacket, he threw it on the armchair. Going into the kitchen, he took a beer from the 'fridge and popped the tab.

He was well into his fifth beer and on his way to a pity party featuring one when a knock sounded at the door. He didn't bother to peek through the peephole but opened the door and gazed a little blearily up at the muscle-bound, big cop towering on his doorstep. "Mike."

"I want to talk to you," Mike began, and then his gaze shifted from Tim's face to the can in his hand. His brow rose.

"Gonna get good and drunk." Turning, Tim walked a little unsteadily back to the stool he'd been slouched on at the kitchen counter.

"Really." It was a statement, not a question. Mike shut the door and followed him into the kitchen, glancing at the empty tins of beer lined up on the counter. "I saw your lights on and knew you'd be up."

"On the way home from work, huh?" Tim took another swallow and emptied the can. Reaching for an unopened can, he popped the top. "Can tell." His voice slurred a little as he angled the can towards Mike. "Got your uniform on."

"Good detection." Crossing to the kettle, Mike filled it with water and plugged it into the socket.

"I'm drinking beer," Tim said.

"I'm drinking coffee."

"I noticed. Make yourself at home."

"Done deal." Mike studied him calmly. "Rough party at your mother's?"

"Rough party every time I go there." Tim burped.

"So why go?"

"Jeez, you're the second. Third? No, second person to ask me that." Tim hiccupped. "Sado-sadomassshim-sadomater - something bad, anyway. I like to hurt myself."

"You don't say." Mike spooned coffee into a large mug.

"Yeah, I do." Tim downed half the beer in several swallows. "Turns out my love life sucks." He pointed a wavering finger at his friend. "Aunty told me."

"She'd know," Mike agreed easily.

"Mummy issues. How gross is that?"

"Gross indeed."

"And then Cindy…" Tim squinted at Mike. "You gonna rip my balls off and nail them to the wall?"

"That had been my original plan." Mike shrugged. "I'm having to reassess. Or wait until another time."

"When I'm not shooooo drunk?"

"That'd be it." Mike pulled the milk from the 'fridge. "You don't get drunk as a rule, Tim. You don't like being out of control."

"Tonight." Tim blinked owlishly. "Tonight is a shep - special occasion."

"Uh-huh."

"Tonight my Aunt told me to sort out my love life." Tim waved the can in the air, sloshing the beer inside. "I don't need a love life. I need sex."

"Right." Mike turned off the kettle and poured hot water into the mug.

"I have shex - sex whenever I want. I don't need good girls like Cindy - oops." Tim held one finger to his lips and winked - unfortunately with both eyes, which rather destroyed the effect he was after. "Mustn't mention Cindy."

"Really." Stirring the milk into the coffee, Mike kept his gaze on the spoon.

"Yep. She's off-topic, off-limits, off everything." Tim's goofiness faded away and he stared morosely at his beer. "She's mad at me."

"Oh."

"Yeah. 'Cause I told her…aw shit."

Taking the stool beside Tim, Mike swivelled it so he faced his friend.

"Anyway…" Tim swallowed the last of the beer and popped the tab on number seven. "Aunt Hannah says Dad isshh to blame a little for not shhticking up for me with my demon mother." Tim took a few healthy swallows and nearly tipped off the stool at the same time. Mike helped steady him and Tim blinked. "Ssshiiiiit. I think I'm drunk."

"I'm not going to argue that." Mike blew on the surface of the steaming coffee.

Tim looked at Mike, feeling sadness overwhelm him. "Dad loved me."

"He sure did." Mike nodded.

"Took me fishing. And Rick, too." Tim rubbed a hand over his eyes, blinking away the sudden tears that threatened. "Can't cry in front of you. I'm a man. Apparently."

"Apparently." Mike nodded agreement.

"Yeah." Tim clapped him on the shoulder and almost missed. "You're a good friend, Mike. Good friend. Wish you'd been my mother."

"That would've made the medical books." Mike grinned a little.

Tim swallowed some more beer and stared at the table for awhile. He thought a long time had passed, but maybe it hadn't, he didn't know. He did hear Mike get up and make another coffee, but he didn't know when he'd popped the tab on beer can number twenty eleven. Thirty twelve. Ten fifty? "How many beers have I had?"

"That'd be number nine." Mike sipped on his coffee.

"What number coffee ish that?"

"Number two."

"You need to catch up." Tim almost fell off the stool.

Mike steadied him.

"Maddy issh waiting for you?" Tim slurred his words a little more.

"Yep."

"You need to go." But he didn't want him to go.

"She knows I'm here. She's fine."

"You shpoke to her."

"I did."

"I didn't sh - shee - shie - see you."

"Don't worry about it. It's on your phone bill." Mike smiled again.

"You're lucky to have her."

"I know."

"Wsh - wis - wish I had someone." Tim could feel himself listing to the side. "Gets lonely."

"I know." Mike reached out for him.

"Cindy…" Everything went black and Tim slid right off the stool.

When he awoke, his head felt like someone was drumming inside it - hard. The curtains were drawn and he was lying on his sofa with his shoes by the coffee table, the top two buttons of his shirt undone, a bucket by the side of the sofa, and a bottle of water with a glass already filled beside it on the table. A note leaning against it stated simply *Drink. You're dehydrated and hung over.*

Big surprise there. As if he didn't know. The house reeked of booze, he reeked of booze, and he was so hung over he felt like he could toss his innards fifty miles in two seconds.

Gorge rising in his throat, he gingerly took a drink of water.

Jesus, he'd gone on a bender last night. He hated getting drunk, hated losing control. The last time this had happened, he'd been out with some fellow students while in university and had woken up lying in his own vomit. The severity of that event, the realisation that he had no idea what he'd done the night before, and the sobering knowledge that he could have died, had him vowing to never get drunk again. He'd been a little tipsy once or twice, but he knew his limit.

Just look what a few words with his mother and aunty had reduced him to, not to forget his words with Cindy, too.

Women drove him to drink. That bender was proof. He had to start avoiding them.

Standing finally after two tries, he staggered carefully upstairs clutching the bottle of water in one hand. A cold shower had him gasping for air but he manfully ploughed on, padding around in boxer shorts while drinking the water, downing some coffee and forcing himself to eat some toast. Then he opened every window in the house and used the air freshener spray like there was no tomorrow.

The bin in the kitchen was empty, the cans cleared away. Good ol' Mike, the mother hen, cleaning up after Tim and making sure he was all right before he left.

A couple of hours later he felt a bit better. Paracetamol, water, and a shower. He wasn't good to go but he could at least sit without his head banging like bongo drums.

Sit and think. Think about what his aunt and mother had said. Maybe he was sadomasochistic. But he was happy like this, it was the way he chose to live. He didn't need a woman in his life. Aunt Hannah had provided him with love of a motherly kind, while his mother was a right bitch who showed him that maintaining control was paramount if his life was to be his own.

His family was definitely different to Cindy's family. Her mother was tall and held her weight well, wearing what she pleased and totally happy. Her father was kindly but shrewd. Her brothers were protective and while one was a real womaniser, the other was, well, he was a soldier that Tim saw only rarely.

But they loved each other. They were a *real* family. They were what he wished he'd had when he was a little boy facing his mother after yet again disappointing her, while his father had objected mildly and sought him out later to assure him that he was good, that he wasn't a disappointment.

Yeah, his dad was just as much to blame. Memories like that he didn't need, he liked to cling to the memory of the happy times he spent with his dad, not remember how he hadn't backed him fully, stood with him against his mother's disapproval and obvious attempts at match-making to better himself.

His dad hadn't lived long enough to see him make it through university, but he'd encouraged him to follow his dreams. Maybe that was because he'd seen his own smothered under his wife's iron hand.

Having had enough of thinking, Tim switched the TV on and flipped the channels. Nothing caught his interest so he heaved himself to his feet. His headache was a dimness, almost gone. Time to get a pizza and some DVDs and waste the rest of the afternoon watching the giggle box.

Time to forget for awhile.

~*~

The next two weeks Tim spent knuckled down at work. Taking a couple of really sick animals home with him overnights helped keep him occupied and gave him the perfect excuse for not going out.

He certainly didn't want to scrutinize the real reason, which was that he simply had lost any interest in seeking out a one night stand. Or a couple of hours stand, as the truth stood. He'd never spent a whole night with any woman.

When he'd bought the house, he'd spent some money remodelling an area where he could keep seriously ill animals overnight and on weekends. Easy to clean lino floors and a large window for ventilation with a blind that could be pulled down for shade, not that it was needed with the big verandas that surrounded the house. A sliding door led onto a thickly grassed area in the back yard for dogs to be walked. Hooks were on the walls to hold drips, and a large basin had cupboards underneath for water and food bowls. Another cupboard held some blankets, sheets and towels, and a spare heat pad lay on the bottom of the cupboard along with some litter trays and a bag of cat litter.

The heat pad made him think of Al, which in turn made him wonder what Cindy was doing. Probably sleeping with that sleaze, Robert. After all, she'd said she was going to have sex that fateful night of the horror party in Hell. He could only assume that as she'd gone home with Robert, he'd been the lucky man.

Goddamn it. The thought of Robert with his greasy hands on Cindy's soft skin made him angry.

Goddamn it again. It wasn't his business, and she'd made that perfectly clear to him.

Late Thursday afternoon found him at home settling a dog on a plastic-covered mattress layered with soft sheets. He hooked the bag of IV fluids on a hook not far above, placed a bowl of water beside the mattress and a second bowl containing some cooked, chopped up chicken.

The dog wagged his tail feebly and took a few bites.

"There's a fellow." Tim rubbed the big, furry head gently. "Keep improving, that's all your owners want. All I want, too." When the dog looked up at him out of liquid brown eyes, and he rubbed behind his ears. "Eat up. I'll take you outside later if you're up to it."

Pulling his shirt off, he slung it into the laundry wash basket and came back out into the kitchen. While pouring himself an iced coffee in front of the open 'fridge door, he studied the casserole dish his trusty housekeeper had left on the second shelf. Sausage and something, by the look of it. Rice in another bowl. Looked like Janet was trying something new. Interesting. He warmed some up and it tasted good. He surprised himself by eating a second plateful. He'd lost his appetite recently but it looked like it was coming back.

He was scrounging in the freezer for some ice cream when the doorbell rang. Placing it on the sink, he went through the lounge and out into the hallway to the front door. Opening it, he looked down to see Cindy standing there returning his gaze steadily.

Man, she looked so pretty. The low-cut blouse hugged her breasts, the little lace edging tickling her bare skin, he'd just bet. The light linen summer pants she wore skimmed her legs before flaring out around the stilettos she wore on her red-nailed feet. Red pants, white top, red stilettos and red toe nails. His gaze drifted up over those luscious curves, following up higher to where her hair was bundled up in some elegant, yet managing to look a little untidy, bun of some kind on top of her head. Errant blonde strands blew in the evening breeze. His gaze finally settled on her face. Blue eye shadow, red lipstick, thick eyelashes, a touch of blush on her cheeks.

She looked so good, so fresh and so confident, that he wanted to fall to his knees right there and rip her clothes off to see that soft skin beneath the material.

One fine brow arched. "Tim."

Reining in his baser instinct, he met her gaze coolly. Or he hoped it was coolly. Arching one brow in return, he replied, "Cindy." That came out nice and level.

Her gaze flicked behind him. "Is this a bad time?"

As in, did he have a strumpet in his house? Little did she know no woman had ever been in his house, except for the vet nurses who came to deliver or pick up animals or things to do with the clinic, Janet his housekeeper, his Aunt, and - well, that was about it. Not even Maddy or Cherry had come into his hallowed sanctuary.

No sir, it was a man's house. His house. Which is why it surprised the hell out of him when the words that fell from his mouth were, "It's fine. Come in."

Standing aside, wondering what had possessed him to say such a thing, he inhaled deeply as she passed. Oh yeah, there was that perfume of hers, stealing into his senses and making him - so not horny. No, never horny. No more. Cindy was hands off. And right now, so was every other bloody female. He was on a crash diet when it came to women. Yeah, a sex fast.

"Go down the hall, right into the lounge, and through into the kitchen," he directed, closing the door.

He told himself he was simply being a gentleman, allowing her to precede him. He definitely was *not* watching the roll of her ample backside and itching to touch it. He kept his hands in his pockets because he was off women and wasn't interested in reaching out to cup those luscious curves. No sirree, he was in complete control.

In the kitchen, Cindy turned to face him. Her expression was calm.

So it should be. She'd been shagging, he hadn't. No bigee, he was on a cleansing, no-women diet. Much more noble.

Jesus, he was such a kid.

Shaking his head inwardly, he asked, "How's Al?"

Immediately her expression softened. "He's got his eyes open and is toddling around. I've shifted him into a kitten pen."

"You've got a kitten pen?"

"I had two made, one for my bedroom and one for the kitchen. Both are on wheels so I can wheel him around the house."

"He needs changes of scenery?" He couldn't resist teasing her just a little.

It was okay, he wasn't breaking his off-women diet by simply teasing.

She smiled. "He likes to know what's going on. Al is a bit of a sticky beak."

"Spoiled."

"Sure." She didn't deny it.

Silence fell between them for several seconds. Cindy glanced away before taking a deep breath and looking up at him. "I want to apologise for my brother the other night."

"Your brother?"

"Marty. At the party."

"Marty at the party. Nice ring to it."

Ignoring his blithe humour, Cindy continued to regard him steadily. "He warned you off me."

"Not really." Tim shrugged. "I believe he was warning me not to hurt you. Big difference."

"Okay." She didn't bother to argue. "He had no right sticking his nose where it doesn't belong. Bad habit of his, we're trying to break him of it but nothing is working so far."

"Maybe you should smack him on the nose with a rolled-up newspaper." Crossing to the sink, Tim picked up the container of ice cream and made to put it back in the freezer.

Immediately, she took a step towards the arched doorway. "I'm sorry. You were obviously eating and–"

"No!" He practically leaped across the distance separating them, just managing to stop himself from grabbing her shoulders. Clearing his throat, he said, "I mean, I've actually finished eating. I just forgot to put the ice cream away."

"Tim, your empty plate is in the sink. There is no ice cream bowl," she replied wryly.

"Okay." He scratched the back of his neck. "Anyway..."

She arched her brow.

"Bugger." He sighed. "Take a seat."

"I don't know if that's wise."

"Please." He patted one of the stools. "Share some ice cream with me."

"Really?" She was surprised.

"Yeah." Turning around again, he crossed to the cupboard and pulled down two dessert bowls.

All the time he was wondering what the hell he was doing. He could feel his no-woman diet becoming a little threadbare.

No, damn it! He was just being friendly, enjoying her company. That was all. Besides, she probably wouldn't stay and–

"I'd love some ice cream."

He didn't know whether to sigh with relief or groan with…well, relief. He for sure didn't know why he had such a silly grin on his face. Maybe the no-woman diet was making him weak.

After spooning ice cream into the two bowls, he replaced it in the freezer and set the bowls on the counter, one on Cindy's side, the second bowl on the other side of the counter. Taking two spoons from the drawer, he picked up a bottle of chocolate topping and took the stool opposite her.

Silently she took the spoon.

Tim squeezed the chocolate topping thickly over his ice cream and handed her the bottle without looking. She took it just as silently and squeezed a smaller amount on her own ice cream. He looked up just in time to see her loop a long strand of gooey topping onto her finger from the bottle, and sticking her finger in her mouth, she sucked it off.

Hell, that just made his shaft sit up and take notice.

Wishing he could smack *it* with a rolled up newspaper to make it behave, Tim focussed on the ice cream.

"Want to talk about it?" She broke the silence.

Oh, brother. "I'm done talking."

"Okay."

So easily dismissed. Call him a contrary old fart, but that annoyed him. He glanced up.

She met his gaze calmly, licking her lips from remnants of ice cream.

"What makes you think I want to talk about anything?" He just had to ask.

He gave himself a mental head slap. He really needed to stop hanging around with the heart-to-heart guys, aka Mike and Rick.

"You invited me to stay."

"Doesn't mean I want to talk."

"Okay."

That niggled, too. So it didn't matter? "Maybe I just wanted some company."

"Okay."

A muscle in his jaw twitched. "Maybe I wanted your company."

"That's nice."

He shoved a bigger than usual mouthful of ice cream into his mouth and swallowed.

Jesus, the ice cream headache he got from that dumb stunt had both his eyes and his teeth clenched shut.

By the time the hellish ice bomb had vanished and he was able to open his eyes, it was to find Cindy nodding sympathetically. However, she didn't say a word.

Good. Fine. He didn't want to talk.

They ate in silence for a bit longer.

"So, I heard you're going into a bit of fostering," he said. It was okay, he was her vet. It was work talk. Doctor and client stuff, nothing more.

"Yeah." She licked her spoon. "I'm looking forward to it."

"You do know there's a chance a kitten or cat now and again may get ill and die, depending on what has happened to them? We don't always know until a few days later if they're sick, there's an incubation time. And you realise that you'll get attached to the little critters, don't you?" That concerned him. The thought of her crying - *steer clear! Steer clear!*

"I know, but I figure a few tears is worth it if I can save some lives and get them a forever home."

A forever home. Oh God, how sweet was that?

"I guess you have some contacts," he continued calmly, without giving away his thoughts.

"A lot, in fact. I'm already putting feelers out." Scraping up chocolate topping on the spoon, she popped it into her mouth. "Spreading the word."

"Good plan." Tim nodded. "Got everything you need?"

"Lara has been a lot of help. She says that you'll…" Hesitating, Cindy dropped her gaze.

Interest sparked, Tim eyed her. "I what?"

"That you'll provide, free of charge, the health checks and worming and stuff for the strays I get from your clinic." She met his gaze. "If it's okay with you."

Hell, yes. "My Aunt is the boss," he stated. "She's a softie for animals. It's something she offers for people willing to foster animals from our clinic."

"I'm perfectly happy to pay for it, though," Cindy continued. "I have the money and don't mind paying, whatever the cost."

He was already shaking his head. "Veterinary clinics are a business, not a charity, true, but we help where we can. We try to re-home cats and kittens, even puppies and dogs, and we've all taken animals home to care for at times until homes can be found. You offering to foster as well takes a bit of the strain off us."

At that minute a whining sound came from the room off the laundry and excusing himself, Tim got up and went to check on the dog. A pat, a bit of reassurance, and he returned to the counter.

"That one of your strays?" Cindy asked interestedly.

"Nope. A patient."

"I remember you mentioning bringing them home when needed."

"Part of the job."

They finished their ice cream in companionable silence.

It felt so natural, so homey. Dangerous territory. Tim slid a glance at Cindy. Very dangerous territory.

Pushing the bowl aside, she regarded him. "I've told my brother to butt out."

"No worries." Tim also pushed his bowl away. "He's just concerned about you. I understand."

Leaning an elbow on the table, she asked softly, "Are we still friends?"

Friends? He stared at her. He'd never been friends with any woman he'd had sex with - ever. And considering what had happened between him and Cindy, he was surprised that she'd want anything to do with him again - ever.

"I guess not." She slid down off the stool.

Like lightening, he reached across and grabbed her wrist. "Wait."

"Tim, it's okay." Gently she tried to prise his fingers from around her wrist.

"No, it's not." He stopped when she looked at him out of big, serious, blue eyes surrounded by thick eyelashes. "I mean, I want to be your friend, but…"

"It's the sex, isn't it?"

She said it so plainly that he blinked in surprise.

"Sex spoiled it."

"No."

"Then what? The fact that I got mad at you?" She tapped his hand and he released her.

"No." Cursing, he tried to explain. "Look, I don't usually make friends with women I've had sex with. I've always walked away."

"And I walked right back." Her smile was tentative, a little - oh God, sad.

That made him feel like a real prick. It also made him a little angry and impatient with himself. Goddamn it, he just had to say it.

Still seated, he growled, "Look, I'm used to being in control, all right? I'm always in control. I control who I sleep with and where." He swung a hand out. "I don't bring any woman here to sleep, this is my place, my sanctuary. I love them and leave them, not the other way around. That's just the way it is."

Rather than scream that he was a vile, insensitive pig, Cindy just regarded him thoughtfully. Right before she surprised the living hell out of him.

Leaning forward over the counter, she touched his jaw with one perfectly manicured nail. "That's the whole point, isn't it? You're always in control. You never trust anyone enough to allow them control. If you think you're going to lose control, you panic and run."

"Panic?" His mouth dropped open in outrage. "Run? *Me?*"

"Yeah, you." She tapped him once on the chin. "You're scared to give up control, Tim Clarke, playboy vet. You don't have what you desire because you're scared it'll mean giving up some of that control you have."

Indignantly, he stood up. "I don't know what the hell you're on about, Lawson, but that's-"

"Control issues, Tim." Rolling her shoulders as though she'd just had a weight lifted off her, she smiled at him. "It's not having had sex with me that bothers you so much, it's the fact that *you lost control*." Before he could get a word in edgewise, she added, "And you know, if you do it enough times with someone you can trust, you might find that you'll like it." She walked briskly over to the door, stopping briefly at it to smile back at him.

Warmly.

Sultrily.

"Call me."

And then she was gone, her high heels first muffled by the carpet in his lounge before clicking decisively along his hallway. He didn't hear the door open and close, but he somehow knew exactly when she'd left.

The house was emptier.

Sort of like his mind, really. Standing there in his kitchen, mouth agape, his mind completely empty of any thought.

When thought did start to return, he realised that Cindy Lawson had just offered to take him under her control.

All he had to do was call her.

~*~

Climbing into the car, Cindy shut the door and buckled up her seatbelt. A twist of the key brought the engine to life, but all she did was sit there and stare ahead.

Had she really offered to take control of Tim? And in what context, exactly? Only now did the thought occur to her.

He took women to their home.

He chose the women.

He had to have control.

For her to offer to control him, she had to be the one to initiate - what? Sex? Oh boy.

Shifting in her seat, she bit her lip. Yes, that was exactly what she'd meant when she'd made that statement. There was no doubt in her mind. However, there was some doubt now because even though she wasn't a virgin, nor was she an experienced courtesan of old, trained to please men in all ways. Okay, she knew several ways, but enough to take control of Tim? Whoo boy.

Mind you, the thought of having Tim under her control, spread out on the bed to do with as she pleased - Cindy fanned herself with her hand. Whoo boy again.

Of course, there was the little matter of…um…her slight body issues. Sure, she was confident, she knew her body wasn't perfect but heck, there were other things that could be worse. And really, she was just a voluptuous babe, right?

Sure as heck, Tim had admitted that he liked her body, that her curves turned him on. However, she wasn't so confident that she didn't have a few doubts now and again, she was only human, but with a sudden shrug, she pushed the doubts away.

In all likelihood, Tim wouldn't be coming around knocking on her door to be taken control of, and she seriously doubted that he'd phone her. Turned on by her curves he might be, but he wasn't besotted with her.

That particular thought made a niggling little pain come to life in the vicinity of her heart.

Oh hell, she was a soppy sap.

Tossing her head, Cindy checked the side mirrors before pulling out into the evening traffic.

But her mind kept working overtime.

Okay, she liked Tim. That was part of the reason why she'd come to apologise to him for her idiot brother. The other part was, well, to be truthful, she missed seeing him. Two weeks and not a sighting of him at the pub she'd been to the previous Saturday. In fact, Tim hadn't been seen in his usual haunts for more than two weeks. Unheard of for the playboy vet.

She missed his eyes that twinkled mischievously, his shirts with their ridiculous sayings, his quirky smile, and his thoughtful expression that she was sure he had no idea he wore when he contemplated things.

Anyone who mixed in similar circles as the Clarke family had heard whispers, the older generation witnessing the way his mother had tried to control Tim from the moment he was born. He had mummy issues, and it had affected him big time. It affected the way he regarded women and was the reason he maintained such tight control over his relationships.

It was why he didn't let any woman get close to him.

So how close did she want to go?

Pulling over into the parking area of a service station, she picked up her mobile phone and was about to dial Maddy's number when a patrol car pulled up directly behind her. In the evening gloom she couldn't make out the exact features of the cops that got out of the car, but she recognised the tall, powerful figure that came striding up to her door. The other cop went into the service station.

Mike bent down to peer at her through the window. "Cindy."

"Hey, Mike." She waggled the phone. "It's all right, I wasn't driving and phoning."

"I know, I saw you." He glanced around and then back at Cindy, his pale-eyed gaze steadily regrading her. "Everything all right?"

"Well, sure." Puzzled, she also glanced around before meeting his gaze once more. "What's wrong?"

"Nothing. Maybe." That unnerving gaze just stayed right on her.

Damn, Maddy had nerves made of steel to be able to meet this gaze head-on and still argue with him. Then again, Mike worshipped the ground Maddy walked on.

Tim certainly didn't worship the ground that Cindy walked on.

Her little sigh didn't escape him and he raised one brow in silent query.

"Nothing." Cindy shook her head. "You said there might be a problem?" A sudden thought occurred to her. "It's not Maddy, is it?"

"No."

"Of course not." Cindy relaxed back in the seat. "Otherwise you'd be with her."

He just nodded.

"So, what's wrong?"

"I'm wondering the same thing."

"You're speaking in riddles, Mike. Just tell me or ask me or something."

Without speaking, he squatted down beside her window and studied her with those stoic cop eyes. "You're Maddy's best friend."

"Yes." Where was he going with this?

"Tim's my best friend."

"Yes." Uh-oh.

"I don't want either of you to get hurt."

"I'm not following you."

"Yeah, you are."

"Mike, I don't-"

"Really, Cindy, do you want to go there? With me?"

No, she didn't, because Mike was all-bloody seeing. "It's not your business." She attempted a small smile. "No offence."

He didn't bat an eyelid. "Tim went on a bender. He never goes on benders anymore."

Actually, in all the pubs and clubs Cindy had seen Tim frequent, not once had he ever gotten drunk. "Why'd he go on a bender?"

"You."

She blinked. "Pardon?"

150

"You." His gaze remained steady. "Since he met you, he's on uncertain ground."

"Uncertain ground?" Dismay filled her. "You mean I'm driving him to drink?"

"Only the once, and I think that was a combination of you, his mother, and a few other issues."

"Oh, my God." She fell back against the seat and stared out the window. She'd just left his house. "He's probably as drunk as a skunk right now!"

"Nope." Mike shook his head. "I know Tim. He won't get drunk again."

"How can you be so sure?"

"I just know."

He sounded so positive that she relaxed a little.

"You came from his house," Mike stated.

"How do you know that?"

"Passed your car there a little while ago while on patrol."

"Oh." Considering what he was saying, she wondered what he thought about that little event.

No, there was no guessing, for as usual his stoic cop face was firmly in place.

"Okay," she finally said. "Are you warning me off Tim? That I'm no good for him?"

"No. I'm telling you that loss of control is a huge thing for him. He didn't have control of his life when he was little, and it's taken him that control to cope with what life has thrown at him. Losing it-"

"Would scare him." She nodded slowly. "I know."

"You do?" Mike was genuinely surprised.

"Yes. So if you're not warning me off him, what are you doing?" She met his gaze directly.

"I'm telling you that Tim isn't a man to blithely hand control over to anyone. His trust needs to be earned, and that will only be by a special person."

"You don't think I'm that person?"

"I don't know. Are you?"

Chapter Seven

She stared at him.

His cop partner came out of the service station and walked back towards the patrol car.

Mike straightened, bending to peer once more through the open window at Cindy. "I'm only telling you this because I care."

"You do?" Numbly, she looked at him.

"You're Maddy's best friend and Tim is my best friend. Friends look out for friends."

She didn't quite know what to say, especially as thoughts were starting to tumble haphazardly through her brain and a sinking feeling was spiralling down through her gut.

Reaching in, Mike patted her shoulder. "You need to talk to me or Maddy, we're there for you." Straightening, he strode away.

Cindy was still staring out through the front windshield when the patrol car pulled out from behind her and drove past her car. Unseeingly, she stared at the red tail lights as they disappeared into the traffic.

Oh God, what had she done? Mike knew Tim so well. Only a special person could win Tim's trust, and she didn't have a clue if she was that special person. Sure, she liked Tim, she missed seeing him, but was there anymore to it?

Was she a special person to Tim?

Did she want to be?

Would he see her as that special person?

Well, hell, she'd told him to call her if he decided to give his control up - *oh hell*! Oh hell, she'd done exactly what his mother had tried to do to him all his life - take his control.

She'd blatantly told him to call her when he was ready to give up his control. The control he'd used to survive his cold-hearted mother's machinations, the control he prided himself on, the control that was a part of him.

And she'd told him to give it up. To call her when he was ready to give it up.

"Oh, bloody hell," she groaned. Now she felt like the worst woman in the world. How could she have been egotistical enough to tell him that? She didn't know him, his secret thoughts, she only knew what she'd seen recently. "Oh, bloody, *bloody* hell. Cindy, what a right royal cock-up you've made of this!"

Wanting the security of her home, she put the car into gear and drove home, cringing inwardly.

Having confidence was one thing, but knowing that she'd boldly told him to do the same thing his loathed mother had tried to do all his young life - oh, that was low.

So very, wrongly, disgustingly low.

Pulling into the garage, she entered the house to relieve her brother of baby-sitting duties. It diverted her troublesome thoughts to find Alex slouched back on the sofa with his feet up on the coffee table, Al comfortably curled up in the crook of his neck.

"Awww." Raising her mobile phone, Cindy snapped a photo.

"Post that somewhere to embarrass me and remember I know where you live," Alex warned her. "And I'm trained to cause grievous bodily harm."

Laughing, Cindy sat down beside him on the sofa. "What are you watching?"

"News."

"All bad?"

"Is it never?"

"True." Leaning back in the sofa, Cindy kicked off the stilettos and propped her feet up beside her brother's on the coffee table.

For several long minutes they sat in comfortable silence before Alex finally asked quietly, "Want to talk about it?"

"Nothing to talk about."

"Okay. Want to talk about it?"

With a sigh, she rolled her head to look at Al on his shoulder. "Have you ever done something you thought was right, only to realise that it was so very wrong?"

Obviously unwilling to disturb Al, Alex looked sideways at her without moving his head. "Yes."

"Did you fix it?"

"I thought I could."

"What did you do?"

"Make it worse."

"That's what I'm afraid of."

"Can I fix whatever it is for you?"

Same protective old Alex. She smiled. "No. It's something I have to do. Or not do."

"Hmmm. Sounds intriguing."

"Anything but, trust me."

"Want some words of wisdom?"

"Please."

"Me, too."

Cindy punched him lightly in the arm and Alex laughed.

Disturbed, Al stirred, lifting his little head and peering around sleepily. Feeling perfectly safe, he gave Alex's earlobe a lick, making him cringe and Cindy giggle, and then he snuggled closer into Alex's neck and went back to sleep.

Life was simple for Al. Cindy wished hers was as uncomplicated as it used to be, before she'd met a certain handsome vet with emotional problems.

"Can I crash here tonight?" Alex asked.

"Sure."

"Thanks."

"Mum smothering you a bit?"

Alex sighed. "She means well."

"But you just want a bit of quiet. To be left alone for awhile."

"Yeah."

"Want to talk about it?"

"Nah."

"Okay."

In comfortable silence, they slouched back in the sofa and watched TV, both of them lost in their own thoughts, Al snoozing happily.

~*~

Early the next morning, Cindy finished feeding Al and after a snuggle and gentle play, she put him back in the kitten pen. Going into the shower, she leaned her forehead against the wall and relaxed as the water cascaded over her hair and down her back.

Sleep had been hard coming the previous night. She'd tossed and turned while trying to decide what to do to rectify her mistake. In the dawn hours she'd come to a decision. There was no way she was going back to face Tim and there were two good reasons for it. One, there was no need, and two, he probably didn't want to see her.

Okay, there was a reason number three, and that was because she felt like a first class fool, but she was sticking with reasons one and two otherwise she'd feel like a coward. So she disregarded number three and concentrated instead on one and two. Nothing like denial.

So that left ringing and leaving him a message on his answering machine while he was at work. He could come home, hear it, wipe it clean and not bother with her ever again.

Why that thought should hurt, she didn't want to dwell on. A clean break, that was it. Go back to what they were, nodding acquaintances.

Yes, that was the right decision.

Having breakfast with Alex, Ruth and Sam in the big kitchen, Cindy chatted about everyday things. Alex volunteered to go out and help Ruth with the heavier things to be done in the garden, openly expressing his wish to do some hard labour without thinking about anything. It surprised Cindy that Ruth didn't argue but then she'd always had a soft spot for Alex, probably because he was a soldier, the same as Sam had been during the war.

Leaving Sam downstairs happily vacuuming the carpets, Cindy went upstairs to the little alcove off her bedroom. Sitting in the chair, she lifted the phone and dialled Tim's number. As she'd expected for this time of the morning, Tim's answering machine clicked on, his voice recording stating 'This is Tim Clarke. Leave a message.'

Just the recording was enough for her mouth to go dry. That and the combined embarrassment and sudden racing of her heart. Five long seconds passed before she finally had the gumption to speak. She'd rehearsed the speech several times so that it would flow smoothly.

Closing her eyes, she said hurriedly, "Hi Tim, this is Cindy. Listen, about last night, forget what I said. I was wrong. Your control is important to you and I should never have suggested that you give it up. Anyway, I guess we're two different people on two different paths. No harm, no foul. I'll see you around sometime." Placing the phone down, she nodded.

No harm, no foul. It had gone well.

The phone rang and she picked it up.

"Cindy?" Tim queried.

Oh shit! Leaping out of the chair, she slammed the phone down and stared at it with her heart pounding. Oh God! Tim had been home! He'd been listening to what she'd said! It wasn't supposed to happen like that! No no *no!* It had been perfectly planned and executed! *Perfectly!*

It seemed not.

Heart in her mouth, she waited for the phone to ring again but it remained silent. Rushing to the window, she peered out at the driveway before slapping her forehead with her palm. Tim wasn't superman, flying from his house to hers in seconds. And anyway, why would he?

She had to get a grip!

Hear beating, she sat on the end of the big bed. Okay, she reasoned, so he'd heard her phone call. So she'd hung up in his ear. Maybe it was for the best. Of course, maybe he thought he'd gotten the wrong number. Maybe he hadn't actually been ringing her. Maybe that was why the phone didn't ring again, because this time he'd gotten the right number.

Yeah, that had to be it. Tim Clarke wouldn't go chasing after a woman who'd told him to lose control, then told him it was the wrong thing to do. Telling him. Oh yeah, he'd just really love being told what to do…not. Oh boy. Cindy cringed.

It was time to step back, say nothing, let the soothing calmness of non contact work its magic.

It was time to go and do some mind-numbing computer work for the family business and forget about *everything*.

Except Al, of course.

She managed to do just that, immersing herself in work, emailing the different companies and dealing with the thousand little things needing to be attended to keep the different smaller companies running smoothly.

An email from Marty informed her that he'd dug around Robert Dunsbrough's deep, dark background, and true to her intuition there was more than met the eye with his dealings. The family weren't buying his chain of home ware shops, but there was another chain of furniture shops that Marty thought looked promising, and he asked her to do some computer background checks and see what she could find.

In-between feeding Al and concentrating on work, the day managed to flit past. By the time she'd finished for the day, Sam, Ruth and Alex had all left, leaving her with the enjoyable companionship of Al.

Steadfastly she concentrated on feeding Al and playing gently with him, taking him downstairs with her to place in the kitten pen in the lounge while she checked the freezer for something to cook.

Sam, bless him, had mince thawed out and she decided to make Spaghetti Bolognese. She'd just gotten the onion out when the front doorbell rang. With a dish towel thrown over one shoulder, she wandered down the hallway to open the door.

"Hi," said Tim.

Her mind went completely blank.

His gaze swept slowly down her, taking in the light sundress that reached mid-thigh, the ruffled apron, and her bare feet. "Good Lord. No high heels?"

"Ummm...no?" What was he doing on her doorstep? She could feel her face flame in embarrassment.

Those brown eyes lifted to study her face seriously. "Red cheeks. Goes well with the tiny flowers sprinkled all over your dress."

Not used to feeling so self-conscious, Cindy shifted uneasily from foot to foot. "What can I do for you?"

"You said to call you. I came instead."

Her mouth fell open.

Standing there in cargo shorts, t-shirt and sneakers with no socks, his dark hair slightly dishevelled, Tim looked relaxed - until one noticed the fine lines bracketing his mouth which wasn't smiling his usual devil-may-care smile, and the guardedness of his normally twinkling eyes.

In fact, Cindy had seen more seriousness in Tim since she'd met him than at any other time.

Oh God, she'd taken away his happiness. Unbidden, a lump rose in her throat.

"Cindy?" He leaned a little closer, his gaze locked on her eyes. "Are you all right?"

"F-fine."

"Because you don't exactly look excited at me taking you up on your offer."

This time she choked, and it wasn't with tears. Her breath caught and she started coughing.

Flapping the tea towel at him, she turned and hurried back into the kitchen, grabbing a glass of water and gulping down several mouthfuls. Once she'd gotten her breath back, she turned to find Tim sitting on the kitchen bench watching her.

"Better?" he queried.

"Yes, thanks."

He glanced at the mince sitting in the bowl. "Cooking tea?"

"Yes." She waited for him to repeat what he'd said earlier, but when he didn't, she raised her brows at him.

"I didn't know you could cook." He looked from the bowl to her.

"Because I'm a spoiled rich bitch?" She couldn't help but ask.

"No. Because you don't look like someone who cooks."

"I look more like someone who eats." Picking up an onion, she weighed it in one hand while keeping her attention fastened on him.

His gaze wandered over her curves. "I didn't say that."

"You didn't have to."

His gaze snapped back up to lock with hers. "I said, I didn't say that."

Why did he have the power to unnerve her when no one else could? She'd faced down bullies in school and walked away laughing. She'd faced snobs who looked down at her style of clothing and her overgenerous, plus-sized body, and she'd walked away laughing. She had friends who liked her, family who loved her, and a kitten who thought she was his mother.

Yet this one man could make her self conscious. And yet again, he never once made mention of her weight, in fact, going by the heat that flared in his eyes before being quickly hidden, he liked her curves.

A lot.

Surely he wasn't really here to make good on her offer? A little tingle shot through her to twirl low in her belly and slip into her nether regions.

Clearing her throat, she raised her head slightly and eyed him coolly. *Stay in control, Cindy. Find out exactly what he wants before you run - either from him or too him. Oh God, where did that thought come from? Concentrate, or you'll make a fool of yourself again!* "So, Tim. Why are you here?"

"You said to call you."

Oh sweet Lord.

"And then you rang and rescinded your invitation." While she waited silently, he plucked an apple from the bowl an arms-length from where his backside rested on the bench, polished it on his t-shirt, bit into it and chewed thoughtfully. "I wondered about that."

"No need to." Picking up a vegetable knife, she skinned the onion, cut it in half and ran it under cold water. "I realised that I was asking you to give up the one thing that has gotten you through this life. I had no right to do that."

He didn't answer straight away, but she heard him bite off another crisp piece of apple. She was cutting the onion when he finally said, "What if I decided that you're right? That I'm too scared to give up control?"

"I'd be terrified that I've given you the wrong information." Scraping the onion into the saucepan with the mince, she added herbs and beef stock cubes. "I have no real idea of your childhood, how you felt, even how you see the world is only my guess-work, and to tell you the truth..." She ripped the top off the tomato paste container and scraped the contents into the saucepan. "If someone had the nerve to tell me what they think I should do, without them knowing me properly, I'd be pissed off. Majorly pissed off." Lighting the stove, she placed the saucepan on the flame, clapped the lid on and turned to face Tim, folding her arms decisively.

He just continued to study her while eating the apple.

Raising one brow, she watched as he finished nibbling around the apple core before he jumped off the bench and strode across to the bin, lifting the lid to toss it inside and letting it swing shut again.

Then, without a word, he closed the short gap between them, grabbed her upper arms, jerked her into him and kissed her.

Hard.

Fast.

Toe-curlingly, achingly *hot*.

His tongue traced her lips with determination, demanding she open to him, and she could do nothing but obey with her heart pounding in her chest, her loins growing damp, and a little voice in her head screaming *Whoo hoo!*

Every line of his lean body was pressed against her curves, his pecs flexing impressively when she rested her palms against his chest.

There was nothing of control rescinding in his kiss or his posture as he bent over her. He kissed her so thoroughly that by the time he lifted his head, she was gasping for air, her eyes were dazed, and all she could do was stare up at him and lick her tingling lips.

Brown eyes already dark with ardour, Tim looked down at her. "I like having control, I want it, I live by it. Then you came into my life and proceeded to tell me to come and see you when I was ready to give up that control. But here's the thing, Cindy. I'm not prepared to give up that control."

She swallowed. "So why are you here?"

"Because I've realised that I'm not prepared to give you up, either."

There was no denying the little thrill that went through her at that announcement, but it was also tempered with confusion. "You never had me."

His gaze strayed over her shoulder to the table behind her.

Cindy's cheeks flamed. "I don't mean *that*."

"*That* was a part of it." Tim's gaze locked on hers once more. "But it started before then, too, this attraction between us."

Heart knocking about in her chest, so very conscious of the warmth of his body against her own, she whispered, "When?"

"Really?" He gave his head a small shake. "Okay, then. Maybe the attraction was earlier on my part and not on yours."

Actually, she had no idea when she'd become attracted to him. No idea at all. The only thing she did know was that she did find him attractive. Somehow, some time, Tim Clarke had grown on her.

God help her. She wanted to rip his clothes off right now and have her way with him. But she was no fool, maybe he was playing with her, he didn't really know what he wanted, he…"What do you want, Tim?" she asked bluntly.

His regard was so steady that she found it almost uncomfortable, but at the same time she refused to look away. She needed to know his intentions.

"I want you."

"That's straight to the point." Ignoring the little whip of heat that snapped through her loins, she added, "But why?"

"Because I'm attracted to you."

"I'm attracted to a Ming vase I saw in a shop, but I don't want to hump it."

A little quirk appeared at the corner of his mouth. "Would you hump me if I was a Ming vase?"

"Tim, you want me because - well, hell, I don't know." Lifting her chin, she narrowed her eyes. "If you want me, tell me why. Why me, when I'm not your type of woman?"

"You're not going to let that comment go, are you?"

"Not when you threw it around enough."

His nod was abrupt. "I give you that."

"Thanks."

"That's part of the attraction you have for me."

Puzzled, she tilted her head.

"Cindy, you don't play nice. You don't sweet-talk me, you don't cosy up to me, you don't play to my vanity. You tell me how you feel, you tell me what you think. You're honest." Expression serious, Tim's hands slid from her upper arms to curl around her elbows, his thumbs gently stroking her inner arms to make her skin tingle deliciously. "You are exactly who you are. I look at you and I'm seeing Cindy Lawson, no pretentious airs, no false modesty. You're a beautiful, curvaceous, confident woman who takes no shit from anyone."

She blinked at the last few words. "Thanks. I think. Wow, you were doing rather okay until that last part."

Tim gave a short, amused laugh. "Honest to a fault."

"But is that enough for you, I wonder?" she queried softly. "Maybe I'm just an amusing enigma right now. You hang around with women you know are ball breakers, that's how you like it. I don't find a good enough reason to trust that I'm attractive enough to keep you interested longer than it takes for the novelty to wear off."

All his amusement fled. "You're more than enough."

Even though she wanted to believe it, she wasn't so sure. "This is a sudden change of heart. Too sudden. Are you wanting the forever after dream, Tim?"

He met her blunt question with an equally blunt answer. "I'm not sure of this forever after business, Cindy. I've not seen it with my own family. I've been hurt a few times, and I've never believed in it for me. But now…"

Silently she waited, refusing to help him, needing to hear it all.

Tim didn't break their locked gazes. His expression was serious, his voice steady. "For the first time in my life, I want to give a relationship a real go. I don't know if it'll work, I don't know if I'll make such stupid mistakes that you'll kick my arse right out the door, but I know that I'm not prepared to just let you walk away without trying." His hands left her elbows to slide beneath her arms and around her waist, his palms pressing against her back as he lowered his head to whisper softly, "Give me a chance, Cindy. That's all I ask. Give us a chance."

Mind buzzing with his words, she stared up at him. This was so unlike him, so unlike the Tim that she knew previously. One part of her wanted to take him up on his offer, to throw caution to the wind, snuggle close and see where it would all go, but another part of her, the cautious part, wasn't so sure it was such a good idea.

Her lust and attraction warred with her common sense.

When the silence lengthened, Tim stated, "You don't trust me."

"No," she replied slowly, and winced inwardly at the slight flicker of his eyes. "To be truthful, no. This isn't like you, and the sudden change is a little hard to take in."

Expecting him to try and cajole her, she was surprised when instead he nodded.

"I understand." Looking over her shoulder, he took a deep breath, nodded at something he was thinking, and then he looked back down at her resolutely.

Taking her arm, he ushered her over to the table and sat her down in a chair. Hooking another chair with his foot, he expertly dragged it out, swung it back to front, and placed it directly in front of her. Straddling the chair back-to-front, Tim sat down and faced her.

Silently they looked at each other, she warily, he assessingly.

He looked so damned handsome, so serious, so - God, she had to rein in her attraction to him and fold her arms to stop herself from reaching out to touch him, to run a finger down the broad forearm and up the swell of his bicep, tracing his beckoning skin with her fingertips under the sleeve of his t-shirt and higher to his shoulder.

She had it bad. Taking a deep breath, she took a tight grip on her errant emotions that had a mind of their own and raised a brow coolly at him. At least, she hoped it was cool. If he guessed how her blood ran hot and her imagination was filled with some R-rated images that involved him, she wouldn't have a leg to stand on.

"I spoke to Maddy." Tim broke the silence.

That caught her off-guard. "What?"

"I did the hardest thing I've ever done in my life and I talked about my feelings." He grimaced a little. "Jesus, can you believe it?"

No, she was floored.

"After you came to my house and pointed out that I like control, and then you invited me to call you when I was ready to give up that control, you had me thinking." He shook his head. "The thought of giving up my control was inconceivable, but then you rang me this morning and apologised, and basically told me goodbye and we'd see each other around sometime. I waited for that feeling of relief, of having been let-off the hook, so to speak, but that elation never came. Instead, I felt…" Tim blew out a long breath.

Holding her own, Cindy waited.

"I felt let down," Tim said. "Dropped. I felt like you'd yanked the carpet out from under my feet and I panicked."

"You?" She couldn't help but be surprised.

"Yeah. I rang you back and you hung up on me." This time both his gaze and his tone were a little accusatory.

"Correct." She didn't think it was the time to confess to her own panic at the time.

His gaze sharpened, but he continued. "You left me hanging, Cindy. My bloody emotions were shot to shit, I didn't know what I wanted, I stood there while my mind went berserk, not knowing what to think or what to make of the stupid *feelings* that were bombarding me, and none of them was relief. And guess what I did?" He didn't wait for a reply. "I actually rang up Rick but he was at work. I rang Mike and he was at work, too, but Maddy was home. Before you know it, I was in her cosy kitchen, eating homemade cake, drinking tea and discussing my *feelings*."

Cindy had to fight the urge to laugh at the mortification on his face, but her heart also did a little tango in her chest at the thought of the unflappable Tim Clarke sitting and talking to someone about his emotions.

About his feelings for her.

"And what did Maddy say?" she asked curiously.

"Maddy has a way of making a man spill his guts." Tim shoved a hand through his hair, the motion leaving a lock of the silken strands to flop enchantingly across his forehead.

Cindy had to fight the urge to reach out and brush it back.

"Before I knew it I was practically blubbering at the table, telling her all about my mother and my ball-breaker dates, as you called them. I was telling her about my control issues, as you'd also pointed out." Tim pinched the bridge of his nose. "She promised me she'd never let Mike and Rick know. I made her promise."

She fought the smile.

"And then I mentioned your name." He looked directly at her. "Just your name."

All amusement faded and she bit her bottom lip.

"I said 'Cindy', and Maddy knew. She just knew." Tim's gaze was unnervingly locked on her, and no way could she break it. His voice deepened, lowered. "She told me what I already knew deep down in my heart. She brought to the surface what I was trying to hide from even myself. Do you know what she told me, Cindy?"

"No." Her answer was barely audible in the room. She wanted to know, though, wanted to know so badly.

"She told me that if I cared for you, that I had to push my past aside and concentrate on the present. If I wanted you, I had to come and talk to you, to let you know." His eyes darkened. "She told me, Cindy, that I had to give myself a chance, and I had to give you a chance to accept me, too."

Nervously she chewed her bottom lip, her own emotions bombarding her. Uncertainty, hope, a thrill of anticipation.

Forearms resting on the back of the chair, Tim held her gaze, allowing the silence between them to lengthen.

And lengthen.

It was suddenly too warm in the kitchen, too confining, too intense.

Intense. So very intense. He watched her intently, heat in his eyes but his face inscrutable.

Waiting.

"Cindy," he finally said. "Tell me what you're feeling, because I swear, your face is so white I'm starting to wonder if I've shocked you into a heart attack."

She swallowed.

"Tell me," he insisted. "I've told you everything, now I need to know if I have a chance."

Oh God. Taking a deep breath, Cindy looked down to discover that her fingers were twisting nervously together. Freeing her fingers from each other, she splayed her fingers out on her thighs and rubbed her suddenly damp palms on her skirt.

She'd always thought she had her emotions under control, that she was cool and calm and collected, that she knew exactly what she wanted and how, but now she was a basket of nerves. A real basket case, in fact. Her heart was pounding in her chest, her cheeks felt way too warm, and her hands were actually shaking.

A sudden movement had her glancing up to see Tim kneeling down before her, one of his hands covering her own. The calloused warmth of his palm was oddly comforting, but the expression in his eyes was mixed. Gentleness, understanding, a little wariness, and a touch of heat. It was a heady mixture.

His voice was patient. "Cindy?"

"I'm not sure where my confidence has gone," she admitted a little shakily. "That's certainly shot that myth to pieces."

"You're fine." A slight smile greeted this, but his gaze remained steady. "Talk to me." When she could only look wordlessly at him, he said encouragingly, "Just tell me how you feel right now."

"Right now?"

"Right now."

Okay, she could do that. "I feel uncertain."

"And?"

"Um…stunned?"

"Are you asking or telling me?"

"Telling."

"Tell me more."

"I don't know about this, Tim-"

"Tell me more." His tone brooked no argument, his gaze sombre.

"Okay," she said. "I feel like I'm standing on the edge of a cliff and I'm wondering if I step off, will someone catch me when I fall, or will I just tumble down and break my neck?"

"Shouldn't that be heart?"

"Damn it!" Exasperated, Cindy made to jump to her feet.

"No, wait." Tim immediately grabbed her thighs, preventing her from moving. "I'm sorry. I was just trying to put you at ease." He shook his head. "That didn't work."

"You think?" Irritation, nerves, and yes, a little embarrassment, all warred within her.

He sighed. "I'm not good at this."

"I agree. You suck at it."

"Give me a chance, Cindy. Give me a chance to *not* suck at it."

"How can I take you seriously when you can joke at a time like this?"

"How can you not take me seriously?"

"Huh?"

Releasing her hands, Tim sat back on his heels and looked up at her. His eyes, usually twinkling with mischief, were grave. Not an ounce of amusement showed on his face.

"Right now, I'm more than serious that I've ever been in my life," he said quietly. "I've done things for you I'd never do for anyone else. I've talked about my feelings, I've swallowed my pride and come over here, I'm listening to my heart and laying it before you. If anyone's at risk of having their heart broken, Cindy, it's me."

The words, spoken with such heartfelt honesty, seemed to hang in the air between them. They slipped through her conscious, reverberating through her, slipping inside her mind and settling in, the meaning becoming so clear, the knowledge that he was right sinking deep into her.

"We know what I want," he continued softly. "You. I know you're scared of taking that step off the cliff, of giving me a chance. Giving us a chance. But tell me, Cindy, tell me truthfully. If I got up and walked through that door, how would you feel? What do you want?"

Closing her eyes, she sought to calm her jittery nerves. This should have been so easy. She always knew what she wanted. She had everything that she wanted, everything except-

A movement at her feet had her opening her eyes and lunging forward in a panic to throw her arms around Tim's neck to prevent him from getting up. "Don't go!"

His arms slid around her, holding her close to him as he assured her quietly, "I'm not going anywhere."

Up on his knees, her movements having put him neatly between her spread thighs, he was able to cradle her against him, one of his hands at the small of her back, the other up higher.

Arms around his neck, her chin resting on his shoulder, Cindy took a deep breath and closed her eyes.

Loss. When she'd thought that he had been getting up to walk away, she'd felt total loss. Loss of one playboy vet, one lean, tall, brown-eyed man who had somehow snuck into her life without her having been aware of it happening, who could make her stomach do flips and make her feel alive, make her feel as no other man ever had in her life.

And if she didn't want that loss…

"I'm afraid I'll never see you again," she whispered. "I'm afraid if this doesn't work out, that you'll leave me behind and I'll never find myself again. I'm so afraid of falling and having no one to catch me. But mostly, I'm afraid if you walk out the door now, I'll never see you again." *And I'll never get over you.*

There was a small movement of his head. "I can't promise you what I don't know. I can't see into the future. But Cindy, I can promise that I'll give this relationship everything I have, that I'll give it my all. I'm not promising to be a Prince Charming, God knows I'm far from it. I just want to be with you, to give us a chance." His breath stirred the hair at her temple. "Please, Cindy, just give us a chance."

His hands ran soothingly up and down her back, and she relaxed against him, allowing his words to sink into her, analysing them through her own fears and emotions.

She feared never seeing him again, she wanted to be with him. To give them a chance, she realised. It had hit her then, when she'd thought he was getting up and leaving. Hit her hard. Tim Clarke had walked into her life and taken a corner of her heart.

Would it last? She didn't know. He couldn't promise. But she could give it a chance, give him a chance, give them a chance. If Tim had felt strongly enough about it to bare his feelings, something he found abhorrent, then surely she could give it a chance.

Love, if that's what it was, was worth a chance.

"Okay," she said softly. "Let's give it - us - a chance."

With a sigh of relief, his arms tightened around her. "You won't be sorry, I promise you that."

"Good. Remember that I have a soldier brother who's been trained to hurt, and I'm not afraid to use him."

Tim pulled back and she saw the grin on his face. "I'll remember." His grin faded. "But mostly I'll remember that you gave me a chance."

Leaning forward, Cindy stopped a hairsbreadth from his mouth to whisper, "You better be worth it, Clarke." And then she kissed him, a soft, sweet kiss that brushed his lips.

The gentleness of his return kiss had her knees shaking at the simplicity of it, the beauty, the caring he poured into it. Tim held her like fragile glass, his kisses gentle, exploring, never demanding more than she was willing to give him.

Cindy was definitely ready and willing to give him more, but she played him, enjoying the gentleness, glorying in the knowledge that he found her desirable, beautiful, that he wanted more from her than just sex.

That he wanted more from her than he ever had from any of his other relationships.

Her kiss deepened and he followed quickly, taking it over within seconds, taking control, and she couldn't help the inward shiver of delight as he demanded entrance, his tongue forging in to sweep through her mouth and drink of her essence.

His desire for her was evident in every kiss now, every touch, his hand at the small of her back slipping down to cup her bottom, his other hand at her breast.

"You better have good intentions towards my sister, Clarke," a voice grated warningly from somewhere at the furthest reaches of her conscious. "Or I'll break those damn hands making free with her."

Slowly, Tim lifted his head and she saw the heat, annoyance and resignation mingled within his eyes before she licked her lips - his taste was like honey to her buzzing senses - and looked over his shoulder to see Marty standing in the doorway with Alex behind him.

Marty was staring daggers at Tim, while Alex was looking at her with his brows raised in silent, polite query.

"Do you mind?" she snapped.

"Only if you do," Marty replied.

"Does it look like I do?" She pulled her skirt back down her thighs as Tim rose to his feet, partially shielding her from her brothers' gazes.

Taking her hand, Tim pulled her to her feet before stepping around to stand beside her, his arm sliding around her waist as he looked at Marty and Alex. "Your sister and I are dating."

A small smile flickered across Alex's mouth. "Really?"

"Yes. Got a problem with that?" Tim glared at Marty.

"Hey, as long as you're doing right by her, I'm fine." Marty glared back at him.

"Excuse me," Cindy interrupted in annoyance. "Since when are you my keeper?"

"I know this jerk's record with women," her brother replied. "You're not going to be another notch on his bedpost."

"You are such an arse. If *I* choose to be a notch, it's none of your business."

"She's not going to be another notch," Tim said at the same time.

"Sure it's none of my business," Marty told Cindy. "My business is breaking his dick off if he does anything disgusting."

"If it was tit for tat, yours would have been snapped off a long time ago by an angry male relative of those women you've bedded like a tom cat around bitches in heat," she returned hotly.

"A slight mix up of the animal kingdom," Tim said. "Tom cats have queens, dogs have bitches."

By this time Alex had wandered into the kitchen and was investigating the contents of the saucepan on the stove. "Spaghetti? And you didn't call me? You know I love spag, Cindy."

"Get rid of Marty and I'll make you as much as you want," she informed him.

"Nah. This is much more fun." Taking a spoon, he stirred the contents of the saucepan. "You nearly burned this."

"She nearly had something else burned." Marty hadn't stopped glaring at Tim.

Tim grinned suddenly and it was enough to have Marty bristling like an anteater.

"Hey." Stepping between the two men, Cindy frowned in annoyance. "Marty, go away. I don't have patience with your holier-than-thou attitude. And Tim, stop stirring."

"I'm not stirring," Tim drawled. "I'm just being friendly to the brother of the woman I'm…"

Marty's nostrils flared.

"Dating." Tim smiled broadly, hooking an arm around Cindy's waist and drawing her back against him so that he could nuzzle the top of her head. "Mmmm, you smell good."

Tim was out to stir Marty and her dumb brother was falling for it. Cindy looked at Alex, the only sensible sibling she had at that moment.

Her sensible sibling was adding more mince to the saucepan.

"What are you doing?" she demanded.

"There's not enough meat in here for all of us."

"Who said you were invited?"

"Hey, you're making spag bog. I'm invited." He started peeling another onion. "You can get rid of Marty, though. That'd mean more for me."

It was obvious that her brothers weren't going to leave her and Tim alone. Tipping her head back, she looked up at Tim. "We have company."

"We could go back to my place," he offered.

That had Marty practically breathing fire.

"Actually…" Tim looked thoughtfully at her fuming brother. "Hold that thought. I think Marty and I need to have a little chat."

Immediately she shook her head. "Oh, no. That's not going to happen. Marty can mind his own damned business. This is between-" But then she was talking to empty air as Tim followed Marty outside and shut the door behind them.

She started to go out after them but Alex grabbed her arm. "Leave them."

"No way. You know what Marty's like."

"Exactly. And I know what Clarke's like. Let them sort it out."

"It's none of Marty's bloody business-"

"He's your brother. He's protective. Let him be." Alex steered her over to the cupboard.

She tried unsuccessfully to pull her arm from his hand. "I'm tired of his attitude when he does the same to other girls."

Alex's expression was mildly understanding. "He also knows Clarke's reputation. Can you blame him for being a little concerned?"

"Well, you don't seem too concerned," she retorted.

"Marty's handling it." Getting out a saucepan, he put some water into it and set it on the stove. "Where's the spaghetti?"

"For God's sake, Alex!"

Her brother straightened, his eyes narrowing a little. "Tim's a playboy. You're our sister. Marty's just having a talk to him, all right? Nothing is going to happen."

A muffled thump sounded from outside, followed by an oath and another thump. Something hit the door.

Cindy closed her eyes and groaned.

"See?" Alex said cheerfully. "Nothing wrong at all."

The door opened and Tim and Marty walked back inside. Tim was gingerly rubbing his jaw while Marty crossed over to the freezer, reached in, grabbed a packet of frozen peas and sat at the table with it held to his eye.

Folding her arms, she looked angrily from Tim to Marty. "All sorted out?"

"Absolutely." Tim dropped a kiss on the top of her head before crossing to the kettle, checking the amount of water and turning it on.

"Top notch." Marty looked at her from his one good eye.

Alex just stirred the mince.

"I give up," said Cindy.

"Wise choice," agreed Alex.

Whatever had gone on between her brother and Tim, it had cleared the air, or so she presumed because who really knew how men thought? Marty was much friendlier and the mealtime was pleasant as they sat around the kitchen table eating Spaghetti Bolognese.

More than aware of Tim sitting opposite her, however, Cindy found her gaze drifting towards him more often than not when she thought no one was watching. He sat so easily, eating spaghetti with a dexterity that she envied - really, how did he manage not to get it on his shirt? - and chatting with her brothers as though he hadn't just given one a black eye.

Both Alex and Marty were big of build, Marty from his love of the gym and Alex from his life as a soldier, and next to them Tim looked lean, yet his strength was there in his biceps that bunched as he lifted the fork and moved. Her gaze slid down a little lower to his t-shirt, and she knew from when he'd held her that his lean build was deceptive. Tim had muscles all right, lean and hard.

It was enough to make her mouth a little dry.

Lifting her gaze, she found Tim looking directly at her, his brown eyes kindling with heat, and he gave her a slow, seductive wink that had her blushing a little and sliding her gaze away. And feeling more than a little heat herself right at the junction of her thighs.

Then she felt it, a slow slide of his sneakered foot up the outside of her calf, and she almost swallowed the mouthful of spaghetti she had without chewing it. She sent him a warning glare - good God, her brothers were at the table! - and he simply winked again and turned to answer Marty's question.

Relaxing a little, she continued eating, but less than a minute later she felt a bare toe trail up the inside of her calf. The man had the legs of a giraffe, long enough to reach her and tease her for his own amusement.

If she cut him off from sex, it would serve him right. When he glanced at her, she mouthed it. *No sex.* His eyes brightened.

Oh shit, he took that as a personal challenge and showed it by giving an impressive stretch that had his t-shirt pulling tight across his rather yummy chest and slouching down in his chair while pushing his empty plate away. Picking up the glass of apple juice, he continued speaking to Marty and Alex while running his toe up higher to play with the inside of her knee.

Cindy nearly spilled her drink.

Marty continued animatedly talking about cars while Alex slid her a shrewd glance but said nothing, a faint hint of humour in his usually sombre eyes.

Shifting a little in her chair, she shot a glare at Tim. His toe retreated and she breathed a sigh of relief, but then it started to run up the outside of her leg. She aimed a kick in his direction but he was too fast, dodging her with ease.

Marty wasn't so lucky and he yelped.

"Shit," Cindy said,. "Sorry."

"Cripes," Marty replied.

Tim smirked at her. Time to change strategy.

While he was occupied talking to Alex, Cindy shifted her legs aside subtly. When Tim shot a glance across the table, she just knew his intrusive big toe was searching for her again.

Marty jumped and yelped again. "What the hell?"

Tim jerked in his chair and sat upright.

Alex just shook his head while Cindy smirked at Tim.

"Hell, man," Marty complained to Tim. "If you want to play footsies, do so with my sister."

"Oops," said Tim.

"You almost had a game of tennis going on there," Marty added.

"Jesus."

"Yeah, you'd need your maker right now if you'd gone any higher, let me give you the tip."

This time Alex snickered.

Cindy demurely peeked at Tim from beneath her fringe to find his cheeks a little flushed from his close encounter with her brother's unmentionables. His gaze when it found her promised retribution.

She couldn't wait.

The atmosphere between them was definitely getting a little sexually charged with anticipation, though the conversation remained light, skimming many topics, and by the time it was over and Alex and Marty were doing the dishes, everyone was relaxed.

Al woke up and demanded his dinner, and Tim took charge of him.

"Aw look," Marty said as Tim attended to the kitten. "Dad's got baby duty tonight."

"Jealous?" Tim drawled.

"That's my nephew you got there, Doc. Just treat him gentle."

Tim rolled his eyes.

"We better get going." Alex placed the tea towel on the rack. "Got an early morning call tomorrow."

"Oh?" She followed him to the door, Marty behind her.

"Yeah. Marty thinks a gym jockie can beat soldier training when it comes to strength and stamina. I'm going to teach him who's boss."

"Your first job will be dragging him out of bed."

"Ha ha." Marty ruffled her hair as he passed. "We'll see who's boss after tomorrows little sweat session."

"I'm so sacred," Alex murmured.

Marty punched him in the shoulder as they walked down the steps.

Alex punched him back, quit a lot harder, sending him staggering into some nearby bushes.

"Shit," said Marty. "That was hard."

"Just a tap, old boy, just a tap." Unlocking the car door, Alex grinned. "A little taste of what you're in for tomorrow."

"You better be able to back up your promises." Marty got into the passenger side.

"I always back up my promises." Alex waved to Cindy as he got into the car and shut the door.

Smiling, she waved back and watched as the tail lights disappeared down the winding drive and out of sight, then she turned and re-entered the house, locking the door behind her.

Walking into the lounge, she saw Tim tickling Al's stomach while Al's tiny paws batted at his finger.

"Tough boy," Tim observed. "He nearly sucked the bottle to death."

"Al loves his milk," she agreed, kneeling down to watch as Al rolled on the fleece sheet between her and Tim.

"He's thriving." Tim glanced up at her, his smile warm. "Thanks to you."

"TLC. It works wonders."

"So they say." He tickled along Al's back, but the kitten was too occupied trying to see around Cindy.

"He's a sticky beak." Grinning, she smoothed under his chin, rewarded by the little purr that sputtered to life.

They spent some time playing with Al, enjoying each others company.

Every time Tim reached past her to pick up a wandering Al and bring him back to the safety of his fleecy sheet, Cindy caught a whiff of Tim's cologne. Fresh, male, it was so him, and she breathed it in deep.

Leaning forward on her hands to roll a small, soft ball for Al, she glanced up to see Tim's gaze on her ample cleavage. That sent warmth roiling through her and she licked her suddenly dry lips.

His gaze followed every flick of her tongue, his brown eyes darkening.

Suddenly the atmosphere was turning from light and pleasant to something a lot more intense.

"Maybe," Tim suggested huskily, "It's time to put the baby to bed."

Chapter Eight

The pupils in Cindy's blue eyes dilated and he watched in increasing desire as she sucked in a breath, causing her impressive bosom to swell.

Jesus, he couldn't wait to get her out of her clothes and have his hands and mouth all over those luscious breasts.

"Are you sure," she asked a trifle breathlessly, "That you don't want another drink?"

"Lady, the only drink I want is from you." Satisfaction coursed through him as her round cheeks with the enchanting dimples in them flushed pink.

Reaching out, Cindy scooped Al up carefully, bringing him to her mouth to nuzzle the top of his furry little head. "Come on, little fellow. Tim wants to go home to bed."

"Not quite what I had in mind," he said.

Her eyes were filled with heat, but they also twinkled with a touch of devilment as well. That was one of the things he found so fascinating about Cindy, she was a mixture of many things - all woman, confident, a touch of uncertainty now and again, mischief, a sense of fun, and with a blunt honesty that attracted him.

Yeah, with Cindy Lawson, what you saw was what you got, and Tim liked what he saw.

Standing, she started from the room. "I'll put Al to bed in the kitten pen in my bedroom. I'll be back soon."

Back? Tim straightened and stretched. If she thought he was leaving, she had another think coming. Tonight he was going to bed the luscious Cindy babe. Yep, he was going to bed her and make love to her until neither of them could think straight.

Maybe he should have another drink to make sure he was well hydrated, shore up his reserves.

Grinning, he had another glass of apple juice, checked that all the doors were locked, and then he went upstairs.

Following the sound of Cindy's voice, he went down the corridor and came to a stop at her bedroom door. She was talking to Al as she settled him for the night but even though Tim leaned against the wall just out of sight, he was disappointed that she didn't at least mention his name to the furry baby.

But the night was young. By the time he finished with her, she was going to be screaming his name.

Grinning to himself, Tim brushed some of Al's baby fur off his shirt. Nothing wrong with a little confidence in ones prowess.

"Now go to sleep," Cindy instructed the kitten. "I'll be up in a couple of hours to feed you again."

Sure she'd be up, because Tim didn't intend for her to actually go to sleep for quite awhile.

Leaning one shoulder against the wall, he crossed his ankles and folded his arms, waiting for her to exit the bedroom.

Cindy walked out, saw him so close and jumped. "Cripes!"

"Hey," he drawled with deceptive casualness.

"Hey yourself." She eyed him closely.

She looked so damned yummy that he wanted to eat her up. Her dress came halfway down her thighs in total disregard for her plump legs which many large women would try and hide, but not his Cindy, no sir. She dressed how she pleased and that was a huge turn-on for him.

But he just knew that even if she was shy about her weight, he'd still want her.

Cindy being so confident just made seduction a lot more fun.

"So." His gaze ran leisurely over her generous curves. "There are a few issues we need to sort out."

"Oh?" Her expression was wary.

"Yeah. Tonight you were a bad girl."

Her brows rose. "Really?"

"Oh yeah. A *very* bad girl."

The corner of her lips twitched. "If this is your seduction technique, Clarke, you're going to have to work harder."

It was his turn to raise his brows in mock surprise. "My, you do have a mouth on you, Lawson."

"All the better to suck you with, honey."

He nearly choked.

She smirked. Hands on hips, one of those angled out cockily, she practically oozed daring.

Recovering himself, Tim managed to maintain a stern expression. "Playing with your brother was not on my agenda."

"It was your toe, wasn't it?"

"Not meant for your brother."

"If it's just your toe you meant for me, I'm disappointed."

"Oh, sugar." He straightened up. "Trust me, it's more than that I have planned for you."

"Good, otherwise I'd have to toss you out my door and go looking elsewhere for…" Moving closer to him, she ran one finger down his bicep, leaving a heated trail in her wake. "Satisfaction."

Hoo boy, she was burning him up. "Trust me, I'm gonna spoil you for anyone else."

"I hope so." Eyes twinkling, she tapped his chest. "Because if you're self promotion is anything like you, I'm going to be disappointed."

Tim looked down at his t-shirt. Yep, he had on his sad cartoon hound with *Sad to the Bone* printed around it. Not seduction material. Glancing up, he grinned crookedly. "I forgot to wear my 'Hot to Trot' shirt."

"Did you maybe think that coming to my door with your sad dog shirt might make me feel sorry for you?"

"It wasn't in the plan, but thinking about it now, would it have helped?"

"Not at all." Sliding her hand beneath the hem of his t-shirt, she hooked a finger in the waistband of his jeans. "So, Mr Discipline, got anything worth showing me?"

Oh boy, did he just. Smiling darkly, he rested his hand on her hip and slid it around to her bottom, cupping and squeezing it before administering a light smack on the curve of one buttock.

Her eyes darkened even more as she breathed, "Spanking, Mr Clarke? I suspected you might be little kinky, going by the rumours I've heard, but I had some doubts."

"And now?" He rubbed the just-smacked bottom with slow, firm sweeps of his hand.

Thick, black lashes swept down to hide her eyes. "I'm having doubts about my doubts."

Dipping his head, he placed his mouth to her ear and inhaled deeply of her scent, closing his eyes as all sorts of warmth swept through his senses at just her closeness and scent combined. "So how far do you want to go, Cindy?"

"How long do you want to play before we get hot and sweaty?"

Seriously, he was going to come in his jeans any second. "Don't you mean down and dirty?"

"Dirty, down, hot, sweaty - why worry about words?" Turning her head, she brushed her lips along his, breathing hotly against the sensitive skin of his lips and making heat skitter through his veins. "I'm feeling a rather interesting bulge against my innocent little body. How long can you last?"

Not much longer...not that he'd admit it. "As long as you need, sugar."

"Really?" A flick of her fingers had his jeans unsnapped. "Really, Clarke?" He angled his hips back enough to allow her fingers to glide the zip of the jeans open and had to clench his jaw against a groan when those dexterous fingers slid inside to cup his rigid length through his boxers. "I'm feeling a little wetness at the tip, Tim." Her breath was hotly damp now, and she flicked her tongue along the seam of his lips. "Now what could that mean?" Her thumb brushed the tip of his shaft through his boxers.

183

He nearly blew his load right then and there, but desperately maintaining control, he grabbed her wrist. "I think Mr Discipline should be in charge."

Her laugh was low, seductive and teasing. "Oh?"

"Yeah. And I've decided that discipline can wait." So saying, he grabbed her shoulders, whirling and pinning her to the wall as he pressed in against her, his lips taking hers.

Those lush lips had beckoned to him from the second she'd moistened them with her tongue. He licked along the seam, feeling the texture of the silky skin before demanding entry, sweeping inside when she obeyed without hesitation. She was sweeter than honey and he had to have her essence, licking deep, demanding more with his mouth even as his hips thrust against hers, her every soft curve a perfect match for his harder, leaner body.

Not enough. Never enough.

Blood coursing through his veins in a hot rush, he turned her from the wall and used his body to crowd her back into the bedroom. A quick glance over her shoulder showed him where the big bed was, and now, with his course in mind, he traced the side of her neck with his mouth, nipping and sucking lightly, his hands already pulling the straps of the dress from her shoulders to lie at her elbows, her bodice following as he pulled it down quickly and expertly to lie around her waist.

The bed at the backs of her knees brought them to a halt, and she shoved the t-shirt up and over his head. Tim obligingly raised his arms so that she could pull it free and toss it aside.

Now he could get a good eyeful of her magnificent bosom in a lacy bra, reinforced with expertise to look both sexy while supporting the generous globes. Purple lace with a pink flowered pattern, no doubt bought from a top end lingerie shop overseas.

God bless top end lingerie shops.

He wondered if her panties matched, and just the thought of that lace cupping her delicious mystery of womanhood had his head swimming and his blood pounding in his ears.

Hooking his thumbs in the dress, he slid it down over her hips to pool at her feet before stepping back to see if his little fantasy might be true.

Oh Jesus, purple satin sprinkled with a pink flowered pattern hid her secrets. His mouth went dry. This pair that Cindy wore wasn't a sexy little thong or brief little scrap of almost nothing. This was a pair of short, flowing, satiny boxers, only so much more fragile and feminine. They flowed around the tops of her thighs, purple lace brushing the tender skin where her bottom cheeks swelled out.

His gaze travelled up slowly, taking in every curve, every dip and swell, his gaze going higher, and with every curve and swell he passed, his shaft grew harder, thicker, longer.

Cindy Lawson was all woman, all curves, all softness and everything a red-blooded man could possibly fantasize about.

His fantasy.

He met her gaze. Standing there in all her glory, the purple panties and bra an open proclamation of a love and desire to wear pretty things, she looked every inch a confident woman, sure of herself. Until he caught a faint flicker in her eyes, a brief hesitation, a slight pink hint in her cheeks.

The fleeting show of uncertainty and self consciousness was gone as fast as it had appeared, and she angled her chin up slightly, once more the confident woman.

But that hint of vulnerability just caught at his heart, made him want to never see that uncertainty again, made him ache to show her how hot she was, how beautiful, how much her body turned him on.

"My fantasy." His voice was dark, sensuous, he could hear it, and he knew she did as well by the darkening of her eyes and the little smile that curled those luscious, plump lips.

One step forward and he was against her, chest to breasts, indulging himself with the tickle of lace as her bra pressed into him.

Holding her gaze, he reached around and unsnapped the bra, sliding the straps down her shoulders and arms, freeing her breasts so that the only thing holding the cups on her was his chest against her breasts.

So erotic, knowing that only he kept her clothed, knowing that she knew it. Her lips parted slightly, the lush pink of them drawing him, but he wasn't finished yet.

Keeping their gazes meshed, he hooked his thumbs into the sides of her panties and eased them down, sliding them over her silken skin, shifting his hips enough to allow them to fall down to her ankles.

Then he moved back enough so that her bra slipped down to join the panties at her ankles.

Another step forward and she was pressed against him, all silken skin, warm, soft, and scented. Her nipples, little nubs of aroused hardness, pressed into his chest and he breathed deep, enjoying watching her eyes close briefly as his chest moved against her.

Bringing his hands around her, he cupped the generous globes of her bottom and pulled her into him. Now he sheltered her, his body bent over hers, surrounding her, and she snuggled closer, her murmur of approval almost a purr. A low, sexy purr that made his shaft jerk.

"Now," she whispered against his throat, turning her face into him so that her breath was warm and damp on his skin, making him shiver with anticipation.

"No," he whispered back, almost a growl, he was so aroused.

Aroused by her scent, her taste, her softness and curves, her body…aroused by Cindy Lawson finally in his arms.

"Tim." She trailed her hands down his spine, nails scraping deliciously, fingers firm as she flattened her palms to slide beneath his jeans and boxers to spread along his firm buttocks. "Please."

He nipped her ear lobe, laving it soothingly with his tongue when she gasped and jumped in his arms. "I have control issues, remember?"

"Work on them later." She squeezed his buttocks.

He laughed, low, deep, dark, and felt the response in the way she nestled against him, drawn by his dominant side even if she didn't realise it.

"I'm not ready yet," he said huskily, and capturing a handful of her luxurious blonde hair, he tugged it gently until she tilted her head back to look up at him.

She looked like sin and sex all rolled into one, heavy eyed with desire, lips swollen from his kisses, eyes dark with need. Voluptuous temptation in his arms, calling to him with a sultry, curvaceous enticement.

"Oh no," he rasped, "I'm far from ready." And he tipped her back onto the bed. A quick yank to get the condom from his pocket and flicked onto the bed, and then he shucked his jeans and followed her down. "Move up, sugar, because I'm going to taste you."

Her eyes widened but she did as he ordered, sliding upward beneath him, her nipples peaking hard to scrape across his chest and upwards, the curls protecting her feminine secrets tickling along his groin and shaft and up against his abdomen.

Tim slid lower, his gaze never leaving hers.

Settled back against the pillows, she licked her lips in both anticipation and nervousness. "You're smiling like the big, bad wolf."

His smile grew. "I'm about to devour Goldilocks."

"That's a cross over of fairy tales." Her breath caught as he used his palms to spread her thighs. "I don't think that's allowed."

"Luscious babe, there's a lot of things I'm going to do to you that's not allowed in any fairytale I've ever read," he promised her.

Jesus, was that growl really his voice? Whatever, it sure turned Cindy on, because her breasts rose in aroused agitation, the pink nipples peaking hard on the trembling globes.

Settling between her thighs, he commanded firmly, "Bend your knees. Let me see what treasures you have hidden here."

She obeyed without protest, her position now giving him full access to her womanhood.

Tim looked his fill, taking in the dewy curls and the sheltering lips already slick with desire. Lowering his head, he ran the tip of his tongue along the outer labia, teasing her with the lightest of traces, feeling her jerk and stiffen.

Chuckling, he blew lightly on the heated folds, enjoying the sound of her sucked-in breath. Lifting his head, he glanced up the length of her body to see her biting her lip, her gaze on him.

One wicked smile, a moistening of his lips that had her eyes widening, and then he lowered his head and licked her.

Hard.

Fast.

His tongue stabbed in low and swiped up, pressing hard against her perineum, sliding easily over the opening of her body, tasting her cream as he came up and over the little clitoris sheltering high, flicking it with his tongue.

One inhalation and all he could smell was her arousal, and it was utterly delicious. Nectar to a man who desired sex, loved the taste of it, wanted it, luxuriated in it.

Nectar to a man who was with the one woman he wanted above all others, the one woman who suddenly made this moment, this time of intimacy, so much more.

He wanted to please her, really please her, drive her upwards and get the rewards of her climax on his tongue. Drink in her orgasm and do it all over again.

Sliding his hands under her hips, he dragged his thumbs into the sensitive area where her thighs met her hip, making her squirm, and he laughed erotically as he slid his hands higher until he gripped the curves of her hips to hold her at his mercy.

And then he devoured her, licking deep, playing with her clitoris, teasing the tiny little bud until it was hard and swollen, sucking the tender flesh into his mouth carefully but firmly, flattening his tongue against it and rubbing.

Cindy shattered and he had to hold her hips firm as she arched on the bed and climaxed hard. He caught the cream that came from her, literally swallowing her orgasm, tasting her as she came, and then he wrung another orgasm from her, refusing to let her come down from the erotic haze into which he'd thrust her.

He worked his tongue around the opening of her body, slipping inside, teasing her, rolling her clitoris until she shattered again.

His shaft was hard, the combined taste of her orgasm, the softness of her undulating body, the sent of her arousal and her whimpers that filled the room bringing his desire to the fore.

His shaft, already hard, was now swollen, demanding, and his hips ached to thrust him home into her body. Seed leaked from the tip and Tim felt as though he'd never been harder or thicker.

He needed her, now.

Reaching out, he snagged the condom that he'd tossed onto the bed and ripped the wrapper off, somehow managing to lift his hips and roll the condom on without shifting too much. Then he moved up her body, watching her shudder as she started to come down from the climax, and satisfaction roiled through him.

Cindy was hot, sexy, and all his.

He just kept moving up until his shaft slid through her swollen labia and lodged at the entrance to her body, and still he moved upwards, sliding in deep and deeper still, and he didn't stop moving until he was lodged firmly inside her body, their groins pressed together.

It felt like hot, sweet heaven.

She opened her eyes hazily as he linked his fingers through hers to bring her hands up each side of her head, burying them in the blonde tresses that lay scattered over the pillow.

He'd meant to say 'Hi' or something just as light to show how in control he was, but what came out was "You're mine, Cindy. All mine." It came out in a voice so deep and dark he almost didn't recognise it. But he knew it instinctively. It was the dominant side of him, an uncovered side.

He might have always been in control, but this dominance was something that only this curvaceous woman brought out in him.

He was going to claim her.

Drawing back his hips, he thrust hard, burying deep, rewarded by her moan and arching up into him, her hips seeking to match his rhythm.

He set a hard pace, fast, the urgency building up inside him. Seed leaked from the tip of his shaft, caught in the protective condom, and he wished there was nothing between them, that his seed could coat the walls of her spasming channel to brand her as his. His fluid inside her, his seed.

Later. Later that would happen, he swore to himself.

Fire burned through his veins, pouring through his body, igniting sparks of heat that burned down to his shaft. His scrotum pulled tight and tighter until he was sure he couldn't last any longer.

His shaft got thicker and he worked to drag it through her channel, glorying in the tight clasp as her body sought to hold him deep.

Hips pounding, he shoved hard, wanting her so badly. The pleasure bordered on pain, sweat dampening his body as he thrust harder, faster, feeling the delicious tension build inside him.

A glance down showed that Cindy was going up that erotic path with him, and he bent down and caught those soft, swollen lips, kissing her deep, wanting them joined in every way as the climax built.

Desire skimmed down through his spine, coiled low, heat burning, and he could feel it, it was so close. So very close. He could feel the power in his muscles, the veins standing out in his biceps as he pushed upwards, breaking the contact of their lips helplessly as he sought the erotic pleasure that pulled at him.

Pulled at his scrotum.

Pulled at his mind.

Pulled at his shaft.

And then it had him. One last, almost brutal shove of his hips and the dam broke, the climax crashing over him, sucking him under, and he heard her cry as she joined him.

He had no idea how long he'd been gone, drowsily and happily floating out in the clouds of spent desire, but when he slowly drifted down it was to find himself lying on his side with Cindy cradled in his arms, her face close to his as they faced each other.

Utter peace and contentment stole upon him. The quiet of the night was beyond the open window, the lamp cast a soft, golden glow around the large, comfortable bedroom, and lying in his arms was the only woman who'd ever meant anything to him.

Life, right now, was bloody brilliant.

Slowly Cindy opened her eyes and the dreamy expression in them made him smile. Oh yeah, true male satisfaction had to be acknowledged.

"Clarke," she murmured.

"Yeah?"

"You were worth it."

"Hot damn, I was, wasn't I?"

Her giggle was tired and satisfied.

Yeah, life was bloody brilliant.

Closing his eyes, Tim drifted off to sleep with Cindy nestled against him.

~*~

To say that Tim was a little quiet was putting it mildly. Cindy glanced towards the kitchen doorway into the hallway. He'd woken her up during the night with some pretty intense lovemaking session, not that she was complaining, but when she'd gotten out of bed this morning and headed for the shower, he'd smiled at her and…well, nothing else.

Had she made a huge mistake? Frowning, she poured herself a cup of coffee. Now that they'd actually made love, was she out of his system? Oh crap, was it what she'd feared?

Surely not. There had been something magical in their lovemaking, something she'd certainly never had with the Italian Stallion. But after the intensity with which he'd made love during the night, the tender words and warm arms that had held her, Tim had been quiet this morning. Thoughtful.

Shaking her head, she took a sip of coffee. She had to get a grip on things and not read more into it.

Tim appeared in the doorway, his hair damp from the shower and an errant lock hanging over his brow. Seeing her, he smiled and walked over, bending to drop a soft, lingering kiss on her lips.

She had to secretly admit to a small amount of relief.

"Mmm," he murmured. "Coffee. I can drink it from your lips."

"Okay," she said, "I don't know if that's kinky, romantic, or even a little ick."

Laughing, he helped himself to a cup and perching on a stool at the kitchen bench, he blew on the steaming liquid and watched her closely.

She could feel the blush on her cheeks, but she met his gaze steadily.

"Well, Miss Lawson," he drawled, "You are a passionate little thing."

"Well, Mr Clarke, you're not so bad yourself," she drawled back.

He grinned. "Okay, you're hot."

She fluttered her eyelashes. "Why, please, do go on."

"Only if you want to end up flat on your back again." His eyes twinkled. "Or on your stomach."

"If you're trying to make me shy it won't work."

"Tart," he said.

"I may be a tart, but you came here sad to the bone, remember?"

"I'm sure leaving wrung out." Deftly catching the tea towel she threw at him, he winked. "In a good way, of course."

"Of course."

Silence fell on the kitchen as they both lingered over their coffee.

Tim broke it first. "So, where are Sam and Ruth?"

"It's Saturday. They don't work on the weekend."

He glanced at his watch. "Unfortunately, I do. I'm on shift this morning."

"A vet's job is never done?"

"Afraid not." Downing the last of the coffee, he got up and placed the empty cup in the sink. "I have to go."

"I'll see you off." She stood.

Sliding an arm around her waist, he drew her with him through the lounge and then the hallway. Nuzzling her hair as they stood at the door, he said softly, "Thanks for last night."

"I think I should be the one thanking you." She shifted and winced slightly. "Not that my muscles will."

His grin was definitely wolfish. "I plan on giving those muscles a good workout *very* often."

"So sure of yourself."

"Well, we could just play safe and go to a movie tonight."

"Really?"

"Yeah. A movie before we boink our brains out."

"You are such a romantic."

"I know, it's all part of my charm."

Seconds later she was waving him off and watching his car disappear down the driveway. Smiling, she went inside and locked the door behind her. Walking into the lounge, she looked down at Al, who was just stirring, his little head lifting. At the sight of her, he pushed up onto his little legs and toddled over towards her, meowing.

Opening the pen, she lifted him out and rubbed her cheek against his. "Men. You all want something."

Al meowed and purred.

Getting his bottle ready, Cindy thought over the events of the night. Now she was alone she had time to think. It was practically mind-boggling. She was dating Tim Clarke. He'd been on his knees at her feet, baring his heart to her, sharing his feelings, and then he'd made love to her in several different positions she hadn't thought of sharing with anyone - *ever* - and now she was dating him.

Would wonders never cease?

Giggling a little, she watched as Al sucked blissfully on the teat of the bottle. Life took some strange turns and she wasn't going to question it.

Then it hit her.

Tim had suggested they go to his place. His house. His sanctuary. The one place he'd never taken any of the women in his life.

He'd been going to take her to his sanctuary.

At the realisation of the magnitude of his suggestion, warmth washed through her. He'd meant what he'd said, he really did care about her and wanted to give them a chance at a relationship.

But he had been quiet when he'd first woken up, and she wondered what that was all about. In fact, she wondered if that was him normally when he woke in the morning. Maybe he wasn't a morning person.

Maybe, she thought impatiently, she had to stop doubting things and looking for problems that weren't there - if they were there at all.

"Seriously," she said to Al, "Sex messes with your head."

He closed his eyes and continued sucking on his bottle.

After putting Al back to bed, she did a quick tidy up of the house, which never really got untidy with just her living in it, and then she went upstairs to make the bed. Just thinking about what Tim had done to her in it was enough to make her blush.

Her one and only previous lover, the Italian man who'd thought her curves so sexy and taught her to accept them, she hadn't allowed to do what Tim had so easily persuaded her into doing the night before, in fact, she hadn't needed a whole lot of persuasion. Tim led and she'd followed.

Hoo boy, had she ever followed.

The phone rang, diverting her thoughts, and she picked it up. "Hello?"

"Hey." Maddy's voice came through clearly. "Want to meet me at Curtis's Coffee Café for lunch?"

"What's the occasion?"

"You tell me."

Cindy looked into the mirror at her image holding the phone. "What's to tell?"

"What's not to tell?"

"This could be a long conversation."

"So let's have it over lunch."

"I don't know. Some things should be kept private."

There was silence for a few seconds before Maddy said, "I want all the details."

Cindy giggled. "I don't know if that's appropriate conversation for a café."

"Seriously, now I really want *all* the details."

"Might make you jealous."

"Mike's my bed buddy. Nothing could make me jealous. Though maybe there could be something he might be able to learn from Tim." There was a low voice in the background, the sound of a scuffle, and Maddy actually squealed. "*Mike!*"

"Do you need to be left alone right now?" Cindy queried.

Maddy was laughing, but a trifle breathlessly. "No, I-stop it! Mike, I - *ohhhh!*"

The voice on the phone changed, becoming deeper, a familiar growl. "Mads can't talk right now, but she'll be able to gasp out a few words by lunchtime."

"Fair enough," Cindy said cheerfully.

"I have to prove something to her."

"Understood, Mr Law Enforcer, Sir."

"'Bye, Cindy."

"'Bye, Mike."

Really, the big lug was besotted with her best friend. Grinning, Cindy hung up the phone. Maddy would be lucky to walk a straight line without bow legs by the time Mike had finished proving his love making prowess to her.

Lucky woman.

There was some stiffness in her own muscles from the exertions of the night before, and she did a few stretching exercises, wincing. Nope, forget that, she'd go for a walk later.

Her gaze fell on Al sleeping peacefully in his kitten pen. She had to find a baby-sitter while she had lunch with Maddy. Her friend wouldn't mind if Al's carrier and bottle accompanied them, but the café would certainly frown upon it.

She rang her mother.

"Oh, of course," Mrs Lawson cooed. "Bring little Al here. I'll take good care of him."

Al was one spoiled kitten, Cindy realised as she got a bag ready for him. Honestly, it was like having a human baby. The bag had some clean rags in it, his formula, bottle and teat, spare bottle and teat, a spare fleecy sheet, and a couple of small, soft balls for gentle playing . She transferred him from the kitten pen to the cat carrier and was ready to go.

Her mother met them at the top of the staircase, eagerly peeking in the carrier and cooing over how much Al had grown.

"You only saw him the other day." Cindy set the carrier on the floor of the lounge.

"Babies grow so fast." Mrs Lawson checked the bag.

"I've packed everything," Cindy assured her.

"Not to worry, I made sure we have some spare stuff here for him."

Cindy's eyes widened. "You bought supplies?"

"In case of an emergency." Mrs Lawson made kissy sounds at Al, who meowed back at her. "Poor baby." She scooped him out and cuddled him close. "Granny's here now, sweetheart."

Cindy rolled her eyes.

"I saw that." Sitting on the sofa, her mother eyed her. "Anything to tell me?"

"No."

"Any grandchildren in the near future?"

"Foster ones, maybe. Furry and with a liking for fish and milk."

"Huh." Rubbing her rouged cheeks along Al's furry one, Mrs Lawson raised one finely plucked brow. "So, Tim Clarke, eh?"

"That Marty's a tattle tale." With a sigh, Cindy sat down.

"He's got a beaut shiner. I understand that's a gift from the Clarke boy."

"Marty needs to grow up."

Mrs Lawson snorted.

"Yeah, wishful thinking." Cindy flopped back in the armchair. "Geez, he embarrassed me last night. I wanted to flog him myself. I mean, who the hell does he think he is?"

"Your brother?"

"He'll be a dead one if he keeps sticking his nose in my business."

"Now, dear, he means well."

"Does he mean well when he's running around the neighbourhood boinking all the girls?"

"I don't want to hear about that."

"Charming their pants off them?"

"Cindy."

"Leaving them bow-legged?"

"Cindy!"

"Geez, Mum, you know what a womaniser he is!"

"He's my little boy. I don't like to think of him like that." With a sniff, Mrs Lawson primly flicked a non-existent piece of something off her powder-blue skirt. Then she spoiled the effect by adding, "He's just like your father used to be."

"Ewww!"

"He charmed my pants off me."

"Mum!"

Totally unrepentant, Mrs Lawson smiled. "I'll always remember the back seat of the BMW-"

"I'm not hearing this." Sticking her fingers in her ears, Cindy started to chant, "La-la-la-la."

"Don't be silly, dear, it's all perfectly natural."

"One's parents don't have sex, you know that. It's an unwritten rule."

"Then you don't want to know what your father and I did last night."

"Oh my God."

"And this morning."

Cindy leaped to her feet. "I have to go."

She collided with Alex in the doorway.

"What's the rush?" he queried.

"Mum's having sex with Dad."

"I didn't hear that."

"All perfectly natural," Mrs Lawson cheerfully called out. "I don't know what the problem is-"

Cindy didn't hear the rest as she and her brother both made for the door.

"Okay," Alex said as they exited the house. "Our parents are easy-going, but there's such a thing as too easy-going."

"At least in front of their kids." Cindy shuddered. "Ew, and ew, and did I mention ewwwww?"

"I believe you did."

Cindy was still shaking her head when she drew up in front of Curtis's Coffee Café. As usual, it was busy. Maddy hadn't arrived, so she slid into one of the high-backed booths and consulted the menu, waving off the waitress who approached.

It wasn't long before Maddy's car pulled into the parking area and her friend exited the car. As she got closer, Cindy could see the glow of happiness on her face. Yep, Mike had well and truly proven himself.

She grinned as Maddy sat down opposite her. "No bow legs?"

Maddy flushed. "No."

"Need any tips for him?"

"Trust me, Mike doesn't need any tips at all."

"Got the love bug all sorted out, has he?"

"No love bug. Love log."

"Okay, I'm trying to decide if that's a wow or an ick."

"Hey, you're the one giving the metaphors, not me." Maddy consulted the menu.

The waitress came over and they gave their orders.

"So," Cindy said. "You got Tim to spill his guts."

"If you mean, did he need to talk? Yes, he spoke to me." Maddy fiddled with the strap of her shoulder bag. "Um…are you mad?"

"Of course not." Cindy sighed. "Though it would have been nice if he'd thought to talk to me."

Maddy looked up in surprise. "Tim didn't speak to you?"

"Well, yes he did, after he spoke to you. I just meant I wish he'd thought to come to me first."

"Honey." Maddy smiled gently. "Tim was tied up in knots. You were the cause of those knots. He needed to speak to someone who wasn't involved to sort out those knots. Trust me."

"You make him sound like a total basket case."

"I've always had my doubts about that bloke's sanity at the best of times, but he's not a total basket case." Maddy grinned a little. "A bit of one, but not a total one."

"What a relief." Cindy leaned back in the booth. "So, were the rumours about his mother all true?"

"Pretty much."

"Total bitch?"

"Cold to the bone marrow."

"What about his Dad?"

"Nice man but weak." Maddy sighed. "Look, Cindy, Tim should be telling you this, not me."

"Tim isn't ready to spill his guts right now. Besides, how can I fight his demons if I don't know what they are?"

"Who said you have to fight his demons?"

"Ever met his mother?"

Maddy's smile faded a little. "Yeah, I've had that dubious pleasure."

"Then you get my drift." Cindy studied her friend thoughtfully. "This isn't some kind of nurse/patient confidentiality crap, is it?"

Maddy accepted the iced chocolate the waitress handed to her and took a sip. "Yummy. And yes, it sort of is a nurse/patient confidentiality *crap* thing."

"Pooh." Cindy knew her friend well enough to realise that she wasn't going to spill too much of what had been said between her and Tim. "Mind you, Tim told me he'd spilled his guts to you."

"That's twice you've put it like that. A bit crass, actually."

"Hey, his words, not mine."

"Okay, then." Maddy waited expectantly.

"He told you about his mother and father and things."

"Yep."

"And then he told you about me." Cindy shifted a little.

Maddy's eyes softened. "This isn't really about his parents, is it?"

"Well…"

"I don't believe it. You of all people."

"What?" Distinctly uncomfortable now, Cindy took a sip of coffee frappe.

"You're always so confident, but you're not totally sure of Tim, are you?"

Trust Maddy to know instinctively what was troubling her. Cindy sighed. "Okay, so maybe I'm a little unsure. A *little* unsure. Who wouldn't be? Tim goes out with gorgeous girls, he's a playboy, and suddenly he's fallen for me and wants a relationship. Wouldn't you be a *little* unsure?"

"You slept with him," Maddy stated bluntly. "You don't go to bed with men you're unsure about."

"Tim's different.'

"How so?"

"I don't know. He's a…a…"

"Must be the t-shirts he wears. You love the weird sayings."

"They're amusing, but no. Mind you, it says a lot about him." Cindy tapped the table thoughtfully.

"So what do you like about Tim?"

"I don't know. He's funny, annoying, kind to animals - that's a big plus, by the way. He likes Al - another big plus, because the man you have the hots for has to love the kids, furry or not."

A smile quirked the corners of Maddy's mouth.

"And," Cindy continued, "I don't know. I feel…really, can I say safe? Because I don't think that's the word I'm looking for."

"Why not?"

"Mads, seriously, would you put Tim and the word safe all in the same sentence?"

"He helped me out one dark night when I was on the highway with a flat tyre."

"You were ready to knock him on the head with the tyre lever."

"I didn't know who he was then."

The waitress came and set their plates of food before them, and they thanked her before she left.

Picking up the fork, Cindy speared some lettuce.

"Do you really not trust Tim?" Maddy asked gently.

"No." Cindy grimaced. "Yes."

"Maybe?"

Chewing on the lettuce, Cindy pushed the beetroot around the plate. "I trust him."

"So what's the problem?"

"How long do you think he's going to be happy to be with someone like me?"

"What's wrong with you?"

"Nothing, but compared to the girls he normally dates… Well, look at me, Mads. I wear tight clothes, bright colours. I make some people wince at the sight of me."

"But you don't care about that, and that's what's so charming about you. You are you."

"I don't want to embarrass Tim."

"Honey, Tim chose you. He likes you just the way you are." Alarm crossed Maddy's face. "You're not going to try and change, are you?"

"Me? No." Cindy laughed. "I am who I am, and I decided a long time ago to just be me. I'm happy the way I am, even though I may not dress the way society thinks a plus-sized woman should dress."

"And that makes you unique." Maddy placed her hand atop Cindy's. "That is what makes you Cindy Lawson. You do what you want, when you want, how you want, and that's the Cindy Lawson that Tim is drawn to."

It certainly eased some doubts that Cindy had, but there was still a niggling little uncertainty that Tim could be happy with her forever.

That sudden thought startled her. When had forever even come into the picture? It was a relationship in progress, he hadn't even promised her forever and she'd known that from the start. She'd been happy with that, or so she'd thought.

Crap.

The thought of being with Tim and then everything not working out, that hurt. A little.

Double crap.

That hurt a lot.

Triple crap.

Heart feeling a little lower in her chest than it should be, she picked up the frappe and took a long drink.

Maddy arched a brow. "Have a revelation?"

"Just a thought."

"Care to share it?"

Cindy smiled. "It's nothing. So, tell me about Mike's love making prowess."

"You're changing the subject.'

"And you're going red."

"I take it this conversation is over?"

"The troublesome Tim one, yes. The hot Mike one, no."

"If we talk about Mike, we talk about Tim."

"Put like that…what are your plans for the weekend?"

~*~

The clinic was closed for the Saturday afternoon when Tim opened the back door and looked out at Mike and Rick. "Hello, ladies."

"You rang." Rick held up a bag. "Brought the nibblies for our little chat."

"Seriously, you two need to get a life."

"We have a life. Now we're just trying to sort out yours."

"I invited you two for a bloke chat, not a ladies get together." Standing aside, Tim waited for his friends to pass him. "But it is you two, so why should I expect anything different?"

Mike grunted and elbowed him out of the way.

"Okay, now that's better." Tim rubbed his abdomen. "That's a *bloke* thing."

"And being a bloke, I'm not going to offer to kiss diddums better," Rick informed him, walking into the vets' office.

"Thank God for small mercies." Tim made to round the desk to sit in the big, main chair, but Mike beat him to it. "Oh, I beg your pardon. Do make yourself at home."

Mike just gave another grunt.

Hooking a chair with his foot, Rick pulled it in place while distributing the iced coffees from the bag.

"Multi tasking," Tim observed. "I'm disturbed. Isn't that a sheila's thing?"

"It's also a doctor's thing," Rick replied, unperturbed. "I can do a prostate exam and talk all at once. Impressed?"

"My anal sphincter just closed up."

Mike grimaced. "Are we here to talk about your arse or your problem?"

"Maybe his arse is his problem," Rick suggested. "Maybe his problem is that he *is* an arse."

"My problem was in being stupid enough to ask you two to come over for a manly exchange of information." Tim twisted the cap off the plastic bottle. "Rick, I think I'm falling for you, man."

In the act of opening a big bag of chips, Rick raised his brows.

"My mother is on an environmental kick. Just using a plastic bottle makes me feel all warm inside." Grinning, Tim saluted him and took a mouthful of coffee.

Rick shook his head. "Always a rebel."

"Speaking of rebels," Mike growled, "What are you doing with Cindy?"

"Ah." Lowering the bottle, Tim eyed his friend warily. "You know about that?"

"Yeah." Mike's eyes narrowed. "So what are you doing with my woman's best friend?"

"Your woman? You sound so - so big and protective." Tim gave a delighted shudder. "Oh my."

"I don't think it's wise to push the big lug's buttons." Hauling out a handful of chips and sitting down in the chair, Rick leaned back, stretched out his legs and crossed his ankles with a sigh of pleasure.

"But it's fun." Tim batted his eyelashes. "And educational."

"Getting your balls ripped off won't be fun," Mike said.

"Now you're just being a bully." Sitting in another chair, Tim propped his heels on the corner of the desk.

They sat and ate and drank in silence for several minutes, Tim enjoying the companionship of his two friends, but uncertain how to word his worry. For sure, there were no other men he'd ever have opened up to, but his problem *was* actually opening up.

So he put out some feelers. "Maddy tell you anything?" He glanced at Mike.

"No."

"Nothing at all?"

"You came, you talked, she tells me nothing of it."

"And that doesn't worry you?"

"Should it?" Mike flexed one big hand.

"I'm getting all faint." Tim placed a hand on his chest. "Really, Mike, you have to stop flexing those muscles around me."

Rick shook his head. "If you want to get some shit off your chest before you prod Mike enough to actually mangle you, I suggest you try to find a way to start."

"Hey, I reckon I've taken a huge step just by getting you ladies here to bloody talk."

"So talk," Mike said bluntly. "Stop pussy-footing around."

"Maddy's right. You are a Neanderthal. Where's your sensitivity?"

"Out the window when it comes to a certain cretin playing around with Cindy and being a shrinking violet about discussing it."

"Shrinking violet? Are you taking florist classes in your off-time now?"

With a sigh, Rick raised the bottle of coffee to his mouth. "This is going to be a long conversation."

"I hope you brought more nibblies, then."

Mike placed his empty bottle of coffee on the table and looked at Tim out of stoic cop eyes. Pale blue, direct, his gaze seemed to burn right into Tim's brain.

As if that was anything unusual.

"All right," Mike rumbled. "You don't call for nothing. What's the problem?"

"Problem?" Tim shrugged. "No real problem."

Rick levelled a steady look at him.

Yeah, Tim had a problem. He sobered. A big one, and for the first time in his life he didn't know what to do about it.

"I can't believe I'm doing this," he muttered.

"Just spill it," Mike ordered.

"I feel like I'm being interrogated."

"You're the one with the confession."

Tim sighed. "Okay. I have a problem with a certain lady."

"Cindy Lawson."

"Yes. Yes, Cindy, okay?"

"We'll see how okay it is in a minute."

Damn, Mike was such a protective arse. One of the likeable things about him, actually. And now that it came to Cindy, Tim was feeling that same protectiveness.

In fact, he felt it so much he scowled at Mike. "Yeah, Cindy is my problem. *My* problem. Okay?"

Mike's expression didn't change one iota, but Rick's eyebrows nearly disappeared into his hairline.

"Yeah." Tim continued to scowl. "I have a lady problem. Happy now?"

"I'm not sure," Rick replied. "I don't have enough details yet."

Frustrated, and frustrated because he was frustrated for the first time in his adult life when it came to a woman, Tim continued to scowl. "I've fallen for Cindy Lawson. I had sex with her." He caught Mike's gaze and almost snarled, "Yeah. I had sex with Cindy Lawson. I slept all night at her house."

Good God, a little voice inside his head said, *you're prodding the beast. Are you insane?*

Yes, yes he was, he decided, because women drove men insane.

"So you slept at Cindy's house," Rick said in a reasonable, calm tone. "And?"

"And I bared my soul to her." Tim flung himself back in the chair and closed his eyes. "I told her I wanted a relationship with her."

"Sounds like you got it."

"No. I mean a real relationship." Tim grimaced. "I'm trying to have a *relationship* with her."

When silence was all he heard, he cracked open one eyelid to meet Mike's steady regard. It was impossible to know what the cop was thinking, so he glanced at Rick. His other friend was thoughtfully contemplating him.

"Any time you want to add something," Tim said.

He felt all kinds of a fool. Tim Clarke had never had doubts about women, had never had doubts about where he stood with them. Now he had a lot and he didn't know what to do about it.

So here he was, the playboy vet sitting with his friends, the cop and the doctor, seeking relationship advice. It was sad. But he was desperate, desperate enough to make Cindy happy, to keep her happy, and to that end he'd sit here like a fluttery fool chatting about feelings yet again. Jesus.

Yeah, maybe he better start praying for divine help.

Chapter Nine

"You love Cindy," Mike stated.

"Love? I don't know about love," Tim replied hastily. "I like her. A lot."

"What are you? Ten?"

"What's that supposed to mean?"

"Tim, you've been around women a long time. You love 'em and leave 'em, you don't love 'em and keep 'em. You want something more permanent with Cindy. Doesn't that tell you that you might like her more than just, well, like?"

"No." He could feel an edge of panic creeping in. More than like was permanent. Did he want permanent?

"I know that look," Rick said. "He's going to faint."

"What?" Tim glared at him. "I am not. What the hell?"

"Just saying, man." Rick shrugged. "You had that fright or flight look on your face."

"Face your fear," Mike advised. "Don't flee it."

"Seriously, are we in some Victorian romance novel?"

"No, we're in your love life," Rick replied. "You can tell by how messy it is."

"I don't have a love life."

"You do."

"You're insane."

"No, you're in denial." Before Tim could reply indignantly, Rick pointed a finger at him. "When you have sex with a woman and walk away, that's just sex."

"So?"

"When you make love with a woman and then try and figure out how to make a relationship last for a longer period, that's a love life."

Oh dear. Tim almost froze in his chair. He had a love life. Freakin' hell. A *love life*.

"Maybe you should have brought the crash cart, Rick." Mike leaned back in the chair and swung his big boots up on the desk.

"He'll be fine," Rick replied. "But if anything happens, you're doing the mouth-to-mouth bit."

Mike grunted and reached for the bag of chips.

Tim didn't know what to think. He knew he wanted a relationship with Cindy. He'd told her, too, and that hadn't changed. But calling a relationship a love life? That opened up a whole new ball game.

The panic started again. He didn't know what love was, not really. Sure, he loved his Aunt Hannah in a non attraction way, and he liked Nancy, and he loved Mike and Rick in a blokey-kind of way, nothing sissy or anything, just really strong friendship, but that was it.

"I don't know anything about love," he finally said. "I don't know if I love Cindy."

Mike and Rick looked at each other.

"Shit." Tim scowled. I don't know, okay? And it's not up for discussion anyway."

"I think I can guess your problem," Mike said dryly.

"It's not what you're thinking. I know *I* wasn't thinking about love when I called you."

"So what is your problem?" Rick asked curiously.

Glad to be back on familiar ground - sort of - Tim exhaled. "How do I win a girl like Cindy?"

"Win? Or do you mean court? Because you have to court in order to win."

"You and your old fashioned romantic notions."

"Much nicer sounding than dating, I always think."

Mike just continued to look stoic.

"Okay." Tim looked at him. "How did you win Maddy?"

A slow grin of supreme male satisfaction crossed Mike's normally impassive face. "I told her."

"Oh great. Like that's going to help me with a girl like Cindy."

"It takes work."

"That's what I'm trying to do!" Tim flung up his hands. "How do I date a girl like Cindy?"

"Well, how do you normally date a girl?" Rick retorted.

"I buy them a drink, boink their brains out and go home."

"You're right, that won't work with Cindy."

"Wouldn't have worked with Maddy, either," Mike muttered.

"Look, Rick, you're married and the big doofus here is engaged, both of you to nice girls. What's the secret?

"No secret. Just be yourself."

"You think that's such a good idea?" Mike actually smirked.

Tim looked sourly at him. "You're really enjoying this, aren't you?"

"Watching you squirm? Yeah."

Tim flipped him the middle finger.

"Now, girls," Rick admonished before growing serious. "Tim, Cindy is a nice girl, but she's different to Cherry and Maddy. Cherry was really self-conscious about her body - which, by the way..." Rick's eyes unfocussed a little as he smacked his lips together. "Yummy."

"But you fixed that," Tim said impatiently.

"Between ourselves, yes."

"And you won her."

"Through patience and sheer perseverance. And boy, is she worth it."

Tim switched his gaze to Mike.

Mike shrugged. "Maddy was confident, but she had issues with family. They knocked her around about in the confidence department, but she was very much her own woman." His slow grin was a little wolfish. "I just gave her that firm hand she needed."

"I'm surprised she agreed to marry you. Neanderthal." Tim fluttered his eyelashes. "That is her nickname for you, right?"

"Yeah, it is. She can call me that." Mike pointed at him. "You can't."

Rick grinned.

"So what's the secret?" Tim demanded. "How did you win Maddy?"

Mike contemplated the desk top for a few seconds before meeting Tim's gaze. "Truth be told, Tim, love is a funny thing. Relationships are funny. Everyone is different. You need to find your own way."

"That's your words of wisdom?" Tim rolled his eyes. "I could have consulted a fortune cookie for that."

"You need to consult nothing. Just be yourself."

"Oh, like that's going to work?"

"You've already been in her bed, haven't you? Who were you then?"

Tim went completely blank, the only thought bouncing around in his head that he'd been his normal horny self, only he'd done things to her that he rarely did with other women.

Because Cindy wasn't other women. Cindy was…special.

"I think he's getting it." Mike turned to Rick. "Thank God. Another few seconds and I'd be trying to punch commonsense into him."

"Here, let me try." Rick crossed one knee over the other. "Now, Tim-"

"Oh great." Tim sighed. "You're going all professional quack on me. If you start charging me by the minute, you're going to regret it. You can't sit with my sneaker up your arse."

Unfazed, Rick linked his hands on his flat abdomen. "Be yourself with Cindy. What you see with her is what you get, and you should honour her with the same thing. She obviously likes your company, she knows your reputation and is still willing to give you a chance. Don't mess it up by trying to be or do something you're not." He spoiled the professional air by scowling and adding, "Idiot."

"Uncalled for."

"But true. Seriously, just be yourself! God knows, if she's willing to go the distance with you as you are, you'll both last through anything the world will throw at you."

"So you think movies, a walk in the park, some hand holding, that'll work?"

"Is that what you want to do with her?"

"Well, heh heh..." No, he wanted to do dirty things with her, make her scream, make her hot and -

"Tim!"

"Sorry. I got sidetracked."

"You don't say?"

"Anyway, I don't know if Cindy will like that kind of thing." He stopped and contemplated for a few seconds. "Mind you, I did say I'd take her to the movies tonight."

"And?"

"She seemed okay with it."

"There you go. Just follow your instincts, and above all, be yourself. Is that so hard?"

"She didn't say we couldn't boink our brains out afterwards."

Rick looked pained. "Please tell me you didn't suggest that to her."

"Heh heh."

"And still she hasn't left him," Rick told Mike.

"No accounting for taste."

~*~

Sitting in the dark movie theatre, Cindy's eyes nearly crossed with boredom. Oh dear lord, how long was this drama story? If someone didn't smack the heroine upside the head soon, she'd do it for them.

Did Tim really go for this stuff? She glanced sideways at him. Or was he just trying to be sophisticated?

Catching her glance, he smiled at her. "Enjoying it?"

"Oh yes." *No.*

"It's very popular."

"Really?" *Amongst the brain dead, perhaps?*

"Seems as though drama is all the go now."

"Uh-huh."

He returned his attention to the screen while Cindy stared at it without seeing, her mind crying out in boredom. The film was a disaster. It was killing her. Intellectual movies just weren't her choice of genre. Now thrillers, horror, sci-fi, that was more to her taste. But she was here with Tim, and for him she'd smile and nod and fake it. Faking it would be a first for her.

She nearly giggled aloud at where that thought took her but managed to control it.

Tim glanced curiously at her, obviously having heard her muffle the sound before it could escape too much. She smiled up at him and looked quickly back at the screen, and he did the same.

That had to have taken all of five minutes. Only another hour to go. *Another freakin' hour!*

And then she felt it, the slide of an arm along the back of her seat. Was Tim really making a move? Finally? Yep, there it came, the subtle shift and his side was now brushing against hers.

Nice. She inhaled the heady aroma of his cologne and soap. Very nice. Leaning into him, mentally cursing the armrest but willing to work with what she had, Cindy laid her hand on his thigh and immediately felt the muscle beneath his slacks jump before tightening.

Seemed as though she'd surprised Tim. Half his luck. She could do with a surprise right then to keep her awake.

She certainly didn't expect the hand that slid down her back and the dexterous thumb that flicked the side of her breast.

Holy Hannah, had she really felt that?

A quick glance sideways showed Tim still watching the screen. Huh. Maybe he'd been so distracted that his hand had slipped and he wasn't even aware of what he was doing.

Another flick, a caress, in fact, and her nipples hardened. Oh man, that had to be deliberate, there was no way it could have been an accident.

Another glance up but no, Tim was still watching the screen.

One way to find out. Cindy slid her hand a little higher up his thigh and was rewarded by his sudden intake of breath. A little higher as she tested his resolve, waiting for him to perhaps stop her.

No, knowing Tim, he'd probably enjoy a little groping at the movies.

With a little sigh of contentment, she settled against him, leaving her hand where it lay high on his thigh while tracing circles on his leg with her nails.

He shifted a fraction. His hand moved, coming around to partially cup her breast.

Hoo boy! And even more titillating, there was a distinct bulge appearing in his pants.

She shifted her hand a little higher up, her nails barely grazing the bugle beneath the slacks.

"Cindy?"

Lifting her head, she peeked up at him. "Yes?"

"Are you watching the movie?"

"Oh, yes."

"Truthfully?"

"Not at all. Bored to tears."

He went so still that she wondered if she'd made a mistake admitting it, and she opened her mouth to apologise when he suddenly swooped down on her.

His arms encircled her and he simply took her mouth in a searing kiss that had her first grappling for purchase on the armrest, then helplessly grabbing his shirt.

Catcalls and whistles erupted around them, interspersed with yells to sit back, stop necking, get a room, and someone threatened to get the manager.

Lifting his head, Tim grinned down at her.

Cindy laughed back up at him. "Oops."

"How about we ditch this joint and find something else to do?"

"You read my mind."

He practically hauled her to her feet, and she hurried behind him as they passed people, nearly sitting on several disgruntled movie-goers' laps as they tripped in the darkened room.

By the time they got out into the foyer, Cindy was giggling and trying to muffle it with her hand. Ginning broadly, Tim slung his arm around her shoulders and steered her past the bored-looking ticket seller.

Outside, he stopped and took in a lungful of air. "Seriously," he said, "That was a crap movie."

"Boring," she agreed.

"What would you have preferred?"

"Spooky, scary, thrilling."

"Well, there's nothing scary or spooky showing, and it's too late for thrilling. How about a drink instead?"

"The night is young."

The beat of a nearby night club drew them and soon they were inside, Cindy letting go to shimmy across the dance floor, laughing as Tim gyrated in front of her.

Several people yelled to her and recognising them, she waved back. Tim was also greeted by name. They danced and drank a few glasses at the bar before once more returning to the dance floor.

She loved it. The music beckoned to her, the beat making her feet tap, and the pure fun of having Tim keeping up with her, his moves quite skilful, just added to the whole experience.

Watching Tim dance was also an experience. Tall and lean, he moved easily, gracefully, and he didn't bother to hide his enjoyment of dancing. He moved closer to her, and closer, until they were dancing up against each other but without holding hands.

"Dirty dancing?" she shouted above the music. "Who'd have thought it of the playboy vet?"

He slid one thigh neatly between her own, grinning devilishly. "Cindy Lawson, the party girl. I thought you'd like dirty dancing?"

One sly rub against his groin, an accidental brush of her hand that had his eyes darkening, and she winked. "I can do more than dirty dance." And with that, she whirled off through the crowd.

Hips swaying, toes tapping, she ensured that she kept a crowd between her and Tim, and it wasn't hard to do considering that the floor was crowded with dancers.

Teasingly, she blew a kiss at him when she caught his eye and whirled away again.

A few shimmies with one man here, a hip shake with another dancer there, an exchanged giggle with a familiar face she knew from other clubs and casual acquaintances, and yet through it all she knew that Tim was searching for her.

She saw him using his dance moves to slide though the crowded dance floor, his gaze consistently finding her no matter where she went, and the dance suddenly became so much more.

From dance to seduction, from innocence to carnal, her moves became slower, more sensuous, and Tim moved closer and closer, winding his way gracefully yet with pure masculine intent towards her.

There was a set to his mouth that was more than wickedness, more than playfulness. His movements had changed, becoming almost like a hunter as he watched her with an intensity that held a touch of rapacity. Brown eyes caught the light, a glitter that was surely from the flashing lights reflected in his eyes.

Closer he came, stalking her in a fluid, effortless motion, and she couldn't help but slow down, swaying as he neared, her heart pounding as the room seemed to narrow, the people vanishing from her vision as her sole attention was captured by the man who stopped directly before her, his arm sliding around her waist to pull her close against him.

She could feel the heat coming from his body, his masculine scent filling her senses, and she looked up to find him watching her with pure sexual hunger in his eyes. Her knees shook a little, her skin tingled, and her lips parted.

In one smooth move Tim whirled them around, his hand sliding down to capture hers, and he led her through the crowd and out of the club, barely pausing to nod to the bouncer at the door.

He didn't say a word and more than conscious of the tension in his body that matched her own, she could only cling to his hand, her other hand curled around his forearm as he hailed a taxi.

It attested to the earliness of a club night when a taxi slid to a stop in front of them almost immediately. Tim opened the back door and she slid inside. Without a word, but his eyes sending her a smouldering message, he shut the door and came around the other side to sit beside her.

When he gave the address to the taxi driver, her head snapped up in surprise.

Catching her startlement, Tim asked huskily, "Do you need to be anywhere?"

"Not for awhile. Alex is baby-sitting Al."

"Good." His gaze dropped to her lips. Picking up her hand, he pressed a kiss to her knuckles, his gaze burning into hers before he straightened and turned to face the front without releasing his hold on her hand.

His thumbs brushed her knuckles and while his movements were gentle, she could feel the tension between them, a sweet, hot, nerve-tingling tension.

Whatever she'd started at the club by making him chase her, now he'd caught her, he was going to finish it.

Lord have mercy, she couldn't wait.

But even more, when the taxi slid to a halt in front of his house, she couldn't stop the myriad of emotions that assaulted her. He'd brought her to his home.

She got out of the taxi while Tim paid the driver, and then stood there as the taxi drove off, leaving her and Tim alone in the quiet street.

Tim crooked a finger at her and damned if that autocratic gesture didn't make a tingle go right down her spine. Silently she walked across the small expanse of road and up onto the footpath, coming to a halt directly in front of him.

His eyes held heat, so much heat, and she swallowed even as her own heart raced in anticipation.

Lowering his head, he kissed her, moving from a brief kiss to something much harder, much darker, and when he lifted his head, breaking their kiss, she couldn't help but whimper and try to follow him.

Framing her cheek with his hand, he rubbed his thumb across her bottom lip in a gentle caress that was a stark contradiction for the heat in his eyes. He moved backwards and blindly she followed, her gaze caught in his. In this way, the tension racheting up between them, he lured her to the steps to his house.

Sliding an arm around her waist suddenly, he turned and unlocked the door, opening it and crowding her into his home using his body, closing the door behind them and clicking the lock into place.

Cindy started to turn around, only to have her whole world swept out from under her.

Plucking her purse from her hand, Tim tossed it aside, grabbing her without any finesse, simply dragging her up against him. He took her mouth, kissing her so deeply it left her gasping for air, and kissing her so ruthlessly it left her clinging dizzily to him, her hands wrapped in his shirt.

Dipping his head, he kissed her throat, his lips seeking, searching, sucking at the tender skin, hot kisses that threatened to be so much more.

Hungry. Tim was hungry, she glimpsed it in his eyes when he lifted his head briefly, his gaze scorching her with the unbridled ardour that glittered within the brown depths. Hungry for her.

Her blood seared through her veins, pooling low as his mouth, his wicked, magical mouth, took hers again, his tongue sweeping in, plundering deep.

His hands moved over her, seeming to be everywhere at once, undoing the clip holding her hair back, unzipping the back of her dress, pulling and tugging quickly, easily, expertly, until she was naked before him.

Through his slacks she felt the hard length of his shaft pressed against her abdomen and she cupped him.

It inflamed him more, his cheeks dark with passion, eyes glittering with fierce desire.

"Cindy." Her name was a hot, damp brush against her lips as he took her mouth again and again, sipping and kissing, taking so much from her and leaving her aching for more.

She wasn't in control and she knew it. Right now the man who had stripped her so expertly, who had aroused her body so skilfully, he ruled them both. Every time she tried to caress him back, he blocked her, taking her hands, holding her, kissing her senseless until she didn't know whether she was coming or going, until all she was aware of was soul-searing carnal heat.

Heat burned through her to pool in her loins, sparked down her back, tingled in every area of her body.

She didn't know when or how, but suddenly Tim's bare skin was against hers, his lean strength surrounding her, strong hands guiding her, sweeping over her body to claim her.

One minute she was standing, the next she was on the floor, her knees bent as he came over her, his muscular thighs nudging her softer ones apart. Biceps flexed as he supported his upper body, lowering himself so that their lips hovered just inches apart.

"Cindy." His eyes burned down into hers.

"Tim.." She sighed, arching up, hearing him hiss as their bodies touched.

One hard thrust and he was buried deep in her body, his shaft driving through her intimate, feminine muscles that clutched at him.

She cried out, but when he stilled, she grabbed his shoulders, begging, "Don't stop. Oh God, don't stop!"

The words unleashed his control and his hips fell into a hard, relentless rhythm as he thrust into her over and over, drawing back fast and driving forward with a rapacious seeking of both mastery and pleasure-giving.

The climax started to build fast, the heat in his eyes, the grated "You're mine, Cindy," only causing the internal fire inside her to flare higher, hotter, brighter, until she shattered, splintering apart even as he continued to thrust, pushing her higher, further, hotter and hotter, shattering her again before she heard her name cried out hoarsely, felt him stiffen, and then she didn't know anything more as the prurience of the moment simply spun her out into Eros.

When she finally opened her eyes, it was to find Tim lying on his side propped up on his elbow with his head resting on his hand, watching her quietly.

She opened her mouth but was unable to say anything at first. On her second try, she managed, "Wow."

His other hand flexed lightly on the gentle swell of her belly, but she didn't feel a shred of self consciousness as she gazed up at him, because God help her if he still didn't look hungry.

Half expecting some witty comment, she was surprised when he said softly, "Welcome home."

"Home?"

With a small smile, he glanced around him. "Well, this is only the hallway, but yeah." His gaze returned to her. "Welcome to the whole of my home."

Pushing herself up on her elbows, she saw his eyes darken as his gaze dropped to her generous breasts that swayed with her movement. "Really?"

His gaze snapped back up to her face. "Yes."

"But you never bring women here."

"I brought you."

And he'd taken her hard, fast, and bloody awesomely on the hallway floor. She couldn't stop the quiver of pleasure that tingled through her belly at just the memory.

His hand on her belly flexed again and she wondered if he felt the quiver.

"This is my sanctuary, my home." Leaning down, he stopped only when his lips hovered a bare inch from her own. "You're the first and only woman I've brought here. This is my home. You are welcome here any time and for any reason."

The statement was almost as shattering as the climax he'd given her.

Staring into his eyes, so close she could see the paler flecks in the brown irises, she whispered, "Really?"

"Yes."

Happiness slipped through her, the joy of knowing that he really cared, that she meant so much to him that he'd opened his home to her.

Reaching up, she laid her hand against his cheek. "You won't be sorry."

"I know."

She wondered how he could even know that, but then he was kissing her again and all thought vanished beneath the tide of desire that once again carried them both away.

Creeping into the house several hours later after the tail lights of the taxi disappeared down the driveway, Cindy still couldn't stop smiling. Tim had dragged her into his big bed and made love to her a third time, and had protested when she'd finally dragged herself back out to return home.

Reminding him that Alex was doing her a favour by baby-sitting Al so she could go out with Tim in the first place, she managed to placate him. Due to the drinks they'd had at the club Tim couldn't drive, but he insisted on calling the taxi and seeing her into it, stopping her at the doorway to kiss her, then again at the taxi, taking her breath away and leaving her tingling in all the right places - at the very wrong time.

"Just wanting to make sure you're suffering like me." He grinned and stepped back.

"Heartless," she retorted, and blew him a kiss as the taxi pulled away.

Now she was at home and still tingling. The night at the movies had turned into so much more than she could have ever imagined.

Alex stuck his head around the corner of the lounge archway and knowingly cocked a brow as he took in her dishevelled appearance. "I take it the night went well."

She could only giggle and say, "Um…yeah."

He rolled his eyes. "Don't tell me. I don't want to know."

~*~

The dog was in renal and kidney failure. There was nothing that could be done and Tim had the awful job of telling the owner.

Old Mr Bertram stood there with tears in his eyes. "Nothing?"

"I'm sorry." Tim ran his hand down the old dog's flank as it lay on the table between them. "He's had a good, long life, but I'm afraid his old body has gone as far as it can go."

A tear ran down Mr Bertram's weathered cheek as he reached out and patted the old dog's head. "He's been a faithful friend all these years."

And even worse, Tim knew the dog had been the old man's closest companion since his wife's death a couple of years ago. It made what he had to say, though truthful, all the harder. "And a faithful friend deserves to pass away in peace, without anymore suffering."

Mr Bertram looked at the drip going into the dog's leg, the outline of the ribs that were starting to show through the skin, the weary way the dog lifted his head only slightly before laying it back down and closing his eyes.

"Yes," he said. "Yes."

Tim watched as the old man continued to stroke the dog's head, feeling the lump in his own throat as the tears trickled down and Mr Bertram sniffed repeatedly before taking out a handkerchief and blowing his nose.

He hated these times, hated when owners had to make the decision to part with their loved furry family members. It was a sad part of his job, but a necessary one, too. He understood how hard it was, and so he said quietly, "I'll wait out the back, give you some time alone with Blackie. When you're ready, let us know."

Mr Bertram nodded and Tim left the room, shutting the door behind him. Going out into the back room, he drew up the solution that would stop the old dog's heart, and then he waited, leaning back against the bench, watching the clock tick away the last few minutes of the dog's life.

Lara touched his arm, empathy in her eyes. "You all right, Tim?"

"Fine."

"You want Margie or Bill to do this? I know how close to Blackie you are."

"Even more reason for me to do it." He smiled a little. "Thanks, Lara. I'll be fine."

"I'll come in with you."

"Thanks, I'll need you." Yes, he'd need Lara for both holding the dog's leg and bringing the vein up, and to comfort Mr Bertram.

Ten minutes passed before another vet nurse poked her head around the door to say softly, "He's ready."

It wasn't long before Tim was carrying the old dog's body, wrapped in a soft blanket, out to the car. Mr Bertram slipped behind the wheel, his eyes dry but red-rimmed.

Tim leaned down and looked into the window. "Are you sure you'll be okay? I can drive you home."

"No, I'll be fine." Mr Bertram cleared his throat. "My son is on his way to the house. He's going to help me bury Blackie." His eyes teared up and he looked forward out of the windshield, taking several seconds to blink rapidly and clear his throat while Tim waited patiently. "Thanks, Doc. I know you did everything." His smile was a little wobbly when he turned his head to look out at Tim. "You were always good to Blackie and me. Always."

"I wish I could have done more." Tim patted the old man's arm. "I'm so sorry."

"I know." Mr Bertram cleared his throat again and straightened his thin shoulders. "Ah well, he'll be with my Mary now, won't he? Playing and jumping around."

Tim squeezed his arm gently. "They'll both be waiting for you."

"Yes." Mr Bertram started the engine and his smile was a little more genuine. "Yes, they will be."

Tim waited until the car had disappeared into the traffic before he went back inside the clinic. Going into the vet's office, he found a steaming mug of coffee waiting for him. God bless Lara.

Sitting down, he closed his eyes and took a deep breath. Losing a patient was always hard, but losing patients he'd treated for years was harder. He knew them so well, knew their habits and particular quirks that made them so individual. It didn't matter if they were animals and birds and mammals instead of people, they each had a spirit, a soul, were individual living beings. He loved them all.

And with every animal he knew personally that died, he grieved. Not as much as the owner, true, but he still grieved a little. And his nurses knew enough to give him some space to regroup before he started consults again.

The day didn't get any better. A battered-looking old cat with one eye was brought in, found, said the rough-looking woman with the raspy voice, in her garden. No one knew who it belonged to and she certainly didn't want the wretched thing around her place.

After checking it out, the cat was found to be a sterilised male, in reasonable health, approximately thirteen or fourteen years old and very affectionate, with a yowl that could shatter ear drums within fifty feet. Lara took it out the back to place in a cage while they advertised him, and hopefully the owner would come looking. A scan had shown no microchip, which made it all the harder.

Tim grinned as the door swung shut behind the vet nurse. The old cat's yowling could be clearly heard, along with the kennel maid's "Good grief!"

The next consult was for a bird with a malignant tumour, again nothing that could be done, and another euthanasia. The owner was a little teary but remained calm.

Then the dreaded call out to another patient, this one to a couple of pet lambs who'd been attacked by dogs, and possibly neighbouring dogs let loose, for the hobby farm was on the outskirts of the city. Another euthanasia, this time accompanied by the crying children who had been helping their parents hand-raise the lambs.

Jesus, the day was just getting worse and worse. The other two vets worked just as hard but it seemed as if Tim's luck was just plain rotten, as he seemed to get every bad scenario.

Another owner who came in and abused them all for the cost of caring and medicating his dog, and a woman who couldn't decide whether to sterilise her cat or let it have a litter so 'the kids can witness the miracle of birth'. When Tim tried to point out the difficulty in getting homes for kittens, she brushed it away and he watched in frustration as she walked out the door, head held high, as she announced that children needed to watch the miracle of birth.

"You should have asked her if she wanted her kids to witness the sadness of watching the kittens put to sleep because no one wants them," Lara said sourly. "Think she'll be back with the unwanted kittens?"

"God, I hope not." Tim scowled. "Then again, better to be put to sleep than dumped. Shit, days like today I don't need."

Sighing, Lara nodded.

Going through the swing door out to the back, Tim heard the old cat yowling and he went into the cat's room and squatted before the cage.

The old cat bumped his head against the cage door and looked up at him in anticipation of a pat. Smiling, Tim complied, rubbing the big head through the cage door, feeling some of his tension slip away as the old cat purred.

But if the owners didn't turn up, this was another cat destined to be euthanised. He sighed. All he could do was hope the owner would turn up or someone would take the old cat, but there weren't many people wanting an old cat and all the health issues that could come with him.

Straightening, he moved onto the last consults of the day. The final consult was yet another euthanasia, this time a dog that had got hit by a car and was so badly injured that nothing could be done except to put it out of its pain. It didn't help that the owner was the one who had been driving the car, and the sobbing woman had to be helped out by her husband while Tim followed with yet another dog wrapped in a blanket to put into the back seat of the car.

Going back inside, he felt that the entire day was cursed. Even the vet nurses weren't happy. Returning to the treatment room, he did a final check of the animals there, all in various stages of recovery from illnesses and operations. And one yowling old cat needing his owner.

"Need anything before I go?" Lara came into the room.

"No, thanks." Tim shook his head. "Let's just pray that tomorrow is much better."

"I hear you." She looked at him. "You look really wrung out. Can I do anything?"

Again he shook his head, but he managed to smile. "I'm fine. Go home, go out, whatever you do, just have a good time."

"If you're sure…?" She hesitated.

"I'm sure. You all did a good job today."

She smiled. "No worries. I'll see you tomorrow."

"I'll be here." *And please, God, let it be a much happier day.*

The clinic grew quiet as the nurses and the other remaining vet left, and Tim did one last, final check of the animals and locking of doors before returning to his office.

Walking in, he took one look at who was waiting at his desk and the weight on his shoulders seemed to slip away. Cindy smiled at him, eyes warm, not saying anything, and then she straightened from where she perched on the edge of his desk and opened her arms.

Without a word Tim strode straight into them, gathering her close and resting his chin on her shoulder, breathing in deep of her soft, sweet scent.

She gently smoothed one hand over his hair while her other hand ran up and down his back soothingly.

The tension eased from him, slipping away as he allowed her comforting, undemanding presence to soothe him. It was as though she knew what he needed, saying nothing, just being there for him.

No one had ever been there for him except for his friends, but there were some things he couldn't tell them. But with Cindy, he felt as though he didn't need to tell her anything, that she just knew.

And she accepted him. Closing his eyes, Tim snuggled her closer, feeling her softness resting against him, feeling the inner strength in her, her calmness in his storm of emotions, her comfort in his sadness, her quietness in his clamouring.

He needed her, not sexually, but just to be there for him, and she was, asking for nothing and giving him what he needed.

For two months they'd been going out, having fun, chatting about different things. She never complained when late-night call-outs took him from her, he didn't complain when she had to go away for a meeting in another city with her father, brother and a business investor. Neither complained about the sometimes odd hours they kept - he for his work, she for hers.

He'd learned a lot about Cindy Lawson in the short time they'd been together. The party girl worked hard, often from home, her agile brain and computer skills a useful asset to her family's business. People disregarded the bubble-headed, giggly blonde to their own detriment, especially the business sharks cruising around looking for opportunities. They zeroed in on her father and brother, while she circled the permitter, looking into their backgrounds, gleaning information, using contacts in both the computer world and her own acquaintances in other countries and cities to find out about the business sharks. Her family took her advice and reports seriously, and she was just as serious about doing them.

Yeah, Cindy was made up of many fascinating facets. Party girl, giggly blonde, luscious babe, steel trap minded business woman, a soft heart for the animals, and a quiet understanding of Tim.

"How do you do it?" His voice was muffled in her hair as he turned his head to press a kiss to the side of her throat.

"Do what?"

"You seem to know what I need before I do."

"I read people well. Part of my job."

"So I'm just a part of your job?"

"The worst job."

He gave her a squeeze.

She laughed softly. "But I can handle it."

"You're going to have to prove that one day."

"Uh-huh." But she didn't move, just kept holding him.

Because she knew it was what he needed.

Relaxing against her, he allowed his thoughts to simply drift away, filling himself instead with the scent of Cindy, her softness, her calmness. He couldn't imagine a better way to end a horrible day.

His mobile rang and with a sigh he straightened, but he didn't move away from Cindy, holding her against him as he leaned to the side and picked up the phone from the top of the desk. "Hello?"

"Tim?"

"Yes. Who is this?"

There was a light laugh. "It's Sassy."

"Sassy?" He searched his memory without success.

Cindy's hand on his back went still.

"Sassy. We met at the pub, remember? It was awhile ago. I manage Petite Creations?"

"Oh yes, Sassy. Of course. I'm sorry." Tim raised his brows as he looked out at the darkening night beyond the window. "What can I do for you?"

"I was wondering if maybe you'd like to go out for a drink tonight?"

"Tonight?" Tim ran his hand up Cindy's back. "I'm sorry, no."

"Oh. Okay." There was a slight hesitation. "What about tomorrow night?"

"No." Tim smiled down at the blonde strand of hair he was twining around his finger, feeling Cindy standing so still against him. She knew there was a woman on the other end of the phone. Her breasts pushed against his chest with every breath she took, and he felt it when she took a particularly large one. "I'm afraid I'm seeing someone, Sassy, but I thank you for asking anyway."

"You're going out?" Sassy sounded puzzled. "Really?"

"Yep." Satisfaction oozed through him. Oh yeah, he was going out with a luscious babe who took all his attention, sexual and otherwise, and boy was he glad.

"I see." Sassy sighed. "Well, I guess I'll see you around."

"No doubt. By the way…" He frowned slightly, a sudden thought occurring to him. "How did you get my mobile number? This is a private line."

Cindy started to pull away and he tightened his grip, keeping her in place.

"Oh, Cindy gave it to me."

Tim pulled away just enough to look down into Cindy's face, taking in her red cheeks in one glance. "Oh? Cindy? Really?"

"Yes. She gave it to me the night we met. I thought she was considering breaking up with you."

"Really?" His hand slid down to Cindy's ample backside. "Well, fancy that." Amusement went through him, especially when Cindy looked away. "Well, like I said, I'm seeing someone."

"Sure. 'Bye."

"'Bye." He clicked the phone off and tossed it back on the desk. "So."

"So." Cindy rested her hands on his forearms and eyed him as closely as he was doing to her.

"You gave Sassy my number. My private number."

"Hey, I didn't know it was private."

He flexed his hand on her bottom. "How did you get it? Back then I wouldn't have given you the time of day."

"Oh, that's harsh." A twinkle appeared in her blue eyes.

"You were an irritating bit of goods that night, if I remember." He delivered the lightest of taps on one generous buttock.

"Hey, I was saving your life."

"You were dropping me into the manure, and you knew it."

She fluttered her eyelashes at him.

"So how did you - oh geez." He remembered her going back to Rick and asking him something, right before they left the pub. "You got it from Rick, didn't you?"

She laughed.

"And then at some stage you passed it on to Sassy."

"Guilty as charged, sir."

Another light tap on her bottom. "You devious wench."

"Just trying to help you out."

"I bet." Tim grinned. "You knew she was after me." Another thought occurred to him. "Hang on. It took her this long to call me?"

"Oh, baby." Cindy smoothed down his jacket collar. "Are you upset? Sassy found herself another man, but they've broken up now." She winked. "You're the rebound."

"You know, that would have made me happy once." He tugged gently on the blonde strand of hair still around his finger, tipping her head back. "I could have boinked her without worry."

"You're such a romantic." She tapped him on the cheek, a little harder than warranted. "And not something you should be saying to me, your girlfriend."

Tim's grin widened. "Luscious babe, you're all the woman I want or need."

Her brow rose haughtily. "Now you're just trying to regain favour."

"I swear I spoke without thinking." He raised one hand. "Scout's honour."

"You were never a boy scout."

"Hey, I'm always prepared. There's a condom in my wallet."

"Oh well, I guess that's proof." The twinkle in her eyes spread to a sparkling smile. "So, Playboy Vet, I guess I'll keep you for awhile after all."

"How about forever?" The words fell out before he thought about it, and she laughed.

So did he.

And then they looked at each other. Tim's breath caught, his eyes widening as he realised what he'd said.

Cindy's gaze searched his eyes. "Tim...?"

"I didn't mean-" he began at the same time.

His mobile rang again.

She glanced away. "You better answer it."

He didn't know whether to be relieved or not as he picked it up. "Hello?"

"It's me." His mother's voice came through, cold and clipped. "I want to see you at the house."

"What?"

"Now."

Tim released Cindy, feeling the loss of her warmth as she moved away. "What's wrong?"

"Something we need to discuss. This can't wait, Timothy."

It had to wait. The vibes he was getting from Cindy's stiff back wasn't good. "Not now."

"*Now.*"

He cut her off and walked up behind Cindy, stopping just behind her, feeling the warmth of her body through his white coat. "Cindy, I-"

Turning, she looked up at him, a small smile on her lips but her eyes serious. "It's okay, Tim. This is too soon for us to talk about forever."

"I know." Too soon. Way too soon. She wasn't ready, he wasn't ready.

The mobile rang and he ignored it.

"That sounds important," Cindy said quietly.

"It's my mother. She can wait." Reaching for her hand, Tim said quietly, "I didn't mean to upset you."

"I'm not upset." She gave his hand a little squeeze. "We've only been going out a short time."

The mobile phone started ringing again.

"It's not important." Tim shook his head when she glanced at the mobile. "You are."

Warmth seeped into her eyes and she moved forward to lean against him. Automatically, his arms came around her waist.

"That's sweet," she said. "But she's just going to keep ringing you."

"I can turn the whole phone off." He did so. "See?"

"Rebel."

Relaxing as the familiar companionship fell between them again, he sought safer ground. "Thanks for coming here tonight."

"My pleasure."

"Did someone phone you?"

"I was driving past and decided to call in on the chance that you wanted to go out for pizza." Cindy's arms around his waist tightened. "I met Lara on the way in and she told me you'd had a hell day. So I came in here to wait."

Dropping his forehead to rest against hers, Tim smiled. "And you knew just what to do."

"Peace and quiet never hurt anyone."

Dipping his head to kiss her lightly on the lips, the taste of her strawberry lip gloss filled him. Lifting his head, he licked his lips. "Mmmm. Yum." And he kissed her again, this time coming up to smack his lips. "Oh yeah. Now I want to lick you all over."

She giggled. "I don't taste like strawberry all over."

"True. Strawberry at the top, cream at the centre." He felt a little surge of heat at just the thought. "My taste buds are tingling."

"Maybe it's your guilty conscious at not talking to your mother?" Devilment danced in her eyes.

"Not likely." He started to pull her skirt up. "I've had a hellish day and now here you come, all dessert and-"

She smartly stopped him from pulling her skirt the rest of the way up. "No."

"No?"

"We're meeting Mike, Maddy, Rick and Cherry for tea."

"We are?" Totally unconcerned, he resumed trying to tug her skirt up.

"At the Pizza Place." She smacked his hand away. "In ten minutes, actually."

"Ten minutes?" He reached for her as she backed away. "I can work with that."

"Pizza now, dessert later." She picked her car keys up from the hook by the door.

Tim sighed. "Promise?"

Cindy smiled widely at him. "Yep, and I'm going to enjoy every minute of it."

"You?"

"Oh, honey." She winked at him. "Do you really think you're the only one who can give oral?" And she walked out the door.

Stunned, Tim stared after her, the meaning of her words filtering through him, followed hard by heat.

He started for the door in determined strides.

"Pizza first!" she called out from the reception area.

Damn it, he knew that tone. Hands on his hips, he frowned. But if he put his mind to it, he could change her mind. Grinning, he started for the door again.

"And if the on-call vet comes in and finds us doing anything, Tim, you'll get nothing from me," Cindy added. "Zilch. Zip. In fact, you'll be going home alone. Just you and your hand."

He knew her enough now to know that it wasn't an idle threat. With a sigh, Tim shrugged out of his coat and hung it up, pocketed the mobile and picked up his car keys.

As he walked out into the reception area, Cindy smiled approvingly at him.

"Don't say it." Unlocking the door, he pushed her outside gently.

"Good boy?"

"Exactly."

"Oh honey." Her smile was pure sin as she got into her car. "I promise you, it'll be worth it."

Chapter Ten

Her silky tone and darkening eyes had his shaft hardening, and placing his hand atop the hood of the car, he leaned down to peer into the window at her. "Sure we can't skip the pizza?"

"No."

"Trust me, Rick and Mike won't even notice us not being there, not with their ladies there as well."

"No."

"Are you sure?"

"Yes. Now get into your car and go home. I'll follow and pick you up."

Hot damn, he still had a chance. Tim drove home quickly, got out of the garage and shut the door, and then leaned against the fence and looked at her, one brow raised. "Want to come in for a quick cuppa?"

She laughed outright. "Get in the car, Tim."

When they pulled up in the car park at the Pizza Place, he said, "I'm on fire."

"Think cool thoughts."

He watched her get out of the car, those luscious curves now out of range of his hands, but not his sight or imagination. "Not going to work."

"Hopeless." Coming around, she opened his door. "Come on, princess."

"I hope you know that it's all your fault that I'm half crippled." He used the motion of getting out of the car to rearrange the front of his slacks.

Amused, she grinned.

"Boy, are you in trouble." Wrapping his arm around her waist, he deliberately dropped his hand to clutch her bottom. "Wait until later."

Reaching behind her, she deftly moved his hand higher. "You want oral, you behave yourself."

Tim nearly tripped going into the restaurant.

Mike and Rick saw him because, of course, they were sitting in the chairs facing the doorway. Sitting in the chairs opposite them, Maddy and Cherry had their backs to the door.

Seating Cindy in a chair at the end of the table, Tim sat in the remaining chair opposite her. "Evening ladies." He nodded to Cherry and Maddy before turning his gaze to Mike and Rick and nodding again. "Ladies."

"Hey," replied Rick.

Mike grunted.

"So let's have the pizza and blow this joint fast." Tim held his hand up for the waitress.

"Tim." Cindy said warningly, but laughter lurked in her eyes.

Rick knocked his hand down. "You haven't looked at the menu yet."

"I'm only interested in dessert." Oh boy, was he. Dessert. Tim eyed Cindy hungrily. Yeah, only dessert.

Ignoring him, Cindy turned to Maddy and Cherry and started talking to them. How she could do that knowing what was to come back home, he didn't know. All his attention was pretty much focussed on it.

"Put ice on it," Rick advised.

"Huh?" Tim looked at him.

"Man, you're looking at Cindy like you could eat her up."

"Heh heh."

Mike frowned. "She's a lady. Knock it off."

"You have no idea what she taunted me with." Tim reached for the menu. "Not exactly what I'd call lady-like."

"Don't care. Get a grip on yourself."

Rick grinned. "Good day at work?"

"Shit day, but the ending is going to be bloody awesome."

"I'd say so, going by your shirt."

Tim stuck out his chest. "Oh yeah, baby."

The picture on his shirt was of a cartoon bull with steam coming from his distended nostrils and a set of huge balls on the other end. Printed beneath the picture was *Get Balled by the Master*.

"Impressive," Rick said. "Turns on all the girls, does it?"

"Only one I want to turn on." He glanced over top of the menu at Cindy, sure she was deliberately ignoring him, until she glanced at him and winked. Hoo boy.

"Just don't do it here." Rick turned his gaze to Cindy. "She doesn't seem very turned on, though."

"She will be."

Mike glowered at him.

"Sorry, precious." Tim blew him a kiss. "Am I upsetting you with my rude, crude words?" He fluttered his eyelashes. "Want to spank me for being naughty?"

"Pound you into the ground, more like," Mike replied.

Maddy glanced at him and his scowl dropped away to be replaced with a small smile.

"Jesus," said Tim. "Whipped."

Mike returned to frowning at him.

"What are you talking about?" Cherry looked at Tim. "Who's being whipped?"

"Mike."

She glanced at Mike.

"Tim's being feral," Cindy explained. "Ignore him."

"I wasn't this feral until you came along," he said.

"Crap."

"She's right," Rick said. "I'm surprised you grew up without having your head ripped off."

"I don't think he actually grew up," Mike growled. "Dragged, more like it, and not very successfully."

"You're just jealous." Tim pulled the ringing phone from his pocket and clicked it off without looking at it. "You didn't grow up, you just appeared as the surly, scowling, big bear you are."

The waitress came and they ordered the pizzas and drinks before settling back to laugh, joke, and chat the evening away.

It was pleasant and Tim relaxed, his eyes lingering often on Cindy as she laughed and chatted to their friends. Looking around the table, he thought how much had changed in their lives. Rick had Cherry, Mike had Maddy, and he had Cindy. And they were all friends. Life was good. No, better than good, it was great.

Watching the closeness between his friends and their women, he saw the ease with which they talked to each other, the warmth in their eyes, and he wondered if he had the same with Cindy, if she looked at him the same way. He glanced across the table and in that moment Cindy glanced back at him, and the warmth in her eyes hit him full on, seeping through him and lower, pulling at little strings of not only desire, but pure contentment.

Yeah, she had a similar look in her eyes. His heart leaped a little. Very similar to the way Maddy and Cherry looked at their men, as though they were the only men in the room, as though they would never tire of gazing into their eyes, as though—

"Hey, Tim." Rick kicked him under the table and handed him his mobile phone with a puzzled expression. "Your mum is on the phone."

"What?" Tim looked at the phone.

"Your Mum. On my phone."

Annoyed, Tim put the phone to his ear. "What is it this time?"

"Tim." Dr Clarke said, "I need to talk to you, but you've got your phone switched off."

"Look, I'm with friends at the moment."

"It's urgent."

He sighed. "How urgent?"

"Please."

That had him frowning. His mother never said please.

"This is important, Tim. Come and see me."

Loath to do so, but now a little worried and more than curious, he glanced up to find Cindy looking at him with concern. Rubbing the bridge of his nose, he sighed. "Tomorrow. I'll come tomorrow."

"Tonight."

"Surely-"

"Don't make me beg."

"You never beg. That'd be beneath you." When there was silence on the other end, he sighed again. "Okay, fine. I'll come. Half an hour." Hanging up, he handed the phone to Rick. "Thanks."

"Everything okay?" Maddy queried.

"Fine." He forced the frown from his brow.

"Your mother?" Mike asked.

Tim shrugged. "Hounding me for awhile. Guess I better go and see what she wants that's so urgent."

Cherry looked troubled. "If its urgent, shouldn't you go now?"

"Knowing Mother, anything urgent will be only to do with her." Tim picked up his glass of Coke and took a sip. "Trust me, it can wait another half hour."

It wasn't long after that the group broke up, the couples going their own ways with plans to meet up again for another evening out.

Cindy watched as Tim fastened his seatbelt. "Off to the evil witch's castle?"

"Afraid so." He glanced at her. "Unless you prefer to drop me off home and I can get my car."

"Nah. What would be the fun in that?" She started the engine.

He smiled at the words, though the thought of meeting his mother didn't make him happy.

"What do you think she wants?" Cindy pulled the car out into the traffic.

"Not a clue." Tim sighed and leaned his elbow on the window sill, resting his chin on his hand as he gazed out at the street lights flashing past.

"If you don't want to go, I can just turn the car around."

That did produce a bit of amusement. "And have you facing the wrath of the evil witch?"

She shrugged. "No skin off my nose. I'm not related to her."

"You would be if you stayed with me."

"Still no skin off my nose." She smiled. "It's a name, not a blood relation."

He laughed but grew serious as the silence fell between them again. The road hummed beneath the tyres and he lost himself in thought, wondering what his mother could possibly want, for she never summoned him by choice.

By the time Cindy pulled to a halt in front of the mansion, Tim was really curious. He got out, only to look back into the car. "You coming?"

She nodded at the four cars parked nearby. "This might be a family affair."

"There's no other family. And you're not waiting out here like some chauffer." A sudden thought struck him. "Um...did you want to go home? I can get a taxi."

"What? And leave you here?" She got out of the car and looked at him across the roof. "We're in this together."

"Really?" Warmth washed through him again.

"Sure. But I'll be waiting in the hallway." She closed the car door and set the alarm. "I'll be your heroine, waiting in the background to save you if needed."

"My heroine." He grinned as she rounded the car and came up beside him.

"Just remember that." She winked as he slid his arm around her waist.

Climbing the steps, he felt for the first time as though he wasn't alone while entering the evil den. Cindy walked beside him, quiet and confident, patient and unquestioning.

They stopped in the hallway.

"I'll wait here." She gestured to one of the regal chairs.

"What about the kitchen? You can have a coffee or tea while you're waiting."

"Nah, I'm good." She touched her belly. "Though I have drunk a lot of Diet Coke. Where's the nearest bathroom?"

"Sure you're not just nervous at the thought of the evil witch being close by?" He nudged her with his elbow.

"Could be, but I'll never admit it." She nudged him back.

Feeling better already, he pointed her in the direction of a nearby corridor. "Straight down to the end and turn left. First door on the right."

"Good man." Reaching up suddenly, she slid her hand around his neck and urged him down. Brushing a kiss across his lips, she murmured, "If you need help slaying the dragon, just yell. I'll be right here."

Oh yeah, Cindy had a way of making him feel so much better about things he didn't want to face.

He kissed her back, resisting the urge to tighten his hold and take her out of the house and back to her place, a place he'd always felt at home in, where he could relax and laugh.

With Cindy.

Forever.

The word floated through his mind, a brief memory of it being said back in the vet's office, but then it vanished as she pulled away and started for the corridor.

He watched her go before seeking out his mother. He hadn't gotten far when the maid met him and ushered him through into the sitting area. And right into the midst of a meeting of some kind.

The three men wore business suits while the woman wore a grey silk blouse and elegant skirt, a strong of pearls around her throat. As he walked in, they grew quiet.

Dr Clarke looked up from where she sat in a big armchair. Annoyance crossed her features, just as quickly vanishing as she stood and crossed the room. "Timothy."

"You seem to be busy." He glanced around. "What's so urgent?"

"In here." She turned back to the people and smiled. "I'll be back in a minute."

They nodded and the conversation resumed as he followed her out, the door shutting behind them. She led him through into another room further on before turning to face him, her expression cold and displeased.

"This was the urgent matter?" Tim thrust his hands in his pockets. "The disapproval? Seriously? Mother, I get that from you all the time."

"I've been hearing some disturbing news." She continued to gaze coldly at him.

Raising his brows, he rocked back and forth on his heels.

"This tomfoolery has got to stop," she stated bluntly.

"Sorry?"

"This playing around at that second-rate vet clinic."

"We've been over this before." He started to turn away impatiently. "I'm not going to discuss it anymore-"

"You're hanging around with that totally unsuitable woman."

"Pardon?" Surprised now, he turned back to face her.

"Timothy, the Lawsons are not up to your standards. Our standards." Her face was as chill as her tone. "That family makes a mockery of their status."

"Are you kidding me?" Tim stared at her. "They're rich. How can they make a mockery of that?"

"They have their fingers in many pies and they're rich." She nodded. "But they have no class. They lack refinement."

He wasn't surprised by her opinion. "Such a snob, Mother. Always have been, always will be."

"You're a Clarke, Timothy. Our name means something in the social circles."

"This is old ground. Now I have things to do-"

"You've been hanging around with that Lawson girl."

"Cindy?" A touch of anger flickered to life. "She has a name."

"Cindy Lawson isn't in your league."

His response was immediate and sharp. "Cindy Lawson is well out of my league, Mother, and well out of yours, too."

"I'm glad you realise it." She sat down on a straight-backed chair. "Now, I need to discuss my will-"

He frowned angrily. "What you don't get is that Cindy is above our league. Her family is above our league."

Dr Clarke looked coldly at him. "I beg your pardon?"

"The Lawsons are a true family." He swung his hand out. "They stick by each other, they accept each other. We are well below their league."

"Don't be ridiculous."

"Ridiculous?" He laughed just as coldly as her expression. "I'm a huge admirer of the Lawson family, and so are many people."

"Fine." She dismissed his words with a flick of her wrist. "As long as you realise that Cindy is out of your league and you stop going out with her."

"I'm not ten years old, having to do as you say."

"I know more than you realise.'

"You know nothing. All you know is your prestige, your plans, your money and status." He looked around contemptuously.

"Think what you like. One day this will all be yours."

"I don't want it."

"You won't get it unless you drop the Lawson girl."

Fury seeped through him.

"That's right." Dr Clarke nodded. "I called you here to talk about my will. You'll be my sole heir. But if you continue to see that girl…"

He picked up where she left off. "You'll disinherit me?"

"You won't get one red cent."

"Wow." Refusing to show the fury boiling inside him, he looked around. "I'd get none of this?"

"None." Sitting back in the chair, she crossed her legs elegantly.

He looked at her for several long seconds.

She arched one brow. "I see we have an understanding."

"Oh, we do."

"I must say I'm a little surprised. Pleasantly so, I must admit."

"Maybe you don't know me as well as you think you do." Anger thrummed through his veins, beating inside his head as he bided his time.

"Then let's finish this and we can all go about our business."

"By all means." He gestured.

Picking up the phone, she pressed a number. Whoever was on the other end picked up almost immediately. She made the command in a smooth tone. "Come."

Tim watched as the men and the woman filed in to take a seat at the table. The woman took out a laptop and opened it.

"This is my lawyer, Donald Alfster." Dr Clarke nodded to the tall, stooped man in the expensive suit. "His clerk, Leticia." The woman at the laptop nodded.

"And the other two?" Tim studied them steadily.

"Business associates. They're here to act as witnesses."

"A bit of overkill, surely?" When Dr Clarke looked at him, he shrugged. "Fine. Whatever."

He watched as they all settled, the lawyer standing behind his clerk.

The lawyer nodded to Dr Clarke. "Are we ready?"

"Yes." She sat back. "Tell my son what he will inherit."

It was impressive but nothing that Tim hadn't already known. The mansion he now stood in, a beachside mansion on the other side of Australia, a villa in France, land, priceless artwork and antiques, jewellery, bank accounts and investments. The list went on and on.

When the lawyer stopped speaking, Tim found everyone looking at him, studying him as though he was an ant under a microscope. The clerk, Leticia, had a glimmer in her eyes. Envy? More than likely, or possibly wondering how she could snare him.

He turned to his mother. "Is that it?"

"Isn't it enough?"

"No, it's not."

The lawyer blinked, the business associates' mouths fell open.

"It's a fortune," the lawyer protested. "You'd never have to work again. The world would be at your fingertips."

"Yeah," he said, "But I wouldn't have the Lawson girl, would I?"

The complete lack of understanding on his mother's face should have made him furious. Instead, he felt...nothing. For the first time ever, for the first time since he was born and shoved into the carefully manicured, heartless hands of his mother, he felt nothing. No anger, no sadness. Regret, yes. Regret for what could have been, what should have been, but that was it.

"What are you saying?" Dr Clarke frowned.

"What I'm saying, Mother, is quite simple." Tim regarded her steadily. "Inheriting all your treasures pales in comparison to the one treasure I value above all else." He looked around at them all, seeing the uncertainty, the surprise, and the total disbelief in their faces. "That treasure is Cindy Lawson." And he walked from the room.

The stunned silence was broken by the sound of someone in pursuit.

"Timothy!"

"We've nothing to talk about, Mother."

"We do!" She grabbed his shoulder.

Stopping, he turned to face her. "No, we don't." Taking her hand, he distastefully took it off his shoulder and returned it to her side.

"If you choose that girl over me, over everything I offer you, then you're out of the will!"

"No contest. I choose Cindy."

Trembling with fury, her hands clenched, his mother glared up at him. "You'd really choose her?"

"Yep." He nodded calmly.

"What has that fat, outrageous woman got to offer you? You tell me that, Tim! You tell me!"

"For a start," he replied coldly. "You are never to refer to her in that derogatory manner again."

"She's not suitable!"

"She's more than suitable. She's kind, honest, more than you'll ever be or ever were."

"What do you see in her?" Dr Clarke flung her hand out in fury. "She's overweight, she'll never be the kind of woman who deserves to be on your arm. She's not worthy to be a Clarke. For God's sake, Timothy-"

Every bit of answering fury Tim felt was solely on Cindy's behalf. He loomed over his mother, watching in satisfaction as she uncertainly fell back a step. Behind her he saw the lawyer, the clerk, and the two business associates watching and listening with mouths agape.

The gossip mill would be working overtime in society very soon, and he didn't care.

Returning his attention to Dr Clarke, he took a deep breath to steady himself before saying with quiet determination, "Cindy Lawson has the hottest body around, did you know that? Her curves drive me wild. She dresses to please herself, and that pleases me, too. She's everything I want in a life partner, and I'll be lucky if she has me as *her* husband. Lucky and honoured."

His mother paled in shocked horror. "You can't be serious!"

"Oh, but I am, and I have to thank you, Mother." Stepping back, he smiled coldly.

Speechless, she stared at him.

"Your delightful offer has made me realise who and what is important in my life. I was unclear about my feelings for Cindy, but you showed me where my heart lies, and it's not with your riches." He looked at the faces all watching him with varying degrees of shock and awe. "It's with Cindy Lawson, whom I love with all my heart." Then he turned and walked from the room.

He almost ran over Cindy standing in the corridor outside, but he ignored her gaping mouth and bright red cheeks, instead taking her hand and pulling her along behind him, taking her out of the house and into the night.

The cool, refreshing night.

"Timothy!" His normally cool, calm, and collected mother stood at the top of the staircase, her voice shrill. "Don't you dare walk away from me!"

Unlocking the door, he ushered a silent Cindy inside the car, shut the door and went around to the driver's side.

"Timothy!" Dr Clarke shrieked. "If you leave now, you'll never see a penny, not a *penny*!"

Getting into the car, he started the engine.

"If you leave now," she screamed, "You are never to come back, do you hear me? I disinherit you!"

Putting the car into gear, he drove away from the mansion, leaving his mother ranting on the staircase.

The silence in the car was soothing. The wind whipped past the open window and every bit of tension left Tim.

Right now everything in the world felt right. Safe. Just as it should be, with Cindy by his side and his past behind him. The future was spread out, clear and inviting.

"Wow." Cindy cleared her throat. "Okay…"

He flicked a glance sideways to find her biting her lip.

A flick of the indicator and he was pulling them over under the shelter of a tree next to a service station, turning the engine off as they came to a halt. Silently he watched the cars pulling in to fill up on petrol, people going about their lives.

Every word his mother screamed at him, her conniving ways, it was all in the past. No more going to her wretched parties, no more having to listen to her phone calls. That'd take some getting used to, but he felt so free.

So very free.

"I'm sorry."

"Pardon?" He looked across to where Cindy sat in the passenger seat, her troubled gaze on him.

"I'm sorry. About the row…" She tried again. "With your mother."

"Yeah. That was something." Leaning back against the seat, he drew in a deep breath. "And unbelievably liberating."

She stared at him for several seconds before shifting closer. "Tim?"

"Yeah?"

"Are you all right?"

His smile was slow but sure. "Never better."

She glanced away.

Looking at her, he saw the troubled way she continued to chew her lip, the tension in her shoulders. "Cindy, how much did you hear?"

"Um…"

"Shit." Straightening, he reached out to rest a hand on her thigh. "My mother can be such a cruel, thoughtless bitch. Her words were just that, cruel and thoughtless."

"Um, yeah." Still she didn't look at him.

"Cindy, you're worth more than her, more than any of those high society women."

Her gaze dropped to her lap.

"I know her comments about your figure must have hurt, but trust me, it's her opinion only."

Her gaze flashed up. "You think I'm worried about *me*?"

"Well…yes?"

"You idiot!"

Tim blinked.

Unclipping the seat belt, Cindy turned in the seat to face him, the light from the service station revealing the concern on her face. "I'm worried about you!" She smacked his arm smartly.

"What-"

"Your mother disinherited you because of me!"

"So?" Rubbing his arm, he eyed her warily. "It was no contest."

"No contest? Your mother and you fell out because of me!"

"My mother and I were never together as a true son and mother," he pointed out.

"Tim-"

"No." Grabbing her upper arms, he pulled her towards him, leaning across the brake so that they could be closer. "No, you listen to me, Cindy Lawson. A choice between her worthless, soulless riches, and the real, warm, alive you, is no contest. Never has been, never will be."

"But-"

"No buts. I've lived surrounded by cold objects, and they're no substitute for love. I'd rather be a pauper with you by my side than a miserable rich bastard alone in my ivory tower. That's my past now. You're my now, and my future."

Her lips parted. "Really?"

"Really." Leaning forward, he kissed her gently on the lips and immediately her scent filled him. "Only you. Always you."

He drew his head back slightly so that he could look at her.

"Tim," she whispered, "What if one day you regret this? What if you realise you might have made a mistake, the wrong decision?"

"This is the right decision." He needed her to understand, to know how he felt. "I love you, Cindy. I really love you, and it's not the 'maybe' kind, or the 'for now' kind."

Her blue eyes started to sparkle with a sheen of tears.

"This is the 'forever' kind," he said.

"How can you be so sure? Your emotions are shot to pieces, so much has happened in such a short time tonight. You need time to think, to-"

"Seriously?" He gazed intently into her eyes. "You really believe this is a spur of the moment thing?"

"Yes." She nodded, a tear spilling out to slip down her cheek. "I think."

Gently he wiped away the tear with his thumb, tenderness spilling through him, though admittedly tinged with frustration. "You want me to think about this, don't you?"

Unable to speak, she nodded.

"I know I don't have to."

She sniffed, lifting her hand to wipe away another tear.

It was too sudden for her, he knew. Cindy wasn't a woman who acted immediately when it came to something important. She analysed it, studied it, and right now she wasn't sure that he was thinking straight.

And that led to another thought.

Slipping his finger beneath her chin, he titled her head up slightly. "What are you feeling right now, Cindy?"

"I know what I feel."

"Tell me."

"No. I want you to think tonight through before I say anything."

This was an unexpected happening and he released her slowly, studying her. Part of him was a little hurt that she didn't trust him enough to share her feelings, but part of him understood.

Her family was warm and loving, and what had occurred between him and his mother tonight had disturbed her. She wasn't so certain that he knew what he'd been doing when he'd chosen her, when he'd said what he did, when he'd proclaimed his love.

Not quite the happy moment he'd contemplated.

"Give me something," he said quietly, needing it to have hope.

Reaching out, she cupped his cheek and leaned in to kiss him, soft and sweet but too brief. Pulling back, she looked up at him before saying softly, "Take me home."

Without another word he started the engine and pulled out of the service station. He dropped her off at the front door, watching until she was safely inside before he went home.

It was only when he pulled into his driveway that he realised he had her car.

No biggie, he had every intention of returning it real soon.

~*~

He hadn't called. Cindy stared at the phone, her heart heavy one minute, lifting the next. But the time dragged on, seconds to minutes and minutes to hours. Two days and she'd heard nothing, but that meant he had to be thinking, right? Which was a good thing…right?

Echoing in her ears was every word Tim had said, every word she'd heard as she stood in the corridor on her way back from the bathroom. She hadn't been able to help herself, standing there and listening. Her heart falling when it had seemed as though he'd actually choose the inheritance over her, and then the joy when he'd proclaimed his love for her.

But had it been for the benefit of his mother, a knee-jerk reaction to her outrageous demands?

Alex and Marty were sitting in her lounge, eating popcorn and watching a dubious movie that seemed to be more bare breasts than actual story. They cast her a few curious glances but said nothing.

Normally Marty would pry but Alex's presence seemed to help deter him. Or, more likely, Alex had simply told him to shut up and mind his business.

Al raced around, hanging off Alex's jeans and pulling himself up onto the sofa, climbing the back of it with agile precision before scooting along the back of it, his eyes bright and his tail up like a little antennae.

She smiled, reaching out to ruffle his fur. He pawed at her hands before shooting over to plunk himself on Marty's shoulder and sniff at the popcorn he was putting into his mouth.

"Ohhh, baby." Marty made sounds of appreciation as even bigger breasts appeared on the screen. "Let's hear it for corny, B-grade, seventies movies!"

"Sure it's not porn?" Cindy asked.

"No, it's the seventies movies. Bare breasts and -"

"Smut, as Mum would say." Alex happily munched on popcorn.

Cindy returned to staring out of the window. She knew what she felt, she had to admit she'd known since the moment Tim had said 'How about forever?' in the vet's office. She'd laughed before looking at him as the meaning had hit her. But then he'd sort of panicked, his eyes widening as he realised what he'd said, and his hurried 'I didn't mean-' let her know that he hadn't thought about it. Not the forever part, anyway.

Seeing how much her heart had lifted and dropped and basically pinged around in her chest that day, it was a wonder she hadn't had a heart attack.

If he decided he didn't love her, she sure as hell knew she was going to have a broken heart.

Why didn't he call? The only thing she'd heard was from Maddy to say that Tim had delivered an unwanted, elderly, yowling cat to one of her patients, who was utterly delighted with him. The cat, not Tim. Apparently the owner had died and the daughter hadn't wanted anything to do with it, but now, thanks to Tim, it had a new loving home and a doting new owner.

When the phone rang, she jumped.

"Hey." Marty eyed the phone and then her. "Want me to answer it?"

"No." She picked it up, her hands trembling a little. "Tim?"

"No, it's Maddy."

Her heart fell in disappointment. "Oh, hello."

"Turn on the TV."

"It is on."

"What channel?"

"I don't know. Alex and Marty are watching some smutty show."

"Turn it on to channel 3."

"Why?"

"Just do it. And don't turn it off straight away, okay?"

"Well, okay, but-" She stared at the phone as Maddy hung up. "Okay."

"What's wrong?" Alex asked.

"Maddy said to change the TV to channel three."

"What?" Marty practically whined. "But it's boobs, sis, boobs!"

Alex simply grabbed the control and flipped the channel.

Curious, Cindy came up behind the sofa and leaned on the back of it.

"An ad for chocolate." Marty huffed in disgust and folded his arms. "Big freakin' deal."

Tossing the remote back onto the table, Alex resumed munching on popcorn.

Cindy watched as Al stuck his nose in the packet of popcorn and proceeded to pull one out, tossing it through the air to land on Alex's socks.

Laughing, Alex grabbed the kitten just as he was launching himself after the popcorn and picking up one of the toys from the basket beside the sofa, he tossed a tinkling ball across the floor. Diverted, Al took off after it.

"Hey!" Marty reached back to tap Cindy's arm. "Isn't that Tim?"

She glanced at the TV. "No, it can't be. It-" She stopped, her eyes widening in surprise.

Yes, it was Tim. He was standing before a blue screen with little hearts and kittens all over the back of it. In his hand he held a small box. His normally happy face was serious, his brown eyes seeming to stare directly at her. Instead of his usual t-shirt with the racy sayings on it, he wore a white button-up shirt with the sleeves rolled up to his elbows.

The man looked sexy as sin. Her heart bumped in her chest and she actually pressed a hand to her chest.

"Hi, I'm Tim Clarke," Tim said, his voice steady, even, not a tremble of uncertainty evident. "And I'm here to tell the world that I love Cindy Lawson. I love every luscious bit of her, her kindness, her gentleness-"

"Is he talking about our Cindy?" Marty gaped.

Alex elbowed him in the side. "Shut up."

"Her sexiness and her total hotness," Tim was saying.

Cindy's mouth dropped open in disbelief, her heart thundering. He was on national television, telling *everyone* he loved her! Oh God!

"My life wasn't complete until Cindy came along," Tim continued, his gaze seeming to look right at her as though he could actually see her. "I made a choice, Cindy, and it was the best - the only - choice I could ever have made. I chose you then, and I choose you now. I love you, Cindy. Marry me." He opened the little box and there was a glint of a ring.

A huge heart swelled to fill the screen along with romantic music, and he disappeared from sight.

"So we sit and wonder what the answer will be!" came the voice over. "Will Cindy Lawson, our local Party Girl, accept the proposal of the local Playboy Vet, or will she break his heart forever? We can only wonder! Now back to our regular scheduled viewing."

Just like that it was over, a movie reappearing.

Cindy stared at the TV, her mouth open.

Alex and Marty stared at her, their mouths open.

"Holy shit," said Marty.

"Got that right," Alex agreed.

The door bell rang, and when it rang for a second time while the siblings remained staring at each other, Alex started to get to his feet.

"No." Numbly, Cindy placed her hand on his shoulder. "I'll get it."

Leaving the lounge, her mind whirling in disbelief, she could only shake her head. He'd actually asked he to marry him in front of the *nation*. Everyone would know - his mother, her parents, their friends, everyone who watched the television at that time. And those who didn't know soon would, for this kind of thing jumped into the gossip circles like lightening.

Every magazine and newspaper would be ringing her.

Still in a daze, she opened the door.

"So," said Tim. "I've thought about it."

She could only stare at him. He looked so good in jeans and sneakers and one of his ridiculous t-shirts. The cartoon horse on it had buck teeth and crossed eyes, and it was down on its knees with its front hooves crossed. Printed underneath was *Please Say Yes*.

"I thought a lot, actually." He moved up the steps until he was standing directly in front of her.

"You went on TV," she finally managed to whisper.

"And I thought, how can I convince my luscious babe that I really want her?" He took another step forward and she took one back.

His brown eyes held an intensity she'd never seen before, but there was also a light, tenderness. Determination. A heady mix.

Reaching out, he cupped her nape and drew her to him, while taking another step forward and making her retreat in time with his progress.

"And I thought," he said softly, "Let's make it known for once and for all, to everyone in the city, the state, hell, the whole country, just who it is I love. Who it is. So I asked myself, how could I do that?"

They were now in the hallway and he moved further in, guiding her backwards.

"You went on TV." Heart thundering, her blood racing through her veins, Cindy could only look incredulously up at him.

At the man who meant so much to her, the man with whom she'd fallen in love.

"So I went on TV," he agreed. "I went on there and I bared my soul. I told everyone that I love Cindy Lawson, and I asked her to marry me." He kicked the door shut behind him, the dimness of the hallway surrounding them in cool quietness. "I didn't want there to be any hesitation, any doubt, as to whom I love. So now I'm waiting…"

Her hands actually shook, her breathing uneven as emotions swirled through her. Love, warmth, so much she wanted to say.

His eyes softened, his hand sliding down from her nape to her shoulder and further down to capture her hand. "Will you marry me, Cindy Lawson?"

"Yes." It was a small whisper in the air, but he heard it.

With a smile so big it practically lit up the hallway, Tim lifted her hand and slid a ring onto her finger.

And then he kissed her.

She clung to him, wrapping her arms around his neck, pressing close, kissing him back almost desperately.

"I love you," she whispered against his lips. "I love you so much."

"Ditto," he whispered back, and then he grinned.

She giggled.

"Whoa," said a voice.

She looked around to see Marty and Alex standing in the hallway, Al bouncing around their feet.

"Welcome to the family, I'm guessing?" Marty had his eyebrows raised.

Cindy leaned her head against Tim's chest, snuggling up to him as his arms cradled her close. "You're guessing right."

"Okay then." He strode past her. "That's our cue to go, I'm also guessing."

"Yeah," said Tim. "You guessed right again."

Alex picked up Al, winked at Cindy and followed his brother. "We'll take the nephew with us to Mum's."

The door closed behind them, leaving Cindy and Tim alone in the hallway.

He seemed more than content to stand there with her cradled in his arms, his cheek on top of her head.

"Tim?"

"Yeah, luscious babe?"

"You really told everyone, didn't you?"

"Yeah, I did." The supreme satisfaction in his voice had her giggling.

"You do know you'll have to face everyone at work?"

"Yep."

"And your Mum will know."

"Yep."

"And?"

"Don't care. I've got you."

"Mike and Rick will know."

"Shit." He shrugged. "Okay, not panicking. Nope, still don't care."

Leaning back in his arms, she looked up at him, her love feeling as though it was going to overwhelm her. "I love you, Tim."

"I love you." He rubbed the tip of his nose against hers.

She wanted him so much, his love, his scent, his body, his soul. "Come on." Stepping back, she tugged on his t-shirt. "I'm hungry."

"What?" His brows shot up in surprise. "You want to go out? *Now?*"

"No." She smiled sultrily. "I promised myself some dessert the other night. Tonight's the night."

He looked blankly at her for several seconds before his eyes darkened. "Oh, yeah, now I remember. I like the sound of that."

He made to go past her, but she grabbed his hand. "Wait a minute."

"What?"

"You have to follow me." Moving forward, she threw over her shoulder, "I've got total control over dessert."

"Really?" Amusement tinged with heat swirled through his tone. "I'm game."

"Really?" She grinned wickedly at him. "Hold that thought, playboy."

~*~

The bedroom was swathed in shadows, the lamp she clicked on as they entered casting softness on the furnishings.

Cindy led him to the big bed, turning to face him with her hand held out.

He raised a brow.

"Condom."

"My aim is to please." He deftly plucked the little foil packet from his pocket and placed it in her hands.

It was her turn to arch a brow. "So sure I'd give in to you that you brought a condom?"

"Like I said, boy scout." He wiggled his eyebrows.

"Tim."

"Okay, let's just say I was hopeful." He flashed a grin.

She tried to look stern but failed, her eyes twinkling with a mixture of laughter and heat.

Tossing the condom on the bedside table, she proceeded to slowly circle him. "You're a bad boy, Tim."

"Oh, baby, you have no idea." His hands went to the snap on his jeans.

"You made me wait to hear from you." She was behind him now, he could feel her warmth as she leaned forward, the brush of her breasts against his back, but when he started to turn she slid her fingers into the back of his jeans. "Don't."

Stilling, he waited, half holding his breath, partly amused but also partly aroused.

"Take off your shirt." Cindy spoke softly.

He obeyed, tossing it aside easily.

"Nice." She ran a finger down his spine, making it tingle. "Now the jeans."

"Quite the little dominatrix," he mused, sounding calm but feeling totally the opposite. In fact, his heart was starting to pound and the tingle from her nails scratching lightly down his spine was joined by a spark of heat when those nails trailed lower, following his descending jeans to cup one taut buttock.

"Nice again." She breathed it in his ear as his jeans fell to his ankles. "Now the boxers."

Shucking them took a matter of seconds.

Curious and aroused, he glanced over his shoulder but she'd already shifted, coming around his other side. He turned his head to see her sit on the bed. Lazily she leaned back on her elbows, her gaze sliding slowly over him, leaving a hot trail he swore he could feel.

Shaft hardening, he reached for her.

"Oh no." She held up one finger. "Stay right there, playboy."

"Cindy-"

"I'm in control this time." Her eyes glittered in the dim light. "Remember?"

"How about next time-" Bent over her, he froze when her hand wrapped firmly around his erection and slid smoothly up the length.

He nearly blew a load right then and there. Jesus, the sensation of her palm around his shaft was mind blowing.

Cindy stood slowly, sliding her length up his, softness to lean strength, her hand cupping his erection. Looking up at him, she breathed, "Lie on the bed. On your back. Hands above your head."

It said a lot for his condition that he obeyed. God, he couldn't wait. He felt like a sacrifice laid out for her as he settled on the smooth cover, his arms above his head, hands partially open.

Standing at the end of the bed, she slowly undid the buttons on the front of her dress while running her gaze leisurely down his length. "Spread your legs."

"Keep up that tone and look," he rasped, "And I won't be responsible for what happens next."

Her flash of teeth was pure wickedness. "Like a bit of bossiness, do you?"

"Only from you." And that was the ever lovin' truth.

Tim liked being in control, and the thought of a woman telling him what to do in the bed was not a turn on - expect when it came to Cindy Lawson. Luscious Cindy with her wicked smile and glittering eyes.

The dress fell back off her shoulders and she stood clad in her lacy bra and satiny, feminine boxers. This time they were red as sin.

Sweet mercy," he muttered, his shaft jerking and straining up towards his belly at just the sight of her. "How about we play Bondage Pete next time?"

Resting one knee on the bed, she smiled lazily. "Oh, honey, this isn't bondage. For that I'd have to tie your hands up."

"Not bloody likely."

"I'm telling you right now." Her voice was soft but there was a glint in her eyes as she started moving up the bed, her luscious curves shown to full advantage in the red satin. "You shift those hands just once and you'll be finishing the job I'm about to start yourself."

"Not in this lifetime."

Arching a brow, she stopped moving.

"Okay, just this once," he allowed, his hands already turning to grip the cover without him even realising it.

He could hear his own breathlessness. Seriously, no woman had ever turned him on like Cindy did, she made him feel like he could hammer a hole in a chunk of wood with his dick, he was so hard from just her look and scent, and the wicked smile she had, and when she licked her lips and moved slowly up between his legs, oh sweet mercy, he had to fight the urge to grab her, throw her to her back beneath him and pound into her.

"Not having naughty thoughts, are you?" She moved further up, the nails of one hand scraping up the inside of his knee.

His vision blurred for several delicious seconds, but then a flash of silver had his eyes almost popping in delight. "You're still wearing your stilettos?"

She winked.

"Oh my God." How hot was that? How sexy?

Kneeling on the bed, she placed her hands each side of his thighs and slowly lowered herself, sliding back, giving him a good view of her generous breasts before she settled herself between his thighs, her shoulders above his groin as she languidly reached for his erection, curling her fingers around it and bringing the tip back level with her lips.

Her lips were so moist, glossy with her lipstick, and then she smiled up at him and licked the head of his shaft.

Sweet heaven! Colours burst behind his eyes and his hips arched upward helplessly as fire swelled in a delicious ball from his shaft to his scrotum and back, leaving hungry trails of need coiling low through his belly.

When nothing more happened, he came to with a panting sound which oh, how apt, was actually him.

"Hold on, honey," Cindy purred, and placing her lips on the very end of his shaft, she slid her mouth down, his length disappearing into moist, hot heat.

Sensation burst, his scrotum tightening as her mouth worked him wickedly, sucking and nibbling, her tongue licking the head, the sensitive underside of his shaft, over the tip and before once again she engulfed him in her mouth.

Head pressed back into the pillows, Tim gritted his teeth, the only part of his brain working in the distance warning him not to reach for her, not to let go of the bedcovers or she'd do what she threatened, and by God, there was no way he was finishing this glorious stunt she'd started.

Fire in his veins, pouring out to smoulder his nerve endings. Shivers of delight, shudders of ecstasy, but when his seed started to come, when his orgasm was upon him, she stopped.

"Cindy!" he gasped. "Cindy, no!"

A slide up his body, satin on his skin, a hot, open-mouthed kiss, but when he reached for her she laughed low and throatily and slid back down, her luscious curves fuel to an already raging fire.

And then she was there, her mouth on him, working him harder, higher, her lips searing on his skin, her tongue a hot lash that whipped his carnal heat higher until he exploded, his seed spurting forth.

She milked him, swallowed, her mouth like magic, throwing him out into a fiery inferno that seemed to go on and on as her mouth drove him up and over into the shattering heat.

He didn't know what happened, when his eruption had stopped, when she'd released him, but by the time he finally opened his eyes enough to catch a glimpse, it was to find her lying beside him with her head propped up on her hand.

"Hi," she said lazily, and licked her lips. "Yum."

"Jesus," he said, feeling his shaft stir. "Wait a minute."

She laughed, genuine pleasure on her face.

"Just a minute. Or two." He closed his eyes. "Maybe three or four."

"How about we give it ten?" She moved beside him.

Reaching out quickly, he dropped his arm over her waist, too wrung out to do anything else but growl, "Don't move." At least he liked to think it was a manly growl, but in all likelihood it was a weak gasp.

Cool fingers smoothed down his arm, the touch soothing rather than erotic. "Poor baby. Was I too rough?"

"Yeah. Oh God, yeah." He smiled. A giggle greeted this, and he opened one eye to look at her. "Payback's a bitch."

"Hmm?" She looked innocently at him.

As if a luscious woman wearing red satin undies and silver stilettos could look innocent. "You look like sex personified."

"I think that's a Mike word."

"Sex?"

"Personified."

"I've been hanging out with him too much. Next thing I'll be calling you a lady instead of my luscious babe."

"But aren't you glad I'm not a lady?" Teasingly, her nails dragged lightly over his abdomen, causing his muscles to twitch and tighten.

"Oh, you're a lady all right." He felt himself come to life again and it wasn't just his ardour. Tiredness vanishing, he opened both eyes and moved fast, rolling a squealing Cindy beneath him and covering her face in kisses. "My wicked, naughty, sexy lady."

She giggled and struggled. "Wait! Wait!"

"What?" He nipped and nuzzled her ear.

"I have to take off the stilettos-"

"No way, luscious babe, they stay on." His hand dipped to the waistband of her satin boxers. "These, however…"

"I could scratch you with the heels-"

"Injuries in the line of duty." Catching her hands, he held them in the tangle of her blonde hair which was now scattered across the pillow.

"Duty?" She pouted. "Is that all I am?"

"Oh, luscious babe, you are much more than duty." Heat still burned in his veins, but looking down at her beneath him, so soft and pretty and mischievous, he felt contentment sweep underneath the heat. "You're everything I desire."

She stopped the playful struggling, her breaths coming deep and a little unevenly as she looked gravely up at him. "Really?"

"Oh yeah. You're my desire. My every desire come to life."

"Oh, Tim." She practically melted beneath him.

"Of course, I'm not going to inherit lots of wealth. I do have some money." He raised his brows consideringly. "A fair bit, in fact. But not as much as I would have gained later down the track." He lowered his gaze to meet her soft blue eyes. "I'll have to work hard, be a kept man even."

"You'll have to work hard," she agreed seriously.

"I better get started then."

"Think you can keep up with me?"

His grin was pure wickedness. "A challenge!"

She squealed, her bra went flying, her girly boxers followed, but the stilettos stayed on.

#####

Big Girls Lovin' trilogy

If you missed "Doctor's Delight" and "Cop's Passion", books 1 & 2 of the Big Girls Lovin' trilogy, they are available at http://www.lulu.com

Biography

Angela Verdenius lives in Australia where she is ruled by her cats, adores reading, and thinks a perfect day is writing and drinking Diet Coke, followed by reading or a good horror movie.

To date, she has written 20 novels, 2 novellas, and several short stories, including a zombie story of which she's especially fond. Her books have won many reviewers' awards, as well as having been on the Fictionwise best-seller list, winning the Golden Rose Award and being twice nominated for an Australian Romance Readers Award.

Visit her website http://www.angelaverdenius.com for more information on her books, and her blog http://angelaverdenius.blogspot.com/ to read her not-so-serious view of what life is throwing at her!

Made in the USA
Lexington, KY
15 November 2012